BALANCE MUST REMAIN

A SIRIANS SERIES NOVEL

K.M. DAVIDSON

Copyright © 2025 by Sirian Ink LLC

All rights reserved.

No part of this publication may be reproduced, stored, or transmitted in any form or by any means, electronic, mechanical, photocopying, recording, scanning, or otherwise—except in the case of brief quotations embodied in critical articles or reviews—without written permission from its publisher.

The author expressly prohibits using this book in any matter to train artificial intelligence (AI) technologies for the purpose of generating text, including works in the same genre or style as this book.

This novel is entirely a work of fiction. The names, characters, and incidents portrayed in it are the work of the author's imagination. Any resemblance to actual persons, living or dead, events or localities is entirely coincidental and not intended by the author.

K.M. Davidson asserts the moral right to be identified as the author of this work.

Cover Design by Nikkita Bell (@nikkitabell)
Scene Breaks Illustrated by Marta Riva (@marta.intotheforest)
Edited by Sophie | Wonder and Wander Editing
Karasi Portraits by Janene O (@neneja_literart)
Brand & Karasi Portrait by Hanna (@sovana.art)

N
W
S
E
The Scorpio Palace
The Black Lake
The Red Raven
The Scorpion Lake
Ghita
Cerelia
Main Town
The Forbidden Island
Crylly Tower
Orion's Lake
The Great Karasi
The Clips
Saros
Vega
Castle of Andromeda
The Red River
Rian
The Rocky Points
Heartlake
Tieslin
Saros Tower
Salo
The Ravens Wood
Elvi
Mariande
Lolis
The Southern Beaches
Etherea
Chim bridge
Eryphus
The Sand Dunes & Beaches
Rigel's Keep
Blood Lake

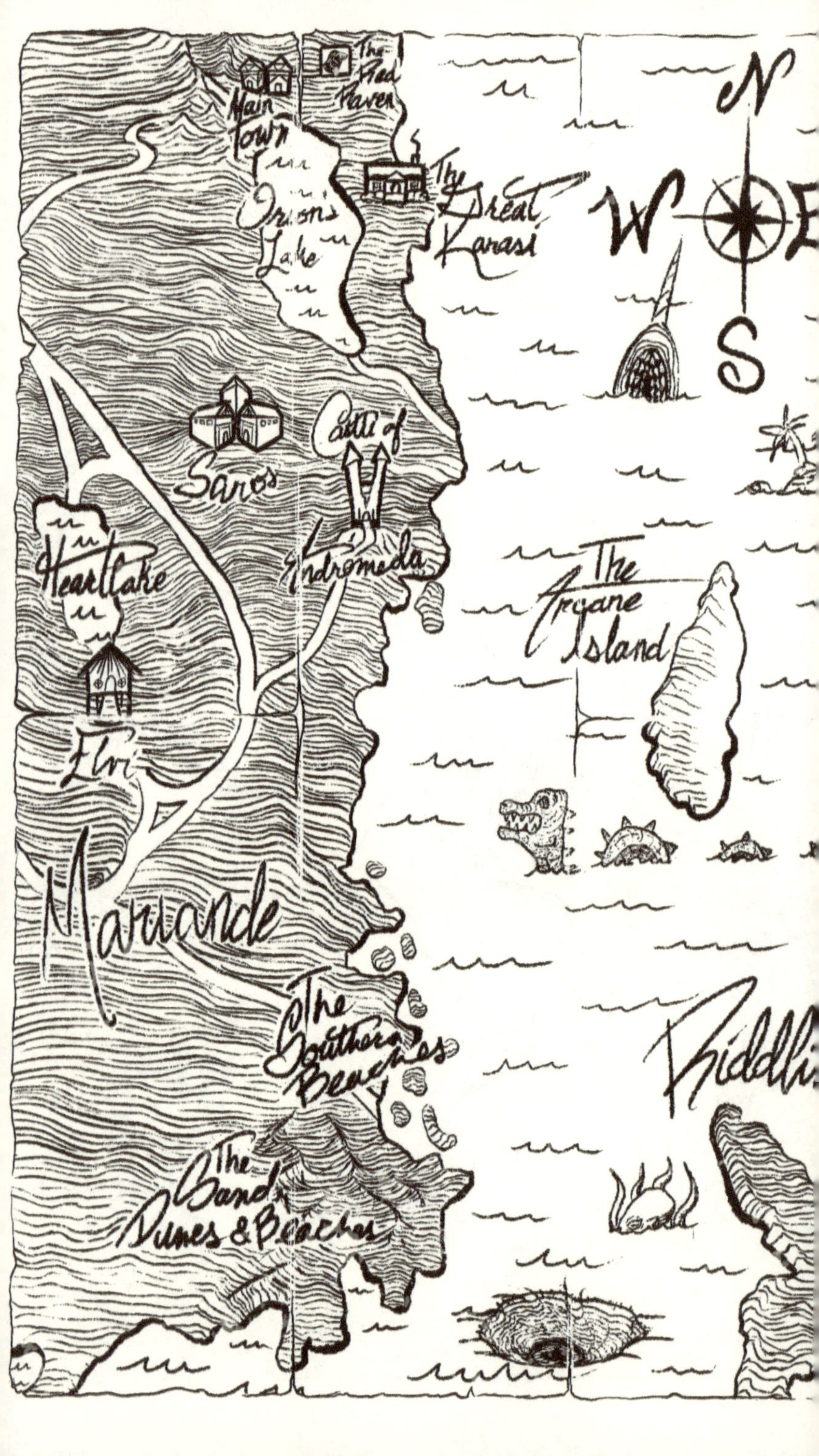

Main Town
The Red Haven
Orion's Lake
The Great Karasi
N
W
E
S
Sanos
Castle of Andromeda
The Arcane Island
HeartLake
Elvi
Mariande
The Southern Beaches
The Sand'n Dunes & Beaches
Riddlli

DEITIES & THE GODS

DEITIES

KUK
The Darkness, the Abyss, Dark beings

KHONSA
Choice, Magics, the Light

GODS (CHILDREN OF KUK & KHONSA)

DOLA
Goddess of Destiny & Fate

MORANA
Goddess of Death & Magic

DANICA
Goddess of Nature & the Energy of All Things, The Morning/Evening Star

ROD
God of Family, Birth, & Humanity

DEMI-GODS

CHILDREN OF MORANA

SYBIL
Magic, Founded House of Echidna

CHILDREN OF DANICA

PHOEBE
Sirian – Gravitational Energy Manipulation

TARANIS
Sirian – Lightning Manipulation

ASTERIA
Sirian – Heightened Energy Manipulation, Stars & Galaxy

DIONNE
Sirian – Heat Manipulation Variation

CHILDREN OF ROD

BRIGID
Magic, Founded House of Argo

BODHI
Immortal Human

ENKI
Immortal Human, The First King

GARUDA
Magic, House of Nemea

MAGICS & THE HOUSES

HOUSE OF ECHIDNA

Founded by Sybil
Serpent and Dragon Shifters

HOUSE OF NEMEA

Founded by Garuda
Feline and Bird Shifters

HOUSE OF ARGO

Founded by Brigid
Marine Shifters

Content Warning

This adult fantasy novel contains mature themes and content that may not be suitable for all readers. Readers are advised that the story includes depictions of violence, graphic imagery, light profanity, and sexual/sexually explicit scenes. Additionally, the narrative explores challenging subject matters, including but not limited to death, dementia-like mental disorder, suicidal ideation, gaslighting, and psychological manipulation. Please exercise discretion and know that the content may trigger or be unsettling for some audiences. If you have read The Sirians Series up to *Fate Demands Sacrifice*, you know this, but for those who have not yet, please be aware this is not an HEA because the FMC does die by the end of this book.

Please take care of your heart and your head.
This story contains depictions of self-harm that may be difficult for some readers. If you are struggling, you are not alone. Help is always within reach.
You can call or text the Suicide and Crisis Lifeline at **988** for free, confidential support at any time.
You are deeply important. You deserve care, support, and kindness — from others and from yourself.

For more resources, visit **988lifeline.org**

To those who have fought—and continue to fight—their inner demons and emerged not unscathed, but alive, and ready to write the next chapter.

THE GREAT CHILD

To be born a legend—hailed as a blessing amongst your peers—is no gift at all.

Growing up with the knowledge that I was the first and last direct descendant of a demi-god was a burden I didn't want to bear. The world called me a miracle, born to a mother thousands of years old.

The Great Child.

While the world stood back in awe as I carried the weight of my title, my mother didn't see me the same way.

I wasn't meant to be, and Sybil only saw my birth for what it truly was.

Fate ushering in change.

Sybil watched the world rise and fall, millennia after millennia, from the moment she was made until her final breaths—everything in the name of Fate. Her prophetic powers were always a blessing and a curse to her. She was granted abilities that rivaled the Goddess and her aunt, Dola.

But she had not foreseen her own child, which scared her more than anything in the world.

At least until Tyra Korbin came.

The older I got, the more restless Sybil became. My mother was always beautiful, stuck at an age that never progressed. Still, a frantic energy clung to her as my own prophetic powers developed. As the world hurtled deeper into chaos, she sensed her final time approaching.

A time when the world would no longer need her, when the clock ticked too fast to keep the Gods' secrets.

Secrets she never shared because the past was not mine to see. I could only see what Path laid before us, even if I never knew when it would come.

My prophesying was not as potent as hers. Sybil saw epics in grim detail, while I only caught glimpses and glimmers of the future. Neither of us could explain why the outcomes made sense or how we could interpret them based on the startling differences in which the future came to us.

It felt like a sixth sense—a flicker of light rising, just barely, over the horizon.

With that knowledge came a balance to maintain. My mother always taught me that Fate required sacrifice, though she never elaborated far beyond that.

She would only explain that it had been decided long ago, a prophecy given to her before I was born.

The powerful must be few for balance to remain.

This prophecy was drilled into me nearly as much as the only advice my mother ever gave me, if it could even be considered that.

Observe and remain silent. Quiet action can speak louder

amidst the noise of the loudest voice.

This lesson carried with me from the first moment my mother uttered it until the very last days of my life. Even when I ached to scream, to warn those I cared for, to shift the future Fate had carved for me…

Because I was the chosen one.

The Great Child.

The Great Karasi.

And greatness was required of me.

THE MAIDEN

*She learned too young that
eternity was a lonely thing.*

THE FIRST PROPHECY

816 A.V. | AGE: 9

I twirled the bottom of a black braid around my finger, rubbing my thumb along the bronze band that held it together. The carriage jolted, ripping a breath from me as I tightened my grip on the braid and my other hand dug into the cushioned seat.

"Relax, *mi fidi*," Sybil drawled, inspecting her nails before dragging her gaze to me. "What has you bound?"

"He is the Cruel King, is he not?" I asked, folding my hands in my lap.

Sybil's hand snapped out, gripping my cheeks between her thumb and forefinger, the edges of her nails digging in. "You do not repeat those words again, do you understand? We were invited to rectify the relationship between the Korbins and the Magics."

"But Mother—"

She leveled me with a glare that could've burned men to ashes.

I pressed my lips into a tight line to suppress my questions, opting for the silence she spoke so often about. I moved my fidgeting to the marigold and purple dress

Sybil had sewn for me just for this momentous occasion, tugging at the bow that wrapped around my waist.

Sybil cleared her throat, drawing my attention back to her. She raised a single, perfectly shaped white eyebrow, her chartreuse eyes and vertically slit pupil boring into me. They stood out menacingly against her deep, ebony skin. She opted for a glittery silver dress and cloak, exuding etherealness, especially with the two white braids hanging over her shoulders.

Sybil may have only been a demi-god, but she was the closest to a Goddess on Aveesh.

The carriage came to a rattling stop, and my head snapped to the door.

"Remember what I told you," Sybil demanded in a hushed tone. "Observe—"

"And remain silent," I finished just as the door swung open.

I peeked through the doorway, but I could only see a mob of people hurrying about behind the guard standing before the door. He hesitantly accepted Sybil's hand, but the hungry glint in his eye didn't get past me as he roamed her body.

"If you wish to keep those lovely eyes…" Sybil stepped down. She stood at full height, just an inch or two shorter than this man. She leaned into his space, and though she whispered, my enhanced hearing picked up her words. "It would be in your best interest to cease ogling in front of the Great Child."

His head snapped to where I hovered in the carriage

doorway. When his eyes met mine, I narrowed them and cocked my head to the side.

He cleared his throat, shifting uncomfortably under my scrutiny as he waited for me to clamor down the stairs alone.

It seemed the fear of the Great Child outside of Eldamain was far greater than the enrapturement of Sybil.

"Come, *mi fidi*," Sybil snapped, extending her dainty hand. I slipped mine into hers, allowing her to drag me behind her as I gawked at the castle before me.

While I'd been to Eldamain's grand, beautiful castle multiple times, something about Etherea's castle crawled beneath my skin.

The walls were made of the same cream-toned stone as Eldamain's, but where Aggelos Palace back home was adorned in natural ivy and flowers scaling the walls, this castle was stripped bare—no ivy, no flowers, not even grass. It was a mix of stone walkways and gravel.

Even the sky darkened the mood, a gray haze casting as far as the eye could see. A chill raced down my arms, and my vision blurred as I stumbled before the grand entrance.

Sybil whipped her head at me, her braids smacking against her shoulders. She hissed under her breath, too quiet for mortal ears. "Karasi… What ails you?"

"Nothing ails me, Mother," I whispered, gazing at my feet. My vision continued to waver, as though I'd opened my eyes under water, and my stomach churned. "I'm just parched."

Sybil pinned me with narrowed eyes, their green luminescence nearly glowing as she scrutinized me. With a huff, she resumed our journey, filing into the castle with the rest of the guests arriving.

After Crown Prince Leif's marriage ceremony, all in attendance funneled into the grand ballroom for refreshments and small plates of food that floated about the room on the hands of servants.

I kept close to Sybil as we entered, marveling at how the crowd seemed to naturally gravitate away from us, keeping a small berth of space. Despite the number of people collectively huddled, Sybil knew exactly where she was going.

We approached a man decorated in an elaborate maroon and gold uniform; various pins were attached to both sides of his broad chest. He had stark gray hair tied back into a bun, the brown skin on his face drawn back from the tension.

"Sir Michael," Sybil hummed as we approached, holding her hand out for him. "It's fascinating to see you again."

Sir Michael startled slightly at the sight of Sybil, but something warm passed briefly across his face as he accepted her outstretched hand.

"I'm relieved to see your journey was not too arduous," he said, bowing as he pressed her hand to his forehead. His gaze landed on me, and he raised an eyebrow. "This is the Great Child."

"My daughter," Sybil confirmed with a stiff nod, ushering me forward with a hand at the small of my back. "Karasi, this is Sir Michael. He's an old acquaintance of mine that has found himself in quite a prestigious position amongst Etherean royalty."

"Pleased to meet you," I recited, blinking up at him.

Sir Michael studied me for a moment, and I tried not to shift on my feet at the intense scrutiny. Then, he painstakingly dragged his gaze to Sybil, still squinting. "How old is—"

"You would do best not to finish that question," Sybil suddenly snapped, but she collected herself quickly.

I frowned up at her, rarely finding her disheveled by anyone other than myself.

"Well"—Sir Michael cleared his throat, waving his hands at four boys beside him—"let me introduce you to the four youngest Korbins."

The boys standing before me all looked to be siblings. While they had minor differences, far more similarities marked them as brothers and Korbins.

Sir Michael introduced the first two: Erling and Yorrick Korbin, one of the two sets of twins amongst the twelve siblings. While the other two boys with them had chestnut brown hair, these two had a slight auburn tint.

The next one was Grimm Korbin, who appeared as though he would rather be anywhere but here.

"And this is the youngest prince, Brand Korbin,"

Sir Michael introduced, gesturing to the boy who stood before me with his head cocked to the side.

I pursed my lips as he openly examined me with pure curiosity glistening in his eyes. Something about him intrigued me, even if he was the most mortal boy I'd ever seen.

Maybe that's why he was so fascinating to me.

I was used to a world surrounded by Magics with strange characteristics and Sirians wielding the Light. This boy, however, was *so very mortal.*

He had the robin-egg, turquoise eyes like the rest of his siblings and they stood out against his sun-kissed skin. Brown locks hung in a wild mess before his forehead, a slight wave to the ends.

It wasn't his looks that captivated me. The foreign glint in his eyes mixed with that unabashed curiosity tugged at something deep within me.

The compassion he exuded made him stand out against the rest of his brothers like a beacon. It softened his features and made his stature less intimidating. While he was the spitting image of his father, it was hard to compare them when they held themselves drastically different.

"I've never met a Magic with eyes like yours before," Brand interjected, jutting his hand out between us with a wide grin that lit those eyes from within. "It's nice to meet you, Great Child."

"Karasi," I blurted, immediately slipping my hand into his. A strange sting shot up my arm on contact, buzzing in my chest. I gasped at the sensation but quickly shook it off upon feeling Sybil's burning gaze on me. "My name is Karasi."

Brand's smile thinned, but the light never left his eyes. He dipped his head as he firmly shook my hand, slowly releasing his grip.

"I see you've met some of my children," a deep, rumbling voice spoke, slipping between Brand and me as we unlocked our hands. Sybil placed both of hers on my shoulders, her nails digging in as she quickly turned me to face the source.

I knew him to be King Alrik Korbin because I'd identified him during the marriage ceremony. While his brown hair was a shade or two lighter than Brand's, I wondered how much of that was because a lighter gray grew in at the roots and was sporadically mixed within. It was cut similarly to the other men in the room, whisked back to reveal a square jawline and cheekbones that made his fair skin slightly sunken. His mustache and beard were well-groomed, mostly gray rather than brown.

And those robin-egg, turquoise eyes couldn't be missed.

"I'm pleased that you could make the journey, Sybil," King Alrik said, extending his hand toward my mother. She offered him her fingers, which he brought to his lips. They barely brushed her skin before he released her, wheeling his attention on me. "It's even a greater pleasure to finally meet the child we've heard so much about."

He bent at an angle, bringing us to eye level, and

while I knew the action was to make me feel less intimidated by him, I found myself sinking back into Sybil as my head lowered. She jabbed her bony knuckle into my lower back, keeping me from folding any further into myself.

King Alrik presented both of his hands before me as though he were moving to pick up a younger child. I was far too old to be held anymore, so I assumed he wanted my hands. I cautiously slipped them into his, and the moment they connected, that nausea from earlier returned.

"If I understand correctly, this is your first journey from home," King Alrik began, but his voice was fractured as he spoke, splitting between my ears. I blinked rapidly, my vision swimming with fog. I caught him frowning as I swayed. "It appears you may have exhausted her with a long carriage ride, Sybil."

"*Mi fidi?*" Sybil kneeled beside King Alrik, her voice muted by the unfamiliar heartbeat echoing in my skull. It was entirely out of sync with mine hammering against my ribcage. I felt her cold hand against my skin, but my vision disappeared behind a milky haze. "Dear Heavens—"

That foreign heartbeat continued to pound in my head, and I found mine slowing to sync with it until they reverberated off one another, clopping like horse hooves.

I didn't see images across my eyes, but in my head, like I conjured them from my imagination.

Except it wasn't my imagination that brought them.

They dropped into my mind like apples from the tree of Fate, rolling inward.

Sirians screamed. Darkness climbed over marble.

A whisper behind blue eyes. Quill against parchment.

Bodies burn. Heads roll. Kingdoms crumble.

A laugh spreading across mountains and plains and oceans—

I gasped as my vision returned with a single blink. Sybil guarded me from the others as her own eyes illuminated, her intake of breath echoing mine.

"What have you seen?" she whispered, only a conversation meant for the two of us.

I opened my dry mouth, closing it to wet my lips with spit. I searched around Sybil, noticing Sir Michael studying us intently, Brand hovering with a foreign look of concern, and King Alrik staring at me with greed directly behind my mother.

[The Korbin Legacy.]

It whispered in my mind, the sound of a million voices and yet somehow just one.

The images that invaded my mind were seared into me somehow. While I only saw strange glimpses, a feeling within my gut translated them into sensibility. It reminded me of the same crawling sensation I felt when someone was watching me from across a room.

"You," I whispered to King Alrik, our eyes connecting.

Because it was his prophecy I bore witness to—my first prophecy.

And it was dark and brutal and chilling…

It would change our future forever.

"You're—" I hissed as Sybil's fingernails dug into my forearm, the intensity of her gaze urging me to stay silent.

"Don't mind her," Sybil explained, rising from the floor to full height. She brushed out her dress and faced King Alrik with her back to me. I glanced past her as she spoke. "It seems the Gods have chosen to pass down my gift of prophecy to my daughter just as my powers seem to weaken."

King Alrik's gaze snaked between Sybil and me, something dangerous warring with the front he kept up. "And was that your first, Great Child?"

"Yes, Your Highness," I mumbled, my voice small.

A feline grin spread across his cheeks as he gently pushed Sybil away, standing before me once again. He fiercely gripped my chin, tilting my head so our gazes locked.

"And what have you seen?" he asked, nearly repeating Sybil's earlier request.

The voice returned, uttering a single command.

[Lie.]

Even though it was my first prophecy, a peculiar instinct took over. My face released any tension and emotion, and I was a stone wall as the words left me beyond my control. "*You will achieve what you seek to accomplish. The world will fear your name for millennia. Darkness will come again.*"

His grin faltered at the last sentence, frowning as he

tilted his head to the side. "What do you mean by that?"

"*When Darkness comes again, Marks will be revealed,*" came out of my mouth. At the mention of Marks, he clenched his jaw, hot anger burning behind those bright irises.

"But I will succeed?" He urged, his grip pinching.

I whimpered but managed a quiet, "Yes."

"That's all that matters." He released me, nearly shoving my head aside as his entire facade returned to the joyous father celebrating his son's marriage.

I peered at Brand, whose skin had paled as he gawked at me. It wasn't fear *of* me that took over his face, but fear *for* something.

When I dragged my heavy-lidded gaze to Sybil, she looked like she'd seen Death itself.

I frowned at her, stepping closer as the attention averted from us, and patrons who'd stopped to watch the spectacle moved on to more exciting things. "What is it, Mother?"

"You spoke of Darkness," she whispered under her breath, her eyes scanning the crowd as she lifted a quivering hand to her chest. She rolled her neck and closed her eyes. "What possessed you to speak such a simple word with such malevolence?"

"I'm not sure," I muttered, noticing that Brand still watched us from where he'd been pulled away by one of his brothers. "The words I spoke came out of me against my will. But Mother, that's not the extent of what I saw. I saw more, but something told me—"

"Speak of this no more." She grabbed my face between her hands, hunching over so our noses nearly touched. "We'll speak when we are home. I must teach you the ways of prophecy. Until then, remember what I have instructed you."

Observe and remain silent.

The Unlikely Friend
818 A.V. | Age: 11

I thought the winters back home were cold, but The Northern Pizi winter had an even sharper bite. It pressed through my skin, digging deep into my bones. I wanted nothing more than to keep the heavy fur coat on throughout the marriage ceremony, but Sybil chastised me about showing my elaborately adorned dress to give the impression that we belonged.

I wasn't sure why we had to be the ones to repair the relationship of Magics with the royals, and why it had to be King Alrik we focused our energy on.

It could've been something Sybil saw in her own prophecies, or maybe it was from her years of experience—even if I didn't know exactly how old she was.

"*Karasi,*" Sybil whispered harshly beside me, pinching the sensitive skin at the back of my neck. My hands fell straight to my sides away from the embroidery I'd been picking at. "If a single thread is out of line on that dress, you'll spend the rest of winter locked in our home."

"That would be warmer—" I hissed as her nails dug

in. "I'll stop."

Sybil's hand fell away, but I felt her staring at me from above. I peered up with a frown, unsettled by the strange shadow in her eyes. "Remember what I've said about needing to make an impression with those in higher status than us."

"Yes, ma'am." I sighed, letting my gaze flicker across the ballroom where couples spun together to the elevated melody.

Bodies twisted and hopped about, partners exchanging partners as every patron moved in a circle about the room. I tilted my head at the glimpses of auburn hair I caught, trying to count how many of the Korbin princes were amongst those in the dance.

Prince Esben was off to the side observing the prancing with his new bride, the Crown Princess of The Northern Pizi. He looked far too much like King Alrik, but that wasn't surprising considering a majority of the Cruel King's sons resembled him.

"Sybil," said a familiar male voice. I whipped my head beside us to find Sir Michael before my mother, his hands clasped behind his back. Beside him was another familiar face that sent excitement fluttering wildly in my chest. "Prince Brand has requested a dance with the Great Child. While they're occupied, I would ask if you'll accompany me on the dance floor?"

Sybil narrowed her eyes at Sir Michael, pursing her lips. Her gaze bounced between him and Brand standing beside him with that open expression, eyes blinking. I intertwined my fingers together in front of me, trying to suppress the jitters tickling my legs.

She noticed though, and I expected her to be upset at my misbehavior. Instead, my mother's face softened to a degree I rarely glimpsed before she sighed. "I suppose it doesn't hurt to mingle amongst the others." She slipped one hand into Sir Michael's, then pointed her finger at me. "Behave yourself. Don't stray too far and stay with Prince Brand. Understood?"

"Yes, Mother!" A fervid grin spread across my cheeks, and I immediately grabbed onto Brand's outstretched elbow. I didn't look back once as he guided me to the dance floor, keeping close to the edge, away from the whirling adults. "Prince Brand, I've never danced before."

"No worries at all," Brand said with a grin. He held his hands palm-up between us, wiggling his fingers. "I'll teach you. Besides, I don't know as much as everyone else does, so we can make up our own as we go."

"Well, how do we do that?" I frowned, hesitantly placing my hands into his.

His long fingers wrapped around my cold ones, warmth seeping into my bones. "Listen to the music and follow your heart. I'll lead, but don't be afraid to take over. Are you ready?"

A thrill like nothing I'd ever felt before rolled through me, and I nodded enthusiastically with that grin still stuck on my face.

The next song began, and I followed Brand's lead.

The dance first started with us swaying our hands

between us like the swing of a pendulum, letting the music absorb into us. Slowly, our bodies moved with our hands, rocking back and forth to the beat of the music. I raised my eyebrows when he added a sidestep but immediately understood when he stepped back to where I was again.

On the next crescendo from the violin, I urged him backwards two steps, then pulled him back with a giggle. We both laughed again when he took an extra step too close, nearly tripping over each other.

We tried to keep up with the music and dance we'd created, but it grew too fast for our movements. Before we knew it, we were jumping back and forth with our hands together, spinning around and doing whatever moves we pleased—utterly ignorant to the tempo.

"Come with me," Brand said over the music, tugging on my hand as he started guiding me toward a side door.

I resisted at first, scanning the crowd for Sybil, but the room had become far too congested. "Prince Brand—"

"You don't have to call me that," he said warmly, shaking his head. He didn't pull me any further. "You can just call me Brand, like you told me to call you Karasi. I figured we could go somewhere else. There's something really cool I found that I want to show you."

"Why?" I frowned, but I let him tug me along without resistance.

He shrugged as we entered the hallway and traveled deeper into the castle, the music fading behind us. "I think you're very much like me, and I really like it, so

I thought maybe you would. If you don't like it, that's okay, though."

The corners of my lips tugged as I let this prince bring me to a room tucked deep within a dark hallway of Castle Ashe. He gently pushed against the mahogany door, peering around the edge. Brand glanced over his shoulder with me and wiggled his eyebrows before slipping us both into the room.

There was nothing spectacular about this room. There were a few settees and chaises scattered about and an entire wall of cabinetry that glistened with various decanters and glasses. Two elaborate chandeliers hung from the ceilings, but they were unlit, making the room appear haunted.

Except what caught my attention was precisely what I knew Brand brought me here for.

A grand window that stretched nearly floor to ceiling revealed a clear winter night beyond the castle, but it wasn't just any sort of view.

This view was of the Northern Mountains, the two large peaks reaching high into the night sky. Stars littered the darkness, and the moon glowed enough beside one of the peaks to illuminate the room. The snow-coated peaks gleamed like beacons in the dark.

It was silent at this part of the castle, and something about the mountains looming before us made me feel like it was just Brand and me in a land only found in fairytales.

"Do you like it?" Brand asked cautiously, standing close beside me. "It makes me feel like I'm in a different world."

"Like a story," I answered, nodding my head. "It's the most beautiful thing I've ever seen. And I live by the Black Avalanches."

"I've seen those before." Brand grinned, gesturing to the mountain view. "These are magical, and you're Magic, so I thought that would be another reason you like them."

I giggled, turning my head to him. He chuckled, too, but my vision wavered the longer I looked at him, my mind swimming. I tried to blink it away, to rid myself of the prophecy trying to ruin my moment of peace.

"Karasi," Brand said, his voice muted. "It's okay—"

I fell to my hands and knees before him and my vision vanished.

Familiar blue eyes blend in colors. Faces morph.
Ever changing. Ever evolving.
Hair grows and shortens, curls and straightens.
Faces slow, colors warm, hair darkens.
Golden eyes flicker. A woman with her head held high—

"Karasi." Brand's voice cut through the image, the cacophony of whispers silencing as my vision cleared. He kneeled before me on the ground, his hands clasping my head. "You have seen a vision?"

I blinked at his touch on my cheeks, using his bright turquoise eyes to anchor myself. I quickly realized I didn't need to, though.

I wasn't sure how I knew this, but his touch single-handedly pulled me from the vision and sent the voices to the recesses of my mind.

I nodded once, letting him grab my arms to lift me from where I'd been on the ground. He wrapped an arm around me and guided me to the nearest settee. We sat down side-by-side, and when he went to remove his arm from around me, my hand latched over his to keep him close.

"Please," I whispered softly, dipping my head and averting my gaze. "It's helping the voices stay away."

"Okay," Brand gently agreed, and he scooted closer, so that our sides were pressed together. "I'm here if you need me."

Something strong settled between us that I never felt with another before.

Connection.

It was a connection built on compassion and kindness, and I knew at that moment Brand would be one of my very best friends.

The Unruly Dark

823 A.V. | Age: 16

When King Alrik formally called Sybil and me to appear before him in private, I had long since mastered the gift I'd inherited from her.

It wasn't difficult, given that I couldn't speak a prophecy unless Fate willed it. At least, that's how I'd come to interpret it, and that's precisely how Sybil told me it worked.

Sometimes, a prophecy was just images playing in my head. Other times, it was accompanied by an ethereal voice—or *voices*. Most of the time, I knew what the vision meant, while other times, I only knew the words.

Sybil said that was because some Paths could still shift. I was only seeing the outcome of the current Path an individual or the world was headed down.

I had yet to receive a prophecy unprovoked, though. It was always related to a particular individual. Sybil had once received prophecies for people *and* the world. They came unexpectedly, so she said I should always be prepared for the day that would happen.

When I found myself being escorted through Rigel's

Keep within Etherea, I stayed close to Sybil. I kept my face stoic despite the restlessness that stirred in my chest.

Since Prince Leif's wedding seven years ago, we had attended three other Korbin weddings with King Alrik in attendance. Every time, there were more glimpses into what he had planned for this world.

At this rate, he was halfway through the initial glimpse I received at Leif's wedding, his sons now in line to be kings of The Northern Pizi, Riddling, and Teslin.

The only thrones untouched by a Korbin were Mariande, Eldamain, and The Clips. I knew he would be successful in taking every throne, but I still hadn't seen how.

Especially because I had yet to glimpse the future of the Carraphim throne—the family that ruled in Eldamain.

My home country.

My restlessness intensified as the guard told us to wait outside the throne room, only able to peer through a slim crack in the doors. My heartbeat echoed in my skull, pulse throbbing at my temples. I mindlessly dug a clawed nail across my forearm beneath my black sleeve, hissing when I cut too deep.

"Would you stop that?" Sybil snapped under her breath, snatching my arm in her hand and yanking my sleeve down.

A drop of dark red blood slid under the rolled-up fabric, the wound already crusted over. My new mark sat beside an angry line from this morning and a line of lighter brown from last night. By tomorrow, the fresh ones would vanish, and the oldest would fade to nothing.

"Why do you mar your skin?" Sybil shook my arm, her grip tightening. "What is the purpose?"

"It keeps me grounded," I mumbled shamefully under my breath, ripping my arm from her grasp and tugging my sleeve back down to my wrist. "It helps relieve the disquiet and pressure building in my body from the prophecies and the voice."

Sybil stared at me with those beady green eyes, her nostrils flaring. "Well, stop."

I set my jaw and rolled my eyes at the same time the lock on the throne room door unlatched, and then both doors swung inward to reveal King Alrik sitting alone on a pure golden throne.

It was only the one throne at the end of the long rug, poised perfectly in front of the large window looming behind it.

"Your Majesty," a guard stationed beside the door interjected. I almost looked back at him, but Sybil dug a nail into my lower back. I kept my eyes trained on the ostentatious crown perched on King Alrik's head because I couldn't muster the courage to look him in the eyes. "I introduce Sybil and the Great Karasi of Eldamain."

I hated that title as much as I hated King Alrik Korbin.

"It's a pleasure to see you both, as always," King Alrik greeted, his voice carrying across the expanse. "My Gods, Great Karasi. You truly are no longer the Great Child. You are blossoming into a beautiful woman."

Bile rose to the back of my throat at the way King

Alrik's gaze dragged from the top of my head and down my body, lingering on where my breasts had been developing and my hips were taking shape.

"Thank you, Your Highness," Sybil responded as we stopped on the rug before the throne, shooting me a flashing glare from the corners of her eyes. "There are still many things she needs to learn before she's truly ready to answer the calls of the kingdoms on her own, as you may be able to tell."

King Alrik chuckled, the sound sharp, scraping against my nerves. I schooled my face into supplication, bowing my head as I curtsied and repeated Sybil's mantra repeatedly.

Observe and remain silent. Observe and remain silent.

"I find myself curious about how your kind conducts themselves," King Alrik began, and I nearly flinched at the way he said *your kind.* "As you know, royalty arranges marriages often based on the most powerful political advantage. Do you find Magics organize marriages based on powerful advantages?"

"Forgive me, Your Highness," Sybil choked out, and I glanced up at my mother as she faked a cough to suppress her surprise. I narrowed my eyes at her, pursing my lips. "There isn't much of a powerful advantage amongst Magics. What we once were capable of is no longer possible. Those abilities weakened after the Gods left the world behind. As far as I know, my daughter and I are the two most powerful Magics on Aveesh at this moment in time. We would offer an advantage to any level of Magic if we were to reproduce or marry."

"Is that how she came to be?" King Alrik slid his gaze from Sybil to me, raising an eyebrow. "What I'm asking is, was her father mortal or Magic?"

My gaze bounced between Sybil to King Alrik, lingering longer on Sybil each time as I waited for her to answer the king's question. Something foreign passed over her face, the corner of her eye twitching at the corner with irritation.

"Magic."

I couldn't help myself. I startled, my mouth dropping as my hands fell to my sides.

When I was younger, I asked about my father once, the first time I'd seen another child with two parents. She chastised me so thoroughly I thought she would transform into the mythological *drakon*.

I never asked again.

King Alrik laughed a deep, hearty sound that bounced off the walls around us. He even clutched at his stomach, his head thrown back. Sybil and I stood awkwardly silent until he collected himself.

He finally spoke, his decorum only somewhat gathered, "I find it quite fascinating that this seems to be news to your daughter. Tell me, child, do you not know your father?"

"No, Your Highness," I answered timidly, casting my gaze at his booted feet. "I didn't know he was a Magic, nor have I ever known his name. Sybil doesn't reveal much about him or the circumstances of my birth."

Sybil tensed beside me at my forwardness with the king, and her body locked up tighter when King Alrik shuffled at his throne. His boots clicked, deliberate, as he approached until we stood nearly toe-to-toe.

Just as he did seven years ago, he gripped my chin between his thumb and forefinger and lifted my head so our eyes could meet. Now only a couple inches shorter than him, he didn't have to lift all that far. He tilted my head side to side and squinted at me with those turquoise blue eyes.

He hummed, bringing my face close enough that his spiced breath tickled beneath my nose as he spoke. "Would you like to know?"

I blinked back my confusion, and my mouth parted as I searched his face.

That voice began to whisper faintly in the back of my mind, but I wanted to know why he asked me this.

I scratched a claw down my arm concealed between us. "It's something I've always thought about."

He raised a graying eyebrow, deepening the wrinkles on his forehead. "Give me a prophecy, Great Karasi, and I will use my resources to find your father."

"Your Highness—" But he cut off Sybil with a hand raised before her.

I swore her godliness buzzed around us as she glared at him, her eyes flashing.

"No tantrums, Sybil." King Alrik swung his gaze to her as he released his grip on me, clasping his hands behind his back as he faced her head-on. "Even demi-gods have their weaknesses."

Sybil balked at that; all the decorum she usually maintained vanished in a blink of an eye. I wasn't sure what he meant by that, but the dread radiated off her like heat, and I couldn't figure out if it was dread for herself or me.

"Do we have an agreement, Great Karasi?" King Alrik said, peering at me from the corners of his eyes as he stayed planted before Sybil. "A truth for a truth?"

[One Truth, one Path, many Truths, many Paths, the True Prophecy—]

Another scratch along my forearm silenced the voice's manic repetition in the recesses of my mind before it could gain momentum.

I swallowed against the trepidation at making any deal with this king, but part of me knew I had no choice. Whether it was my foresight or mortal intuition, I nodded as I maintained eye contact with King Alrik and said, "I will give you your prophecy."

"Excellent." King Alrik approached a door by the window I hadn't caught before. "Although, I should clarify, it's not my prophecy you'll be foretelling."

I frowned at him, my eyes bouncing from him to Sybil, but she seemed just as lost. He knocked twice on the door, and I was even more startled to find Brand stepping out of the room.

And Gods, he looked so handsome. He was much more mature than when I'd seen him at Prince Esben's wedding in The Northern Pizi five years ago. The shadow of stubble was growing along his jaw, and his hair looked like I could run my hands through it.

But I was pulled from my thoughts when he fully emerged with a young girl clinging to his arm, her head dipped while it frantically twitched between Sybil and me.

The girl's terror was palpable, and she held to Brand as if she could fold into him and herself, her shoulders hunched. Long, dark auburn hair hung down her petite frame, her pale skin stark against the deep maroon dress she wore.

"Great Karasi," King Alrik said, but I couldn't look at him as the whispers stirred again in my mind. This time, I waited for them to tell me their secrets. "This is my daughter, Princess Tyra Korbin."

"Daughter?" Sybil's head jerked away from Princess Tyra and to the king. "The rumors… I thought she died in childbirth?"

"You would think a demi-god of your caliber would be above rumors, Sybil." King Alrik chuckled, nodding at Brand.

He whispered something into his sister's ear, ushering her closer to me. As she inched forward, the whispers started to speak more clearly.

[Buried in the Dark…]

A solitary room. A young girl hunching over parchment. Ink-stained fingertips.

My fingers quivered at my sides, a heartbeat joining out of sync with my own. My vision of reality wavered as Tyra neared, and King Alrik's voice was muffled as he spoke.

"What I'm about to reveal to you both shall remain in secrecy. Few know the truth about my daughter, so if this begins to travel the kingdoms, I know only one of us in this room will be responsible."

"Please," Brand whispered to me, and I tried to make eye contact with him, but my head turned heavy, fogged like I'd drunk too much wine. "Don't hurt her."

I could only nod as my gaze slowly slid back to find Princess Tyra looking at me head-on, and I quietly gasped at the Mark in the middle of her forehead.

The Sirian Mark.

Dread washed over me at the thought of this poor girl being daughter to the Sirians' biggest threat to existence. I didn't want to see what Fate had planned for her if it meant having to watch her die by the hands of her father.

But then she blinked at me with those Korbin-blue eyes, and my vision went dark.

[The Dark shall rise…]

Sirians screamed. Darkness climbed over marble.

Slithering from her outstretched hands. Spreading like an infection.

In my corporeal body, I struggled to breathe, and I vaguely registered my knees giving out beneath me.

He whispered into her ear. She stood before a familiar castle.

Darkness concealed her. Darkness obeyed her.

Sleeping royalty choked. A kingdom crumbled.

I was no longer in control of my body, but I might've been crying.

Quill against parchment. Fate sealed in ink as black as night—

I choked as I slammed back into my body, a flash of bright white blinding me. It slowly faded as my heart raged in my chest, and I greedily gulped in air. As feeling returned, I found warm, strong arms holding me as they kneeled with me on the ground.

I expected to find my mother's eyes hovering over me, but instead, I found King Alrik's and Brand's. Their faces couldn't have looked more different.

Brand looked concerned, while King Alrik looked greedy.

A wave of familiarity rippled through me.

"You…" I cleared my throat, reluctantly inching out of Brand's embrace, but he immediately helped me up from the ground until my feet were steady. I nodded once at him as I wiped my sweaty palms on my dress, dragging my gaze to where King Alrik gripped Tyra's shoulders. "What is it you want to know?"

"Is her power permanent?" King Alrik asked, pushing Tyra forward, holding her at arm's length. The girl whimpered, her face twisting in panic. Brand moved toward her until King Alrik leveled him with a glare. "What *is* her power?"

I shut my eyes as the voice snuck into my mind.

[Darkness. The Abyss…]

"She's responsible for the Abyss within the Black

Avalanches," I said aloud, my voice flat and distant. "*The Herald of Darkness.*"

"Darkness?" King Alrik said at the same time Sybil muttered, "What?"

"*They will call her power Darkness,*" I told King Alrik, blinking. I slowly turned toward my mother, my voice returning to normal. "There are rumors that something lives within the Black Avalanches. The Magics in Heridy have spoken of it."

"Why didn't you tell me about this?" Sybil snarled as she closed in, grabbing my arm. Her eyes *actually* glowed then, alarmed.

"I didn't think—" I stopped short as Tyra whimpered again, slowly backing away as she stared at Sybil with wide, frightened eyes.

"You're frightening her," Brand whispered harshly at Sybil, his jaw clenched. "You don't want to—"

My vision pulsed at the edges as the same dark tendrils I saw in the prophecy started to crawl across the floor in every direction, a strange energy crackling in the air. My eyes blew wide as I realized this was the Darkness the voice spoke of—the power King Alrik wanted to know was permanent.

"You must breathe, Tyra," Brand gently urged, lifting and lowering his hands with his own breath. "Breathe, then will the power back."

Tyra kept her eyes locked onto her brother as she followed his breathing, her shoulders visibly relaxing with each moment that passed, and the Darkness stopped crawling across the floor. Once her breathing eased, the black, vine-like power slowly slithered back *into* her body.

"*The Darkness is permanent,*" I suddenly blurted, my voice monotonous again. I met King Alrik's gleaming eyes. "*She will end those you seek to destroy. She will be your weapon.*"

King Alrik looked upon Tyra like she was the world's riches, but the gaze had no depth. My heart ached at the pain in Brand's eyes as he watched his father and sister.

When I finally turned my gaze upon Sybil, my blood ran cold.

In all my life, Sybil never exhibited fear. There was occasionally concern, confusion, or even apprehension, but never fear.

She, too, looked at Tyra, but her skin blanched and face slackened, her hand clenched around her own throat in silent terror.

I sat beside Brand on the edge of the window, our feet dangling over the stone wall that dropped steeply stories below. All those below us—from knights to visiting folk—were miniscule and insignificant from this height.

The ledge was narrow, though, which left me pinned between the stone frame and Brand, the coolness pressing on my shoulder starkly contrasting to the warmth radiating from his thigh against mine. I kept my hands folded atop my skirt as one of his hands braced the frame. The other rested against my lower back, which burned through my dress.

It was supposedly there to steady me and prevent me from falling forward.

"You don't believe Tyra can be saved?" Brand asked, staring out over the expanse of the Etherean kingdom. "This Darkness is irreversible?"

I waited for the sense within me to answer, my voice taking on a level pitch, "*Yes. The damage has been done.*"

He closed his eyes in answer, pressing his lips together as he subtly nodded.

"You care for your sister," I concluded, not because I could feel that truth humming within my mind but because it was evident based on how he reacted to King Alrik's display and the prophecy I foretold.

Brand frowned, enhancing the stubble growing on the edges of his jawline. Those piercing eyes took on a slight glisten to them as he spoke softly, "Tyra has been alone for so long. I'm the only one of our siblings who has spent any time with her. She's been sequestered in her room for most of her life, only knowing our father and mother and her nursemaid. My father found out too late that I'd been sneaking into her room to spend time with her since she could barely walk.

"By that point, she'd grown an attachment to me." His smile dimmed, shadowed by nostalgia, bringing a sad tilt to it. "When you're the youngest of twelve boys, especially when most of them have grand, loud personalities, it's easy to fade into the shadows. You can get away with far more than others."

The Herald of Darkness clung to the only soul who showed her compassion. A farewell softened with hope.

"She will escape your father's clutches," I assured him, my hand slipping instinctively to his knee, squeezing gently. His head snapped to where my dark skin stood stark against his beige breeches, but I didn't remove it. "She'll endure quite a bit of suffering at his hands. He hopes to wield her as a weapon to achieve all he aspires for. And he will be successful with her by his side. He couldn't achieve it otherwise."

"And when she's finally free of him?" He lifted his eyes to mine, searching my face with wonder. "Will she find happiness?"

A cold hand slips into warmth. A first kiss seals a promise.

"She will know love and happiness before her time ends." I nearly choked on those words as that end flashed in my mind.

A reveal. A betrayal. A plea.

But that guiding voice said *no* with a finality I dared not challenge. Brand couldn't know how Tyra's end would come to her.

Whether he saw that I concealed the whole truth from him or felt Fate seal in time, he maintained eye contact as he nodded once in acceptance.

He startled me as his hand twitched at my lower back, hesitating before it trailed up my spine. It sent goosebumps across my skin, a rush of heat settling in my bones.

His hand crested over my shoulder, and his fingertips brushed the edges of my jawline. He followed where my chin came to a point, tucking his fingers under as he tilted my head back just enough so our faces aligned: eyes to eyes, nose to nose, lips to lips.

"There's not a day since Leif's wedding that I haven't thought of you," he whispers, his sweet breath fanning my skin. My eyes fluttered at the sensation inching its way into my chest, swirling.

"That was seven years ago, Brand," I managed, the corner of my lip ticking as I watched his eyes flicker across my face. "We've seen each other at your other brothers' weddings—"

"Except Sorin," Brand interrupted, drawing my face closer to him. "I was instructed to care for Tyra and couldn't attend. I was robbed of your intriguing beauty."

"Intriguing." I hummed, my eyes falling to his pink lips, which curved into a playful grin. "You find me intriguing?"

"Why, yes!" He gasped, as though to counter it was blasphemy. "Intriguing, startling, breathtaking…"

My breath caught in my throat as his nose brushed along my high cheekbone. He inhaled, the predatory ancestry within me awakening in a flare of fervor that settled low in my stomach.

His hand cupped the back of my head with his thumb still tucked under my chin. He whispered against my ear, the ember blazing. "Bewitching."

As he drew back, his lips dragged against my skin, his breath trailing with it. Our noses pressed side-to-side, but our lips still didn't touch, barely any space left between them.

"May I kiss you, *mi leiron?*" he asked, the name enchanting me.

My lily.

"Please," I begged, relishing the silence in my head.

Brand closed the small space between us, his lips gently caressing mine with a featherlight touch against my neck. The first kiss was brief, and I nearly followed him as he pulled back, his eyes heavy-lidded as he gazed down at me.

But I wasn't through with him.

It was my turn to initiate the kiss, and I didn't ask.

I reached for him, my hand wrapping around his wrist. I kept him in place as I laid my other on his thigh to push myself against him. His body shifted back, but only to steady us so we were away from the ledge.

We were feverish with the second kiss. He groaned against my lips as my tongue ran along his bottom lip, pleading for entrance. He obliged, his hands moving to gather me against him with a firm hold on my hips.

Gods, we were only teenagers, my mere sixteen to his fresh eighteen, but we kissed with urgency, like thieves fleeing with a crown that was never theirs.

That's what we were to one another, though; something precious that we knew would be ripped from one another at any moment's notice.

He was the youngest prince of a mighty kingdom, and I was one of the most powerful Magics to walk this world beside Sybil. I was the daughter of a demi-god, and he was the son of one of the most evil men our world had ever seen.

We didn't belong to each other, and that same voice inside me told me we never would, but I was covetous of him.

He was beautiful and kind, overflowing with compassion and curiosity.

I may have been a rarity among my kind, but so was Brand.

THE LAST ANDROMEDAN

825 A.V. | AGE: 18

I quietly knocked on Sybil's bedroom door, her soft mumblings carrying through the wood-paneled door. I listened until she stopped before trying again.

At the second knock, her voice silenced momentarily, and then it continued in a hushed tone.

She didn't scream for me to go, so I took that as permission to enter.

I clutched the bowl of soup in one hand as I twisted the doorknob, peering through the crack in case she threw something at me like she had the previous night when I entered after a beat of silence.

Lately, it had been a gamble with her.

Ever since she lost herself to Madness.

When Tyra revealed her Darkness to us two years ago, Sybil slowly descended into what I could only guess were her final moments. I never knew how old my mother was, but as a demi-god, I knew she was ancient. She sometimes spoke in great detail of historical events or uttered names of long-dead demi-gods with familiarity.

"Sybil," I said, interrupting her pacing by the

window. Her white hair was matted, the ends frayed and thinned from her constant tugging. "I brought you some dinner. Can we sit down?"

She jerked her head at me, her green eyes dull and distant.

She'd gone from being beautifully ageless to appearing middle-aged, with wrinkles framing her eyes, lips, and nose.

"Yes?" I urged, holding the bowl before me as I took a few hesitant steps. Her eyes frantically bounced from the bowl to me. Then, she squinted at me suspiciously. "It's only soup, Mother."

At the use of the title, she softened immediately, a faint smile bringing life to her sallow skin. She nodded softly, scurrying to the small table beneath the window.

I sighed in relief, walking around her bed to place the soup in front of her. I unhooked the napkin from the waist of my skirt, laying it across her lap where her nightgown bunched at her thighs. I frowned at how frail she looked, wondering if she ate the food I left her when she wouldn't let me in.

"The Abyss?" Sybil said suddenly, her eyes searching my face.

I shook my head, slowly lowering to the chair on the opposite side of the table, folding my hands in my lap. "It grows darker. It's as if the peaks swirl with black clouds."

"The mortals?" She sipped on the soup, frowning at the bowl before directing the glare at the spoon.

This is how it was with her over the last few

months—jilted conversations with minimal words. I wasn't sure what to make of it then, but I didn't question her or attempt to lie. Once again, it usually led to her lashing out.

"They still don't sense it." I smoothed my skirt, trying to adopt a tone of casual ease.

"But they're safe?" She kept her gaze on the bowl as she asked.

"Everyone is safe." I let *for now* stay silent so as not to panic her. "The Carraphims continue to call, but Fate will not let me see them to speak of what I know."

"Fate." Sybil stopped her spoon midway, eerily dragging her gaze to mine. "Dola."

"Is that who speaks to us, Mother?" I asked her. She'd never answered what or who exactly the voice was before, so I figured I would take advantage of her loose mind.

She shook her head vehemently. "No."

I pursed my lips, not willing to push my luck. She'd answered the question, even if it still didn't reveal what the voice was.

She lowered her spoon back into the soup, her hands falling limp over her stomach. I slowly reached toward the bowl and tapped the rim. "You can eat your soup, Mother—"

"I must go." She shot to her feet, the chair clattering behind her. I jolted at the abruptness. She paced in front of her empty fireplace, wringing her hands together as she spoke more than she had in months. "They require me to go. They are asking it of me."

"Who is asking you to go?" I clenched my hands tighter in my lap, uneasiness creeping under my skin. I summoned just the tips of my claws so they poked into the tops of my hands, but not enough to break skin.

"The Lyrans," she whispered softly, shaking her wild hair. "The Lyrans. The Gods."

[The Truth will be revealed.]

I let the claws break my skin.

"That name…" I tilted my head to the side. "You said *Lyrans?* What does that even mean?"

"Dola, Danica, Rod, Mother," she listed, counting on her fingers. "Lyrans. The Gods."

[The Gods mourn their children.]

I clenched my jaw as I closed my eyes, begging the voice to hush.

"The others can't be let out." She stopped suddenly, her back to me as she faced the fireplace. She dragged her hand across the empty mantel. "Ascension and endless dusk."

I steadied my breathing in hopes that my patience would follow suit. While most may have dismissed this as the ramblings of a sick, mad woman, I knew better.

Sybil was never just any woman. She was a demi-god, and a demi-god with the power of prophecy.

"There are too many powerful Beings." Sybil spun on her heel, finger already raised, accusing. "The powerful must be few for balance to remain."

At the same time, the voice whispered *Fate demands*

sacrifice, Sybil added, "There must be sacrifice."

"Powerful Beings," I repeated, trying to move past this mention of the Gods and the Lyran label she gave them. "Do you speak of Tyra and me? What sort of sacrifice must occur to restore balance?"

She lowered her finger to her side before slowly dragging her feet across the floor. She hovered beside me, squinting out the window toward the Black Avalanches. "I must go. I am the only one who can keep the Gods locked away."

"Are they in a prison?" I asked, but my voice grew quiet as her face morphed from her manic state to a serene, more peaceful expression. "Maybe it's time for bed."

"A bedtime story," Sybil said as I guided her to the edge of her bed. I threw back the covers and helped her underneath. When I went to leave, she grabbed my arm. "One last story."

I sighed as I stared at the ceiling, my shoulders deflating.

She told the same stories on repeat for a week now. I didn't have the energy to hear the tales of her childhood and what it'd been like to fly in her *drakon* form before the ability was torn away.

"Okay," I relented, sitting next to her feet. "One last story. This one time, okay?"

"I have loved few." She smiled faintly, reaching to brush a braided dread over my shoulder. Her hand cupped my cheek, and she tilted her head admiringly before uttering, "I always loved Mother. There was once a man, so long ago… I couldn't fathom losing him. You lose them all eventually."

The mention of the male had me wondering if she spoke of my father. Unease curled in my stomach as Brand slipped into my thoughts, but I shook it away.

"In all my existence, you, Piers, and Asteria are the only people I've loved so deeply. I believe it may be engraved on my soul."

I bit the inside of my cheek and forced a face of interest, trying to suppress the shock at her words. My heart thundered at the unfamiliar male name, filing it away for the future.

Sybil had never spoken of Asteria before, though. From my understanding, the last mythological tale of Asteria dated over two thousand years ago.

Which meant Sybil was around that age, possibly older.

"Long ago, there once lived two girls, the Brightest Star and the Cursed Child." Her hand slid from my cheek as she reclined against the headboard. "They were both so alone, first of their kinds, and they found solace in the connection… Cousins, of sorts, and yet they felt the kinship of sisterhood between them."

"And you lost her?" I whispered, awed by a new tale. How she spoke of herself and Asteria made sense, and I could see them both being the first demi-gods of their kind.

Sybil the first Magic demi-god, the Founder of the

House of Echidna.

Asteria the first Sirian demi-god.

Real tears rimmed Sybil's eyes, and my heart dropped. Grief washed over her as her shoulders tilted inward. She stared at her hands as she softly spoke, "Asteria never got the chance to be a mother. Her beloved died in a terrible battle against the Lyrans."

"A battle?" The only terrible battle I'd ever heard of was concerning the Etherean War, but that was only eight hundred years ago. "I still don't understand what the Lyrans are, Mother. I've never heard you or anyone use this term before."

"You never will." Sybil's head hitched up, her face stern. "And you will *not* repeat it, do you understand?"

With that, Sybil angrily yanked the edge of the blanket and tucked it under her chin as she nestled against her pillow. She twisted onto her side, facing the door so her back was to me.

I sighed for what felt like the hundredth time in the small moment I spent with her, shaking my head before I rose from the bed and journeyed to the door. But just as I turned the knob, Sybil called my name.

"Never believe the history you've been taught," she said quietly, her eyes locked onto me.

"You were the one who taught me history." I leaned against the doorknob, my other hand perched on my hip. "Are you saying you lied?"

Sybil blinked once, then shrugged. "It is not true, *mi fidi*. Not really. Not all of it."

The following morning, I went to wake Sybil to spend some time in the garden before winter fell, but her bed was empty. I scoured the house and the grounds our home occupied before riding into Heridy to ask if Sybil had been about. There was no sign of her in our town, nor in any other place she might have gone.

I spent the entire day walking in Heridy, roaming the cobblestone streets. I was about to journey to Aggelos Palace to see if she was consulting with the Carraphims when it hit me.

It wasn't a prophecy as much as it was just a knowing.

I stumbled against the nearest brick wall, my back slamming against the harsh surface. I sank to the ground as my heart clenched in my chest, and her soul wrapped itself around me.

Mi fidi.

I don't know where she went or how she did it, but Sybil left this world. I didn't expect to cry for her; our relationship had always been rather complicated.

Tears soaked my cheeks as they silently fell from my eyes. I closed them and pleaded with the sixth sense that allowed me to hear the voice, hoping it would answer me.

A soft, ethereal, yet distant voice snuck into the far corners of my soul. "She rests now, young drakon."

"Tell her I said goodbye," I spoke aloud, and a place

deep within my body warmed—somewhere unreachable, buried within.

Goodbye.

The Turning Point

826 A.V. | Age: 19

After Sybil left this plane, I decided to see the world free of my mother's constraints. I learned I could use my gifts to provide a living for myself, and that nobility preferred house calls for the sake of discretion. No folk from high status during the turbulent times of King Alrik Korbin wanted to test their relationship with him by traveling to Eldamain just to see the Great Karasi.

By this time, I learned Fate had something to do with the inklings I received to go to a specific country. It wasn't the usual whisper or flashes of images in my head, but a quiet and insistent knowing that pulled at my sternum.

After visiting with Mariande's king and queen—who were presently the only kingdom outright denying King Alrik a marriage contract—I knew I had to go to Etherea next. Part of it was that pull from Fate, but the rest came from the thrill of possibly seeing Brand again.

Despite the numerous times I visited Rigel's Keep for a wedding or a prophecy for Alrik, I never had the opportunity to see Eryphus, the capital of Etherea. I found an open inn and spent a few days exploring the city. I told Brand I was in town and that if he required a reading, I would be more than happy to provide one at a reduced price.

I half-expected him not to respond since it had been three years since we kissed. But alas, he answered that he would like to meet at the inn I was staying at the following day before nightfall, that there was something he wished to discuss.

Which is how I found myself in Etherea the day the world changed forever.

I was waiting in the tavern below the inn when a Sirian man came stumbling in, his face gaunt.

"The Arcane Island," he whispered to all present, gasping for air, "has fallen."

Outrage and mayhem exploded in a flurry of shouts, screams, and tears. I lurched from my seat only to feel a wave of dizziness overcome me. I steadied my hand against the table, the other clutching my forehead as pain pulsed from temple to temple.

[The True Prophecy,] the voice hissed in the back of my head. *[The True Path.]*

"Karasi?" Turquoise eyes appeared in my vision, shadowed by a hood. Rough hands caught my shoulders, then cradled my face. "Are you alright?"

"Brand," I said, although it was a sigh of relief and contentment as the voices vanished at his touch. A small smile twitched at the corners of his lips. "What's happening? They said the Arcane—"

"Are you staying here?" He asked, glancing over his shoulder. I nodded, and he slipped his hand into mine. "Let's go somewhere private. I can explain."

I frowned at him but squeezed his hand, guiding him through the crowds of people crying and screaming, asking if anyone knew of survivors. We finally slipped into the stairwell where the sound tapered off the higher we climbed.

"This room here," I said as I ducked around a corner to a concealed door, shuffling in my pockets for the key. Out of the corner of my eye, I caught Brand lowering his hood and forgot what I was supposed to be doing.

The young adult male I kissed three years ago was no longer that. His hair stayed the same length, perfectly curling at the edges of his face, but that face had grown stronger. His features squared off, his pink lips peeking out from the short, dark brown beard.

My hand reached up of its own accord, gently skimming his jaw as I stared in slight awe at seeing him again. Those kind eyes softened further as he gently covered my hand with his own, trapping it against his neck.

"Hello, *mi leiron*," he whispered, his words encasing me in a familiar embrace.

I hadn't realized how much I yearned for someone familiar.

I shook myself out of my stupor and unlocked the door, ushering him inside and checking the hall to ensure no one saw us slip away. I stepped in after him, shutting and locking the door again as he paced back and forth in the small space.

"Brand," I drawled quietly, "what's happened?"

He stopped, slowly dragging his eyes to mine. My heart cracked at the pure despair, and I couldn't stop myself. I closed the distance between us and pulled him into a hug, looping my arms around his neck. He instantly melted into my arms, circling his own around my waist.

"It was your father and Tyra, wasn't it?" I whispered against his ear, and his grip tightened. "I think I saw this."

When I read Tyra's prophecy, I saw the Sirian island decimated, and she stood before them with tendrils of Darkness shrouding her and the unmoving bodies.

"I think you did, too," he agreed, stepping back. "I didn't want this for her. I never wanted him to do this, to force her to use that power for nefarious purposes."

I sighed heavily, pressing my lips together. I wanted to comfort him but didn't know what to say. The voice appearing after the man announced the fall of the Arcane Island to the tavern only confirmed it.

King Alrik wanted to get rid of the Sirians and used his daughter to do it.

"I knew my father disliked the Sirians, but I didn't think he would go this far," Brand muttered, shaking his head. "I must admit, it wasn't his fault he was born without the Sirian Mark while my aunt and uncle both inherited it. His parents didn't help by insinuating something was wrong with him for lacking it.

"But to spend his life punishing an entire race of Beings? To massacre a majority of them, take their thrones by placing my brothers on them?"

"That has been his motivation?" I curled my lip, recoiling. "Over something so... miniscule?"

"To him, it was never miniscule." Brand turned sideways, staring at the small fireplace. "It was his entire existence, his legacy.

[Crows will answer the call.]

I clenched my fists, breathing in through my nose. Brand was lost in thought, either not catching my small moment or simply not acknowledging it.

"Everything has permanently changed, now, hasn't it?" Brand muttered, running a hand through his hair. "What Tyra has done, what my father has done... The Sirians will never be the same."

"*The world will never be the same.*" I tried to add more inflection with my voice, but I swore under my breath at the even tone it maintained. I wanted to be there for him and promise everything would be alright...

But I couldn't.

I was physically incapable of doing so. It was like someone had crushed my voice in their grasp, cutting me off.

"I don't want to push you." Brand twisted on his heel and rushed upon me. I stepped back, but he grabbed my face in his hands, desperation in his gaze. "I refuse to be like the others. I won't ask for your prophecies. I won't force these words from you. I can't stand to see you silent while your eyes plead for words you are forbidden to speak.

"I can see you want to comfort me," he whispered, pressing our foreheads together. I grabbed his wrists, tears burning my eyes as I shut them against his touch. "But it's not your responsibility. You're my friend, *mi leiron*, and being here in whatever way you can is more than enough. The fact that you're here at all is a blessing from the Gods."

"I wish to be more for you." My voice was gentle and soft, hesitant at my admission. "I fear we, too, will never be the same."

"I'm not naive." Brand sighed, brushing my braids over my shoulder and tracing what I presumed was a vein down the side of my neck. "You are the daughter of a Magic demi-god, and I'm only a mortal man. If our lifespans don't separate us, our circumstances surely do."

"So, I'll remain a friend to you." I nodded, and yet we didn't put space between us.

Instead, he took another step into me, our chests brushing, and my breath hitched. My hands splayed across his upper abdomen, my fingers tracing a dip I found beneath his tunic.

"Oh, no." Brand's lips twitched at the corner as they brushed mine, a breathy groan fluttering from me. "You will always be *mi leiron*, no matter what your Fate has in store for the both of us."

I flung myself into his arms, wrapping my arms around his neck as our lips crashed vehemently. He pulled my body flush against him, arching my back as he curved over me and snaked his arms around my waist. He braced a hand between my shoulder blades, his palm flat and fingers splayed across my spine.

The way his lips moved against mine lit something within me, coaxing it from me and silencing the voice, erasing any thoughts that weren't mine from my mind. I tangled my hands in the hair at his neck, twisting my fingers through the silky strands. I rolled my hips, eliciting a deep moan from him that slipped between my lips and dove straight to my core.

"Karasi," he mumbled, both of us panting, "I don't want to—"

"Don't mistake your name for me with my identity." I stepped back from him as I slowly untied the strings of my dress. His eyes tracked every movement, darkening to a hue familiar to me but not familiar on Brand. "You forget I'm far from innocent and virtuous. I am no lady, no princess—just a wild thing that can't be tamed."

I slid my dress over my head, casting it somewhere to the side of the room, only to find Brand an inch before me, roughly clasping my chin between his fingers. I gasped, but heat gathered instantly between my legs at the ravenous gleam in his gaze.

"In this room, in this bed—" he paused to gaze down at my naked body, following his hand back up my torso until he cupped my breast in his hand. He pinched my nipple, and I moaned as I fisted his tunic in my hands. "*I will tame you.*"

The sudden aggression sent a thrill through me. I was so used to others doing as I demanded for the sheer fact they thought me a Goddess, a powerful Being to fear or revere. The realization that this man was more than willing to dominate had me buzzing in anticipation.

"Then command me, *Prince*," I hissed, retreating to the bed without taking my eyes off him. A smirk played at the corners of his lips as I lowered to the thin mattress, reclining back on my hands so I was fully exposed to him, my legs spread open. "Do with me as you please."

As quickly as the mortal man could, he removed his tunic and breeches. When he stepped before me, he immediately knelt at the edge of the bed, his hands gripping my calves. He dragged me to the edge of the bed and spread my legs even wider, kissing a path up my inner thigh.

"I wish to know how Magic *tastes*." His breath was cool against me, and his fingers spread my lips. Eyes on one another, he dragged his tongue from bottom to top.

I threw my head back as I moaned, still angled so that I could look back down as I wished while he continued to rub his tongue along my entrance. Occasionally, his tongue flicked at the top of my clit, circling that bundle of nerves, followed by his lips that wrapped around and sucked.

It wasn't until he plunged two fingers in that I cried out, dripping onto the sheets below. He wasted no time, those fingers moving swiftly as he curled them into me repeatedly. I panted against the rising pleasure spiraling tighter within me as my walls clamped around his fingers.

"I want you to come for me, *mi leiron*," Brand muttered, replacing his lips on that bud with his thumb, circling over the sensitive skin. "I want you soaked when I fill you."

His filthy words wrapped around me, sending me over the edge as release found me. It crashed into my body, and my arms quivered with the effort to hold myself up. Brand was relentless as I continued to pulse, calling his name with every spark of ecstasy.

He watched his fingers as he dragged them from me, and my entire existence hung on him as he drew those same fingers between his lips. My mouth dried at the sight of him, and he smirked.

"Get on your hands and knees," his voice rumbled with the demand.

I knew what he was asking. My stomach twisted with greedy anticipation as I flipped over on the bed, propping myself on all fours and baring myself to him as I arched my back.

I'm convinced to this day that mortal man *growled* at the sight. "Good girl."

The mattress dipped behind me as he put his knees on the insides of mine. I whimpered softly as he pushed against them to spread my legs wider. He slid his cock along my entrance as his other hand drew up the small of my back and deepened the arch with a gentle pressure, so in contrast to how this had gone thus far.

"I want to be deep inside you," he whispered, his

breath brushing the back of my neck as he placed a kiss there. He left another on my shoulder as his hips shifted, his cock suddenly sliding into me. I groaned at the feel of him, relishing in the throb of his cock inside me. "You are intoxicating."

He stayed still for a moment as he moved his hand up my back and over my shoulder to grip the front of my throat. He pulled back at the same time he sunk deeper into me, stars flashing across my vision as I cried out.

"Do you feel how hard I am for you?" he grumbled, tightening his grip on my throat. He rocked his hips back only to slam himself as deep as before. He moved slowly back again, repeating the movement.

It was torture. I wanted him to lose himself, every inch of him grinding within me.

"Gods, Brand." I whipped my head over my shoulder, staring into those bright eyes the best I could as I pleaded, "Fuck me."

"How hard do you want it?" He goaded, that smirk playing on his lips.

"Make me forget," was all I said.

He faltered momentarily; the Brand I was so used to flickered across his face as his forehead twitched. He quickly recovered as he bent to my ear, pinching it between his teeth as he answered, "Happily."

From there, Brand's pace was frenzied but rhythmic, his hips slamming into me with a recklessness that sang to my soul. Our moans chased one another around the room, accompanied by our bodies crashing into each other.

His movements became jerked as my walls gripped him tighter, the head of his cock pressing into nerves that sent heat licking across my skin. When he thrust into me at an angle, I tipped over the edge and chased yet another orgasm while he followed behind me, filling me.

We both breathed heavily as we fell to the mattress side-by-side, laying on our backs and staring up at the ceiling.

"Do you know—" he paused, panting as he turned his head to look at me. I met his glowing eyes. "Do you know how long I have fantasized about that moment?"

I raised an eyebrow as I twisted on my side, propping myself on my elbow. I extended a sharp claw. He watched in fascination as I gently pressed it just above the base of his throbbing cock, following the path of hair north until I was at his sternum.

"You have fantasized about bedding me?" I inquired, marveling at the goosebumps that lined his peach skin.

He wrapped his hand around mine, halting my movements as he stared at me. "I have dreamed about what your wet cunt would feel like wrapped around me. It's been borderline obsessive."

I found myself heating again, smirking as I said, "Such filthy words for such a beautiful man."

"Only for you, *mi leiron*," he whispered, brushing his lips along my knuckles, again that kinder version of him now on display. "Your wish is my command."

"So, if I wanted that again?" I asked, leaning against

his chest as I hoisted my leg over him to straddle him. I rubbed myself against his cock, smiling.

He groaned, his body jerking at the sensitivity still lingering. "I would willingly oblige."

"But if I wanted passionate, soul-shattering love making?" I positioned my entrance just above his cock, taunting. "What would you say then, my prince?"

With a quick jerk of his hips, he seated himself within me again, drawing me down so he was fully enveloped in me. I rolled my eyes, still marveling at the fullness of him within me.

Brand sat up, delicately kissing the column of my throat, and muttered against it, "Then I would show you just how thoroughly you have ensnared me."

As we came together for the second time that evening, I found Brand could be both the courteous, affectionate friend he was in daylight and the demanding, domineering man.

I also found both versions could chase away the visions that inhabited my mind, filling me so there was no room for them or the voice that followed.

And I wondered if Fate found sick pleasure in punishing me with a man made *for* me, knowing I could never truly have him.

The Longest Night

829 A.V. | Age: 22

The wedding of Princess Tyra Korbin tasted like ash and blood, for that is what preceded these otherwise festive events.

Long before it occurred, I knew what would happen under the guiding hands of King Alrik. The true devastation still rippled across our world, and Alrik stood victorious amongst the wreckage.

He got everything he could've ever wanted, and all I could ever do was sit back and watch it unfold, lurking in the shadows, taking quiet action while the loudest voices claimed victory.

I wondered whether something occurred long ago that led to the Gods' distaste of Magics and Sirians. Maybe Sybil even knew.

Only three years after the fall of the Arcane Island and the Sirian Academy, tragedy struck the Sirian community again. Just six months ago, the royal family of Eldamain—the Carraphims—were brutally murdered by *someone* wielding this Darkness the world whispered of. King Alrik immediately called for retribution while

Heridy crumpled under the chaos.

The Council of Eldamain consisted of elderly men without the energy or desire to find some long-distant Carraphim to claim the throne. Not only would it have required time to find this hypothetical heir, but if they were to find such an individual, they would also need to train them to be a leader for an entire country. Without an heir, they knew the likelihood of tracing one meant stretching their fingers across every facet of this world.

Lucky for them, The Clips intervened, offering their help to temporarily own the territory of Eldamain until such an heir could be found. I wasn't privy to all the specifics of the agreement, and even my sources who usually knew were silent since the collapse of Eldamain's throne.

Suddenly, a few months after the Council of Eldamain signed the treaty with The Clips, Princess Tyra's engagement to the Crown Prince of The Clips, Arden Bronte, was announced.

It was all rather suspicious to me, but who was I?

The Great Karasi, the most powerful Magic on Aveesh, a woman with immense prophetic power.

No one asked if I saw this coming. Not that they could have asked me before the events unfolded. Fate wouldn't allow it. But, if anyone were to ask now, I could speak of all I knew regarding how this wedding came to be.

But King Alrik got everything he wanted, and the world wanted to move on.

Besides, according to someone somewhere, Alrik's siblings were the culprits behind the destruction of the Carraphims. No one questioned burning them at the stake, not even when people wondered how the siblings did it when they wielded the Light—not the Darkness.

"Sulking in the shadows was your mother's favorite pastime," a deep voice chided low, chuckling before they continued, "Am I to believe you are following in her stead?"

"Sir Michael." I peered from the corner of my eyes, dipping the lip of my champagne flute toward the male. "I fear, whether or not I wish to follow in her stead, that is what the future will hold for me."

"Something you've seen?" He gave me a dry look, sipping his drink. "Or is that cynicism? You're far too young to be pessimistic yet. A mere child in her early twenties?"

"Child." I snorted, downing what remained of my champagne and placing the empty glass on a passing tray. "As we attend the wedding of a nineteen-year-old princess."

"In her world, that's the proper age to marry," Sir Michael said simply, shrugging. "But in your world, I anticipate you still have a long time to go."

My body locked up, and just for a breath, I questioned if the cinched bodice of my dress was too tight. I inhaled around the stiffness in my chest. "You know nothing of my world."

"You would be surprised, child." I turned to him with

that, watching a different kind of darkness flicker across his features. "I know far more about your world than you may even know."

"Enlighten me, Sir Michael." I grabbed my skirts in both hands, standing fully flush before him. I had no patience for games with royals, even if Sir Michael was only an employee of the Korbin family. He also happened to be one of the few people Brand ever talked about respectfully. "What could you possibly know of my world that I don't? Do you foresee the future only to watch its horrors play out in silence? Do you know what it's like to form relationships only to know you will outlive every last one of them?"

I took a menacing step toward him so there were just inches between where his shoulder pointed at me and my rising chest. I narrowed my eyes at him, curling a lip. "What do *you* know of my world, Sir Michael?"

"There will come a time, Karasi, when you will need my assistance," Sir Michael explained, his face a mask of stoicism. "When the time comes, you know where to find me. Until then, I hope you enjoy the festivities. I fear this may be one of the last where Sirians and Magics can coexist amongst the mortals for quite some time."

With that, Sir Michael bowed slightly before journeying to the side of the room where Princess Tyra stood with her new husband.

While I wanted a moment to process the interaction, I knew that wouldn't happen tonight. Not when I locked eyes with Tyra from across the room.

She wanted my attention.

I took a deep, steadying breath before calling my inner Sybil forward, throwing my shoulders back and straightening my spine. I crossed the ballroom entirely aware of all the gazes lingering as my long, black, velvet train dragged behind me, pearls and diamonds expertly woven to mimic the silver flames once wielded by the long-lost *drakons* that my lineage reigned from.

A reminder to the mortals of what loomed on either side of them, both past and future.

"I believe congratulations are in order, Your Highness," I said in greeting, curtseying before Prince Arden and Tyra. "It was a lovely ceremony, and dare I say, you two truly look like you're in love."

"It may have been a political match," Arden said quietly, his eyes lingering on his blushing bride, "but we have found a friendship with one another, and love has grown fast."

To my surprise, Tyra *smiled*, and I remembered seeing this very moment when I first met the princess. I kept my grin, even if it had tightened with foreknowledge.

Her smile wouldn't last long.

"Might I have a word with my old *friend*?" Tyra asked Arden, squeezing his bicep. The word sounded so foreign on her lips, and I raised an eyebrow. "It's been many years since we've had the chance to catch up."

Arden eyed her suspiciously, but there was no malice behind it. Instead, he nodded once before pulling her into him for a quick kiss on her temple. A soft blush rose to her cheeks as she smiled, but then she turned to me, and all amusement dropped from her face.

Tyra ushered me toward the hallway outside the ballroom, and I followed in step beside her.

I watched her as we walked because this version of Tyra felt familiar and less jarring. It wasn't an understatement that she came alive around Arden, life and light in her face so startlingly drastic compared to how I knew her. None of this was an act, but entirely genuine.

It spoke volumes that, outside of Arden, Tyra never knew happiness.

"Please," she urged, pausing in front of a door where a guard already stood. I warily glanced between the two, but she nodded once before following after me.

The guard shut the door behind us, and Tyra locked it from the inside. I shot her a skeptical glare, but she just pursed her lips. I took a moment to absorb the study, but it appeared to be one of those rooms where royals and wealthy individuals used to accept guests.

"I remember the day I met you quite clearly," Tyra began, pacing around the length of the room with slow, methodical steps. She trailed her finger along the wall, her face lost in thought. "Father asked you to confirm if my powers were permanent."

"If you wish for me to confirm again, Tyra," I slowly lowered myself to the sofa in the room and lounged back, draping my arm over the back, "there has been no change—"

"But you also foresaw my fate that day," Tyra interjected, and my foot ceased bouncing. She must have sensed my unease. She turned her head with a predatory glint in her eye. "My entire life, all I could do was watch and listen and observe."

"I understand that more than you know."

Observe and remain silent.

"Brand tells me Fate allows you to utter prophecies, but there are many times you must omit pieces so as not to change the desired outcome," Tyra continued, her hands clasping before her. She strolled across the room at the same pace until she stopped before me. "Are you allowed to speak my prophecy?"

[Fate is sealed, but the Harbinger must ask.]

I blinked at her, and that was enough of an answer for her.

"What is my prophecy, Great Karasi?" Tyra said, her voice even. She took a deep breath, as though already coming to terms with something I had yet to utter. "What is my future?"

This was a different urge than I had ever experienced. I knew her future, but I didn't want to tell her.

This time, though, Fate *required* me to, and my voice came out in the monotone level I was accustomed to.

"*You will be Queen*," I said, the words pouring out of me. "*You will bear three children, but you will not see them beyond adolescence. There will come a time when the Truth will be revealed, and you will die by the hands of the one you love most in this world.*"

Tyra didn't show any emotion. Her eyes moistened, but no tears were shed. She nodded once in acceptance, flattening her hands along the front of her wedding dress.

I was cynical, but I wasn't evil. This was her wedding day, and she *was* happy.

"Tyra," I said, and I made to stand. She held up her hand. "You should be relishing in your happiness. You look truly radiant, and I believe you deserve happiness, no matter what your… No matter what."

In response, Tyra offered a sheepish grin, shutting her eyes and shaking her head. "You're very kind, and I see what my brother enjoys about you. Unfortunately, I knew Fate would come for me. I have done monstrous things, and no matter the reason behind them or the motivations, I still committed atrocities against innocent people. I deserve my fate. Now knowing what I do about my time left on this plane…

"I will cherish the years left of my life with my husband." She glanced momentarily over my shoulder, some of the light I'd seen in her with Prince Arden flickering back. "Thank you for your time and your kindness, Great Karasi. I believe there is another that wishes to see into his future."

I snapped my head over my shoulder, quickly rising from the couch.

"I'll leave you," Tyra whispered, but I was transfixed.

Brand leaned against the wall with his arms crossed over his chest, his head lowered. He looked up at me through those thick lashes, his jacket discarded over a chair in the corner of the room. His tunic stretched across his chest, the ties at the collar undone to reveal a patch of his chest, his pants clinging perfectly around his legs.

"In any other world…" Brand began, pushing himself off the wall. His eyes dragged down the length of my body as I stood frozen, leaving a trail of fire on every inch they perused. "I would've claimed you on that dance floor the moment I saw you. You are ravishing, *mi leiron*."

That nickname never ceased to melt every facet of my being. It was as if he planted a seed within my chest, and with each utterance of that word, it bloomed anew every time.

"You would not have survived such an endeavor," I hummed, my head trailing him as he circled me, still inspecting. He curled around my right, and I called forward my claws, gently dragging one down the side of his face and neck. His eyes darkened. "I would've eaten you alive."

"I would've let you," he countered, his fingers digging into my waist as he hauled me to his chest. I gasped at the sudden movement, but it morphed into a low moan as he peppered soft kisses along my neck. "Only after you let me have just one taste."

"Filthy tongue," I chided, chuckling as my stomach warmed. I slid my hands up his chest and around his neck. Wrapping my fingers into his hair, I pulled back to look him in the eye. "Show me what else it can do."

We both moved simultaneously, lips crashing

together in a violent, desperate need to be closer to one another. The voices went quiet immediately, and I couldn't help but groan into his mouth.

His hands went to work on the clasps of my dress, frantically pulling them apart as I worked on the strings of his tunic. When my bare back was exposed, his smooth hands laid flat against my skin, his warmth seeping into my bones. I ached to feel the heat of his body against mine, submerging me in the serenity of him.

Brand stepped back long enough for both of us to discard our clothes. I shimmied out of my dress, and when I stood, we faced one another bare in the middle of the room.

We were hungry for each other's touch, the feel of our bodies together. We fell to the floor in a tangle of limbs, and I wanted nothing more than to lose myself in Brand.

I whimpered desperately when he slammed my wrists down on either side of my head, lowering his body and trapping me between him and the rug beneath. A sly grin pulled at the corners of his lips. "It seems you may be at my mercy."

He knocked his knees against mine, spreading my legs wider, and then he sank deep into me. We echoed each other at the connection, and I clenched around him as he filled me. He sighed in pleasure as he jerked his hips, hitting a spot that sent a euphoric sensation through my body. He moved again, repeating the movement, and I wanted so much more.

I locked my ankles behind his back as he rocked into me, granting him access to depths only he could reach. Stars danced across my vision as he fucked me hard and fast, our moans filling the space. My walls tightened with the coil inside me, my hips rolling to urge him toward the spot I knew would send me over the edge.

Instead, he slowed, only inserting himself a few inches before drawing back, teasing at the edge of nerves. I groaned in frustration, my hands flexing for purchase, but he still pinned me down.

"Brand," I whined, arching my back, but he slowed more. I clenched around him, my mind reeling at how close we both were. "Brand, I swear to the Gods—"

"I told you to beg for it," he muttered against my ear, chills racing down my arms, my cunt throbbing.

I whimpered again, twitching my hips only for him to counter it with a smaller movement. "Please, Brand."

"Please what?" He asked, and I heard the smile in his voice.

"Please, let me come," I finally said, my voice desperate.

"That's my girl," he praised, then thrust into me, seating himself entirely, and the coil snapped.

Brand quickly twitched his hips in shallow thrusts to draw out the orgasm, my vision shattering as I came undone beneath him, crying out his name at the overwhelming pleasure that raced through me. He followed shortly after, burying his face in my neck as he finished.

After a moment, he rolled to the floor beside me, and I curled into him with a content sigh.

I relaxed against Brand's chest, his arms and legs creating a cage around me. My head lolled back against his shoulder, and his fingers traced up and down my arm as he pressed his cheek against the side of my head.

"We have only ever been honest with one another," Brand whispered, and my chest bristled. There was no way this conversation was about to be a pleasant one. "We've known our love is forbidden, and we have always cursed the Gods for allowing us to meet, only to one day rip us from one another."

"I love the way you speak to me, your duality of gentleness and depravity," I said, staring at the curtains drawn across the far window, "but I wish you wouldn't pepper me with beautiful words right now."

"I'm to marry Prince Arden's sister, Princess Clarissa," Brand admitted, and my heart clenched. "Tyra wanted me out of Etherea and out from under our father's influence. She had Prince Arden organize the arrangement to help me. I'm to be Lord of Cerelia alongside Clarissa."

I knew this day would come.

There was never a future for Brand and I for more reasons than one, and even more now with how the world was about to change. Despite being the youngest of twelve sons, he was still a prince, and nothing could change that. I may have been all-powerful and desired, but I was still a *Magic*.

Our future would've been brief if there had been one.

"Say something, Karasi." Brand turned me in his arms, forcing me to look at his face. However, I kept my own neutral, like when I foretold a prophecy. "Don't shut me out in these last moments with you. Don't minimize the decade of friendship and the love between us to silent farewells."

I wanted to curse him for using that word again.

Love.

Because that was what broke me.

I knew the moment I left this room, and we parted ways, I would never be the same. Whatever humanity I held onto would go with him in his iron grasp, and I would be left to put together what was left behind, just like when Sybil left.

A tear streaked down my face, and he quickly brushed it away as his own tears gathered. He caressed my cheek, and I leaned into his embrace, enjoying the moments of silence in my head I always had when he was around.

I didn't know if I would ever be able to find someone again that made the voice of Fate silent like he did.

"What would you have me say?" I whispered, staring up into those bright turquoise eyes. "Would you wish for me to beg you to deny the betrothal? To run away with me across the world? I'm not foolish, nor am I naive, Brand. You love your sister. You wouldn't leave her—not like this.

"You're also a Korbin. There's no escaping that name, and there are far too many recognizable qualities about us. We would never be safe."

"Mar my skin," he pleaded, adjusting his position to grip the back of my neck. "Scar me so that I'm unrecognizable. We can retreat to wherever we want. The island is empty, and we could live together there."

"Until you die." He flinched at those words as if it were something he hadn't considered. "I don't know how long, Brand, but I will outlive all who I love. I will soon stop aging for a long time to come."

"As your mother did?" He asked, frowning as he traced where wrinkles might someday form on my face, but not for centuries. "You'll look young forever?"

"I'll look young for a very long time." My voice was soft, my vision blurring. "You will age and wither, and I will look no different from how I do now."

I brushed a stray curl from his face, my fingers playing with the edges. He shut his eyes, pulling me closer to him. I laid my head on his chest, listening to his steady heart that beat in sync with mine.

"I do love you, Karasi," Brand whispered, and my tears fell onto his chest. I pressed my lips together, swallowing a sob. "You're the strongest person I know. Don't let the world harden you. You're not your mother, nor will you ever be. I know someday you will be a fine mother. I don't need a prophecy to know that."

I didn't have the heart to tell him I had no desire to be a mother, nor did I believe I even could.

I also couldn't lie to him. We were built on honesty.

"I love you," I whispered, inhaling a quivering breath.

"You're the only good I've ever known, Brand. It's with you that I know goodness exists in the world, and I greedily held onto you as long as I could."

I held onto him just a little longer for the remainder of the night, even after the wedding ended. When most of the guests had parted, we snuck out to my carriage and journeyed to the inn I rented within Cerelia. We continued our night together in that room until the sun leaked through the windows.

Then, he reluctantly left me, his hand lingering in mine until the distance separated us, and I was left alone once again.

The Unbroken Bond

836 A.V. | Age: 29

News traveled fast in Aveesh when it involved the Korbins but never fast enough when it mattered most.

As I predicted, the Crown Prince of The Clips became King only a year after his wedding, making Princess Tyra a queen. But nearly seven years after her wedding and three children later, Tyra's husband found out she was a Dark Sirian and had her executed for what they deemed crimes against the world. They burned her at the stake, just as they had her aunt and uncle, since it was finally revealed she was supposedly in an alliance with them the entire time to take down the Sirians.

I lost a lot of my faith in humanity that day. So very few knew the truth about Tyra and the Darkness, and I could never shake the image of the poor, scared young girl in the middle of the throne room. Fate handed her a cruel end, and I didn't know the reason then. Even later in life, I still didn't understand why it had to be her.

The moment I heard about her death, though, I knew what I had to do, consequences be damned. First and foremost, we'd always been friends, and he deserved someone who understood the truth about Tyra. He had loved her more than anything in the world.

I slipped my hood off my head, studying the waiting room of the Lord of Cerelia. My attention slid over the intricate, warm wallpaper spread across the walls. Gold designs swirled atop the beige color, glistening in the sunlight sneaking in from the hazy day outside. The plush furniture was a deep maroon, and I dragged my hand along the stitching of a chair the same color.

A faint smile tugged at my lips.

Some Korbin traditions just couldn't be shaken.

"Well, let me see you," a deep, familiar voice rumbled, rattling my chest. I stiffened, my grip wrapping around the back of the chair. "Do you look just as you did the night we last saw each other?"

I inhaled slowly, turning with a practiced grin, but it slipped the moment our eyes locked across the room.

Seven years had passed, and while he teased me about my final parting words, Brand Korbin had barely aged himself.

Of course, he had the typical signs of aging for a man in his early thirties, but there was no receding hairline, no gray strands of hair, just faint wrinkles forming at the corners of his mouth and edges of his eyes.

The evidence of years spent smiling.

While my heart warmed for him, it broke for me because I would've given the world to be the cause of those smiles.

"Gods, you weren't teasing that night." Brand's hands unlocked behind his back as they fell to his side. He stepped forward once but went no further. "I suppose you're here because—"

"I'm so sorry, Brand," I said quietly, because I refused to use his Lordship's title. "I understand if you're angry with me—"

He flinched as if I'd slapped him. "Why would I ever be angry with you?"

I held my head high, my back straightening. "I foresaw this, yet I didn't tell you. You're more than aware your sister came to me the night of her wedding—"

"Karasi," Brand interrupted, rushing upon me and gripping my shoulders. At this proximity, I caught a few silver pieces at his hairline blinking in the sun, but I was more overwhelmed by the warmth radiating from him and the silence in my mind. "I know of your gifts. I know the limitations. I could never be angry at you for something beyond your control, *mi leiron*."

My lily.

And yet, I was in his and his wife's home, and he was gripping my shoulders with the passion we left behind us.

I cleared my throat, inching backward to put much-needed space between us. He frowned, tilting his head.

"Very well." I nodded tightly, and he raised an amused eyebrow at me. "I came here to extend my condolences and to let you know I wished Tyra a happier life. I know she achieved that in her last years, and I hope you two had a relationship not shackled by your father."

Brand's face softened; the ghost of a grin tugged at something buried deep. "Tyra and I were close in her final days. We spent many dinners together with King Arden and her children. I would've given years off my life to spend more time with her, but my father and Tyra were on borrowed time for far too long. She had her destiny, and it pains me."

His voice cracked at the end, tears glinting at the corners of his eyes. I stepped forward to comfort him but then remembered it wasn't my job to do so any longer.

And that was when I truly began to question why I came here in the first place. A simple letter would have sufficed. There was no need for me to have shown up unannounced.

"I should be going," I said quickly, moving toward the door, but Brand stepped in my path.

"*Mi leiron,*" he said gently, and my agitation bubbled over.

I clenched my jaw. "I can't belong to you while you belong to another, Brand. That's not fair."

"I told you long ago I would always belong to you." Brand wrapped his hand around my wrist, raising it between us. "And you'll always be *mi leiron,* even when you no longer wish to be."

"Adultery is beneath you," I snapped, wrenching my wrist out of his grasp. "Don't tell me you have stooped so low in your title and position to…"

The intensity of his gaze faded to something more profound and agonized as his shoulders hunched.

What I saw wasn't remorse. It was grief.

"Brand," I whispered, and it was my turn to take his hand in mine. "Where's Lady Clarissa?"

Reality crashed into me. I'd been so focused on Brand that I forgot this was the home of a lady and lord. It was the lady's duty to greet both expected and unexpected guests. Even though our friendship transcended the standard between Magic and mortal, it was still common courtesy and decorum for her to greet me while we awaited her husband.

"She passed away four years ago." Brand's voice was hoarse. He gazed down at where our hands were interlocked. "She passed giving birth to our daughter."

Our daughter.

A quick image flashed in my mind of a girl with raven black hair, gold eyes, and a Sirian Mark, the one plaguing my dreams as of late.

"It appears I need to extend my deepest condolences a second time," I whispered, sighing. "How haven't I heard of this?"

"We wanted to keep things quiet and private." Brand shrugged. "Besides, the death of a lady in The Clips is nothing compared to the theatrics this world has been exposed to over the last thirty or forty years."

"Indeed." I considered what this possibly meant for me right now. Flashes of our times together ran in my mind, the way he called me his and that I belonged to him…

He wasn't wrong.

Yet it wasn't just the physical connection with him I yearned for. It was just *him*, and I knew—even after all these years—I was still in love with him, and I questioned if there would be a time when I wouldn't be.

"Would you like to meet her?" Brand asked hesitantly, his cheeks pinking. I furrowed my brow, concerned he meant his dead wife, but then he laughed, the sound wrapping around me. "Gods, no. I mean my daughter."

"Oh." I startled, blinking at him. This was territory I was unfamiliar with. I met and interacted with children plenty of times, but never the child of someone important to me. "If you would like me to."

Brand smiled, interlacing our fingers, and it was like we were young children again. "Come with me."

He practically raced through the halls of his home, paintings and portraits flashing by in a blur of colors. I held tightly to his hand, my other holding my skirt as I fought the childlike bliss that worked through me.

We came to a halt before a beautiful sunroom. Despite the winter chill arriving, the sun warmed the room entirely made of glass, decorated with beautiful plants and walls of books and trinkets. A nursemaid sat in a wooden chair, hunched over a small child playing with figurines on the floor.

"Annabelle," Brand called, slipping his hand from mine as he stepped deeper into the room. I followed hesitantly behind him, especially as the nursemaid nearly fell from her seat at the sight of me. "Darling, there's someone I would like you to meet."

The little girl snapped her head at me, and my breath was stolen from my lungs.

She was the spitting image of Tyra; her hair was the same hue as Brand's. The only difference was her eye color. She didn't inherit the Korbin signature, but rather a dulled brown, which must've come from her mother.

"This is a dear friend of mine," Brand began, crouching to her level and sweeping his hand toward me. "This is the Great Karasi."

Her whole face lit up at the introduction, and she scrambled to her feet to get a closer look at me. I raised an eyebrow as she stumbled toward me, standing toe-to-toe as she gazed up from her small height.

"Come closer," Annabelle said in a soft, squeaking voice. She emphasized her urgency by beckoning me lower.

I glanced at Brand for assistance, and he chuckled as he nodded encouragingly. I mimicked his stance to be closer to the child's eye level.

"You have funny eyes," she observed, and I pursed my lips. I couldn't blame her. I supposed they were *funny* to her standards. "Why are your eyes like that?"

"I'm a Magic," I told her quietly. I held my hand between us and ushered forth my claws. She startled, but she didn't back down. "I have many gifts that the creatures of old used to have. The eyes and claws of a *drakon*, and I can foresee the future."

"Can you change into a *drakon*?" she asked, her eyes lighting up once more.

Brand's throaty chuckle warmed something within me, and I consciously reminded myself we were in the presence of *his child*.

"The Gods didn't seem to grant me that gift," I admitted, squinting. "Am I still interesting enough?"

"Most definitely." She smiled, wrapping her hand around my two fingers and dragging me back to where Brand stood. "The Great Karasi will stay for dinner, Father?"

"Only if she wishes," Brand said as he observed me. And when he added the next words, my chest ached. "She is more than welcome. In fact, it would mean a lot to me."

"Me as well!" The little voice below squeaked as she beamed up at me like I was a new toy.

"I suppose dinner after travel is appropriate," I agreed, forcing down the tightness rising in my throat.

I stood by the fireplace of Brand's study, swirling the liquor in my glass as I stared into the flames within.

The dinner had been rather interesting as Annabelle interrogated me about my prophecies. She asked if I could tell her when she would learn to ride her horse or when her father would give her a new mother.

Brand choked around his wine at that, and I couldn't

suppress my amused grin.

The door to the study opened, but I knew it was Brand. I felt his presence, but I kept my gaze on the fire. His presence stirred the air behind me, breath warm against my neck. My eyes fluttered shut.

"Dinner was nice," Brand said, and even though his chest didn't touch my back, his voice rumbled around me. "We don't have guests often, and I think it was good for her."

"She surely had entertainment for the evening," I muttered, and Brand's chuckle shot straight through me.

"It's been a pleasant gift to see you." Brand's fingertips ran along my shoulder and down my arm, the touch featherlight. I carefully placed the glass on the mantle before me, my movements slow. "A gift I fear I don't deserve."

I startled, quickly twisting on my heel. I frowned at him, searching his face, only to be amazed again that I stood before him after years apart.

"Why do you believe that?" I asked, shaking my head. I lifted my hand to cup his cheek, and the caress seemed to pain him. "What are you thinking?"

"How selfish I am for wanting you all to myself again," he whispered between us, his hand overlapping mine. "How I just want you beside me for one night where I can pretend we are young, and free to do as we wish."

I hummed, sliding my hand down his chest, resting above his heart. "Darling, I'm still young and free."

Brand laughed as his hands hesitantly slipped onto my waist, and it morphed into a moan as if my body provided him with a balm for the ache of years lost. "Always such a sharp tongue, *mi leiron.*"

I gripped his tunic in my fist and yanked his lips to mine. He stiffened in shock, but it didn't last long.

We fell into each other like no time had passed, as if we'd been born to do so for eternity. I immediately plunged my hands into his hair, marveling at the familiar feel of him against me. His mouth moved in sync with mine, a rhythm only we knew.

"Come to bed, Karasi," he mumbled against my lips, pulling away to press his forehead to mine. His use of my name weakened my knees and willpower. "One time. Who knows when we will get another chance?"

For the first time in seven years, Fate was silent while his arms stayed locked around me.

I nodded against him, and he slipped his hand into mine once again.

We walked down the hall, and as we approached his daughter's room, he pressed a finger to his lips. Brand stepped slowly and deliberately as he passed, his hand slipping from mine. I mimicked his movements but stopped when I beheld her asleep in her bed, the visions taking the opportunity to steal me while he was not touching me.

Many oddities occur when you live beyond a mortal lifespan. Kingdoms fall and rise, customs change, and religions stretch far and wide until they're but a fragment of the grandeur they used to be.

But I always found lineage to be the most fascinating of them all.

As I looked upon Brand's daughter, I saw flashes of the future ahead for her descendants. Korbins were the sole reason the significance of the Carraphim name was lost to history. Yet, this Korbin line would be the single reason the importance of the Carraphim name would be remembered.

And it all circled back to the child who haunted my dreams, the Sirian with the golden eyes and raven black hair.

The child whose name meant *aster*.

THE TRUE PROPHECY

841 A.V. | AGE: 34

Many years ago, Sir Michael said I would know when I needed him and how to find him.

So, when the sensation to see him came alongside the idea to head to the abandoned Arcane Island—Fate only knew why—I sent a raven on the winds to summon him to The Red Raven in Eldamain.

I waited at the bar top for hours, watching the door from the corner of my eye. My impatience grew with every new patron that wasn't him until he was finally the one to open the door.

He appeared no older than the last time I saw him, and my words at Tyra's wedding felt entirely ignorant.

Of course he was Magic.

Sir Michael hadn't even stepped foot through the door when I directed him back outside to the horses tied up in front of the pub.

"What was it you said about me not being able to understand the burden of Magics?" He raised an eyebrow, and I clenched my jaw.

"Not another word."

We set off toward the eastern shores of Eldamain to a small sailboat that I had acquired, though I had no clue how to man it.

I expressed as much, but Sir Michael huffed once, shook his head, and told me he knew how to man a sailboat.

"So, she just vanished?" Sir Michael asked after I told him the story of when Sybil left. He didn't remove his gaze from the rope he loosened.

I shrugged, staring off toward the land mass slowly growing larger ahead of us.

He scoffed, shaking his head. "Sybil said it could happen one day, but that was… Gods, that was so long ago."

"How old are you, Michael?" I narrowed my eyes, searching his face. He appeared to be middle aged, with gray hair hugging his face and wrinkles deep in the corners of his eyes.

Then again, he appeared to be in his middle ages the *first* time we met twenty-five years ago.

He offered me a sad, sideways grin but kept his attention on the sail. "Ninety-two, Karasi."

I adjusted the shawl around my shoulders. "What House?"

"Nemea," he said, shaking his head as that distant look of many lives lived passed over his gaze. "I didn't inherit many traits except the naturally enhanced abilities. On the other hand, my brother inherited everything, including wings."

"And you knew Sybil personally?" I searched his face, gauging his reaction. I didn't expect it to deepen with grief. "You knew her well."

"My brother knew her," Michael elaborated, a slight frown appearing between his brows. "We crossed paths long ago when my brother and I were young adults. He became infatuated with her, and she seemed… Well, she seemed to enjoy him more than she enjoyed me."

I couldn't envision my mother *enjoying* anyone, even at a friendly level. It made me think of Brand, which only brought a deep, sorrowful weight to the pit of my stomach.

I knew Michael had more stories to tell about Sybil than she ever told me.

"She never mentioned you or your brother," I explained, not unkindly. "Where's your brother, then?"

Michael pressed his lips together, finally dragging his eyes to me. "He was killed thirty-four years ago."

My heart stopped in my chest before picking up a stronger rhythm, and my blood roared in my ears. I blinked away rare tears that burned the corner of my eyes and threatened to leak. "You're lying."

"The day after his death was the last time I ever saw Sybil," Michael said, reaching for me. I recoiled, yanking my hand into my body. Hurt crossed his face. "She never spoke to me again and she never told me she was… I didn't see her again until you came to Etherea for Leif's wedding."

I warred with my emotions. There was the bitter

sting of betrayal because Sybil never told me a single detail about my father and fought anyone who tried. King Alrik once insinuated he would find out who my father was, but after Tyra's prophecy, I had very little interest in communicating with him beyond necessity.

There was also a foreign longing to know the man who sired me—to learn *all* I could about him. A deeper, familiar longing accompanied the immediate thought of telling Brand about this and remembering I couldn't.

"How did he die?" My voice came out harsher than I intended, sharp like a whip.

Michael flinched, but he fussed with the ropes as we neared the northern shore of the Arcane Island. "As I mentioned, he had wings from the House of Nemea. We tried to stay quiet about it, but someone found out, and they tortured him for his tears and ripped out his claws for their healing powers."

I hissed at that, hoping one day the mythologies of the Beings we once shifted to would fade away into existence or become stories only Magics told to their children. With people like the Korbins on thrones, Magics were already far and few, and we didn't need to be hunted.

"Did he have..." I paused, considering. I inherited every single trait of Sybil from her vertical, *drakon* eyes to her explicit, vivid prophecy. "Did I get anything from him?"

"Some of his physical traits I see in you," Michael explained with a wistful smile, gathering the anchor. "It's how I knew who you were when we first met. He was also able to mind walk."

I nearly tipped over at that, snapping my head to him. "Gifts like that are nearly unheard of these days."

Michael nodded solemnly, the anchor hitting the shore with a splash. "Again, we kept it quiet. The only people who ever knew about it were our parents, me, Liam, and Sybil."

"Liam?" I raised an eyebrow before jumping to the sand.

Michael stared at something over my shoulder as he said, "That was his name, Karasi."

I was slightly disappointed that his name wasn't Piers, but I was even more fascinated because it meant two things.

Sybil said she had loved few people in her life, one of whom was a man named Piers.

There were *two* important males in her life, but Sybil never loved my father.

It was the first time I realized how many versions of Sybil may have existed over two thousand years that I would never be privy to.

I walked through the abandoned Sirian Academy, scattered with overgrown foliage and sagging roofs. I silently thanked the Gods that, at some point, Sirians must have traveled here to lay their dead to rest because there were no discarded bones lying about as the bodies had in the prophecy.

My footsteps echoed against the stone ground and remaining walls, the swish of my skirt carrying across pebbles and stones lying haphazardly on the ground.

I didn't know why I needed to come here. I just knew Fate urged me to, so I obeyed.

The longer I walked, the louder the heartbeat that was not my own grew within my mind, the hushed voices of Fate indiscernible. It wasn't until I stumbled into an open courtyard with grass reaching my waist that a high-pitched scream blared around and within me. I staggered back against a pillar, blindly reaching for anything to steady my balance as a flash of white overtook my vision.

I gasped at the air ripped from my lungs. My hand flew to my chest, my heart rate slowing to a dangerous beat. Knees buckled beneath me, forcing me to the ground where the gravel bit into my skin. I caught myself with my free hand before the rest of my body plummeted to the ground, rocks scratching my palm.

The strength of the vision was nothing like I'd ever felt before. The rhythmic thrum pounded in my ears, and I lost control of my body as I was shoved into the endless depths within my mind. The white expanse blended with streaks of neutral colors: grays, beiges, and browns. The sound of wind rushing past my head accompanied the heartbeat, clouding my senses. It morphed into a mother's wailing and a father's vengeful scream, as though their hearts were being ripped from their chests.

Bright, ethereal figures thrashed in total darkness.

[The Gods will mourn their children…]

Tendrils of Darkness broke through the sky, shrouding the ethereal Beings behind a thick, black smoke.

[Buried in the Dark.]

A bright, white-gold flash like the Sirian Light sent a spark of pain through the middle of my forehead.

A man in a black cloak carried a strange bundle through a shadowed forest, frantically twisting his head over each shoulder.

[The Stars will come back home…]

Scaling a stone tower on an isolated island, a single window. A child curled into a ball in the far corner, her eyes squeezed tight, her face scrunched.

[Orphaned by the past.]

Black smoke cleared the child from sight, shouts of men and women echoing as ghosts battled with swords and shields.

[When Darkness comes again…]

A young woman with dark, raven-black hair stood still as others rushed past her: a stranger with emerald eyes and a hut, another young woman with a ruby necklace, a sickly young boy. All the while, the Mark upon her head stood against her tanned skin.

[Marks will be revealed.]

The night sky hung ominously above, stars slowly blinking into existence, two figures dancing under the sky in my peripheral.

[Fate demands sacrifice…]

My heart stopped for a few seconds, the tightening in

my chest deepening to a blinding pain. I tried to inhale, but a heavy force sat upon my chest.

[The Great One will fall.]

I registered my lungs greedily breathing air as my heart rate normalized, and my vision continued to waver into the next scene.

Different thrones sat upon daises, with various materials like gold, wood, and bronze. Flashes of crowns upon new, unfamiliar, and somehow recognizable heads, sneaking behind walls and corridors, hiding amongst books.

[Chaos will govern thrones…]

Boats sailing to distant shores, filled with Sirians, Magics, and humans, ravens soaring in the sky above them, the same girl with the blue-black hair at the front.

[Crows answer the call.]

The girl at a dinner table with an open box full of letters, fire dancing in her hands, a king with blond hair handing the girl a letter, her sitting in a dark library with a large parchment splayed out before her, another woman with white-blond hair grinning mischievously—all one after the other.

[The Truth will be revealed…]

Familiar black tendrils climb up a dais, wrapping around one of the thrones from earlier, a scream penetrating the air, echoing around.

[Abyss claims a King.]

My mortal vision returned instantaneously. I was shoved out of my mind and the sudden change made me expel the water and food I consumed that day.

After my body finished emptying of anything and

everything, I fell to my side on the rocky ground, rolling onto my back with a groan.

The sky loomed above me, the sun hidden behind a layer of hazy, gray clouds. I willed my breathing to a normal rhythm as the images I saw danced like shadows above me. I questioned whether I was trapped in my mind or brought back to existence.

I shot a claw from my nailbed and scratched it across my arm, hissing at the pain that sprung to the surface. I sighed in relief at the corporeal sensation, my arms falling slack to the ground beside me as a trickle of warm blood burned a trail down my cold, clammy skin.

This was nothing like I'd experienced before, and yet the extra sensation within me allowed me to understand it for what it was.

The True Prophecy.

My soul felt it.

This prophecy was the first and the last—a prophecy connected to those which had come before and the trajectory of the world.

Some of the words were familiar, and I realized this prophecy had haunted me through my entire life thus far, sneaking in through other Paths I'd foreseen. It was connected to people I had met who had influenced—or would influence—the future.

I knew all the visions I had foretold until this point laid the Path for this one to be revealed.

Because this was not just a prophecy for the entire world, applying to key individuals already born and yet to be conceived…

This prophecy was directly my own.

[Yours.] That voice scratched against the edges of my mind. I winced at how it grated against my nerves, clenching my jaw.

No, this was not just my future within these words.

It was my responsibility to ensure it unfolded precisely as it needed to.

This prophecy was mine to *enact*.

THE IMMORTAL WAKE

879 A.V. | AGE: 72

The manor in Cerelia had barely changed since I visited it nearly fifty years ago. Time was beginning to blend as I outlived those around me, whether by an untimely demise or old age.

In this case, my old friend was reaching the natural end of his life, and I was summoned to his bedside by the very daughter who once insisted I stay for dinner.

I waited in the receiving room, pacing the length of each wall as I studied the paintings and tapestries, all hung on patterned wallpaper. It all made the space feel loud, yelling the reminder that I didn't belong. I curled my lip at it.

I didn't need a reminder.

"My Gods," a melodic voice said, interrupting my stand-off with the wall. I quickly twisted on my heels, my arms clasped behind my back as I raised an eyebrow at the aged woman before me. "Father said to expect you to look the same as my memories. I didn't truly believe you would look *exactly* as you had forty-three years ago."

Annabelle.

The child who had summoned me, and the line from which the *aster* I dreamt of would descend.

I tilted my head as I studied her, my heart clenching at how much I felt I was looking at Tyra if she had the opportunity to age.

"It is nice to see you again," I said as I bowed. "You are now Lady Annabelle, yes?"

"Indeed." She sighed, taking a few steps into the receiving room. She held out her hand and beckoned me. "We aren't sure how much longer he has these days, so I hope to bring you to him to at least give him peace. We believe he's been waiting for this moment."

I couldn't help the slight smirk twitching at the corners of my lips. "I have no doubt he has."

I followed Annabelle through the hallways adorned with various paintings of her and her family and unfamiliar faces that looked similar to Brand.

"I regret to say I find it difficult to keep up with the affairs of the kingdoms over the last fifty years," I admitted, toying with the bracelets hanging on my wrists. "Did Lord Brand ever remarry?"

Annabelle nodded, a ghost of a smile flitting across her face. "He did a few years after you visited. She was a commoner who dedicated her life to teaching. Until she met my father, of course. She bore him two more children—my twin brothers."

"It would only be right that the Korbin family continued to birth twins." I chuckled under my breath, shaking my head. A braid slipped over my shoulder, and

I flicked it away as I peered at Annabelle with narrowed eyes. "And having brothers… Has that complicated things for you regarding the manor and *ladyship*?"

Annabelle smirked at that, holding my stare. "Father made sure it didn't, and there were plenty of documents to support my inheritance of the title. It helps that I've married and had my own children. Nonetheless, he made sure long before they were born."

"I expect nothing less from Lord Brand." I slowed as we approached a slightly cracked door, the light from a window illuminating the gap.

Without Annabelle saying a thing, the voice in my head whispered to me, *[Here.]*

"How old is your father now?" I asked her, my heart clenching in my chest. If Annabelle was nearly fifty years old and I was seventy-two, that meant Brand had to be—

"He's seventy-four," Annabelle answered quietly, her hands tightening at her waist. "He's lived a long, mundane existence compared to some of my uncles. I like to believe he was happy with it and that was all he wanted out of life."

"It was," I assured her, my gaze lingering on the sliver of light beyond the door. "I have known your father since childhood, and we always shared a special bond."

"I know of your bond," she said not unkindly, her brow furrowing as she followed my gaze. "I can't begin to imagine the love he always had for you and you for him, and how painful it had to be not to have one another because of this world. I don't know all the details or nature of your relationship, and I know he loved my mother dearly… Well, at least he learned to love her…

"But for what it's worth, I have never held any resentment toward you because of his memory of you. I just remember when you came to our home, and you told me stories."

More than anything, I wanted her words to mean something. I wanted to believe that was what I desired—that Brand's daughter did not harbor resentment toward me for always holding his heart.

The harsh truth was that I couldn't be roused to care in the slightest what this significant—yet insignificant—woman believed of me. It was not that I didn't respect her for who she was to the world or the future or Brand, but I simply lost the ability to care.

Relationships grew increasingly difficult for me because of my gifts. Those who looked beyond my title were few and far between now.

Brand was the last one who did.

"Thank you," I said in an even voice, nodding once before heading through the door. I gently pushed, and it creaked on its hinges.

The body on the bed dragged a heavy-lidded gaze in my direction, and when I connected with those softly haunting turquoise eyes, I nearly fell to the floor on shaky knees.

Brand always looked just like his father, and with age, there was hardly a difference.

The only change was that Brand had wrinkles at the

corners of his eyes and mouth from his life of smiling and laughing, whereas Alrik had frown lines and sunken cheeks.

His mouth ticked up into a brilliant smile, his hand rising from the mattress, extending to me across the expanse.

"*Mi leiron*," his voice was huskier than it used to be, but he was still Brand. "You are a dream."

"I've always been real." I took hesitant, quiet steps forward, fighting the voice in my head that chanted *death* repeatedly, like a whisper on the wind. "And you look old."

He laughed then, that same musical laughter that seemed to tune my soul to his, and I couldn't suppress the grin that pulled up my lips.

I sat beside the stretch of his legs on the mattress. I went to take his hand in mine, but he stopped me, beckoning me closer. I bent so that his hand could grip my chin between his fingers as he'd always done, and my eyes fluttered briefly at his touch.

For a brief moment, I wondered if I'd made a huge mistake not letting him grow old with me. If his touch was still so freeing, would fifty years together have been worth it?

He squinted, tilting my head from side to side as though he were searching for something. "Not a single wrinkle on your beautiful skin, but I believe your eyes hold more weight than mine."

"I've still watched the same world evolve as you, even

if it doesn't appear so," I whispered between us, leaning my face into his palm. "I've also seen far into the future beyond our time."

"And how does it look?" he asked, but it was full of mirth. I rolled my eyes with a small grin, and his brow furrowed. "You're different."

"Says the bedridden old man," I teased, but it came out flat.

"You grin as if it pains you." His thumb pressed against the corner of my lips, my heart warming. "You're no longer wild and untamed but civil and reserved."

I hummed at that, removing his hand from the side of my face and cupping it between mine in my lap. I brushed my thumb over the veins and soft wrinkles on the back of his hand.

"Karasi," Brand whispered, pulling my attention to him. I looked up through lowered lashes, raising an eyebrow. "It's just you and me again."

Tears sprung to my eyes as I inhaled sharply, squeezing his hand in mine. I frowned as I tried to blink them back, but one escaped down my cheek in a rush, falling on our hands.

"Are you prejudiced against an old man?" He chuckled under his breath, but it morphed into a cough that had him clutching his chest. My heart cracked, my lower lip quivering. "The Great Karasi will shed tears for a lowly mortal man."

"Don't be foolish," I snapped quietly, laying his arm on the pillow beside his head. I sprawled across the small space at the edge of the bed, curling my body into his.

I rested my head into the crook of his shoulder, staring up at his face as I placed my hand on his chest. I could feel his congested breaths and the slow beat of his heart. Another tear slipped free as the arm beneath me curled toward my back. His other hand laid on top of mine as he drew me closer into his body.

The voice remained silent, and for the first time in ages, I took a deep, freeing breath, inhaling him.

"The voice will never be silent without you," I whispered, searching his face as he angled his head. "How am I to stay sane?"

"You seem to have managed without me the last fifty years," he explained, not unkindly. "You're far stronger than you realize. You are the most powerful Magic in our world, the daughter of a demi-god, if rumors are to be believed."

I huffed a breath of laughter, burrowing deeper into his soft body, so different from the honed man I used to know, but still unmistakably him.

"Do not feed loneliness, *mi leiron*," Brand pleaded quietly, brushing another rogue tear from the edge of my jaw. "Find those who can understand you and accept you as I have, who do not require your gifts, but your love."

"That is quite difficult when my gifts are all I'm known for." If there was anyone to whom I could always speak my mind and feelings, it was him. "I don't know how to form relationships with people who don't understand that I can't share everything with them. They will use me for what I am."

"Karasi," Brand interrupted, squeezing me closer.

"You don't understand, Brand." My voice fluctuated in speech, quivering at the panic gripping me. He was slipping through my fingers for a final time. "Fate continues to lead me toward people who have this great influence on the future, and I have to be cautious on what I say and how much I fight the voice of Fate. Even *you* have come to play a bigger role in the future of the world, and your daughter is the ancestor of a girl that I believe will mean something to me, something like a daughter but I didn't birth her—"

"Karasi—"

"She's part of this huge prophecy, The True Prophecy. When I received it, I had a visceral reaction to it. It's going to undo all your father has set out to accomplish, and yet it's going to usher in something big; something my mother and the other demi-gods sought to hide—"

"Karasi!" The rasp of Brand's voice pulled me out of whatever state I'd been in, and I connected with those blue eyes at the same time we both realized what had happened.

I just told him about the future.

The voice was letting me tell him because he would die today, and there was no one he could tell.

I would be here with him when he died.

"Tell me everything," Brand begged, his grip on me tightening as he tucked my head beneath his chin. "Tell me everything you couldn't before and everything you know to come. I want to hear about this world and what will come of it before I go. I want to know what will come of you.

"But most importantly, I want to give you that reprieve one final time."

A genuine smile broke out across my face, and I laughed around the tears soaking his nightshirt. I rose upright in the bed and readjusted him so that his head laid in my lap as I leaned against the headboard.

And I told Brand Korbin everything I couldn't when we were growing up.

I told him how this gift of prophecy worked, about The True Prophecy, what each stage of it meant for me, and what I saw.

I told him about how his direct descendancy would bring the Carraphim family back from the shadows, that there was an heir out there somewhere, how his line and their line would usher the one to reintroduce Sirians again.

But most of all, I told him how much I had loved him, and how I believed I would never stop.

At one point, Annabelle came to check in on him. While he rested, I asked her to gather all those who wished to say goodbye as he would pass before the day ended.

When he was awake for the final time, Annabelle and her family came in, and his grandchildren sat with him and told him the town gossip. His two sons came in, and

I was surprised at how much they looked like him. They brought their families with them since they all lived in Cerelia.

They all wanted to stay close to him.

I buried my joy for his sake as I let him have his time with all of them. Brand created the family he always wanted, full of kindness, love, and devotion. One where siblings adored each other and spouses weren't in competition for his acceptance, where they would continue to share how wonderful of a father he was for generations, and they would mean it.

So, I decided I didn't regret not keeping him for myself. I would've never been able to give him any of this, and the wrinkles lining his face were all carved from the joy brought by the people around him.

"I'll be waiting for you." He held me tighter to his chest as we laid there. "It was always you…"

Just before midnight, Former Prince Brand Korbin took his final breath, passing peacefully, surrounded by those who loved him most.

While he left me hollow, a shell of the woman he loved, I knew deep down a piece of him would always remain with me. I would fight Fate, time, and even my own stubbornness to always share with the world what Brand believed it deserved.

Compassion.

THE TRUE PROPHECY

The Gods mourn their children,

Buried in the Dark.

The Stars will come back home,

Orphaned by the past.

When Darkness comes again,

Marks will be revealed.

Fate demands sacrifice,

The Great One will fall.

Chaos will govern thrones,

Crows answer the call.

The Truth will be released,

Abyss claims a King.

THE MOTHER

She sacrificed, not for herself, but for what must be.

WOUND OF STARS

1184 A.V. | AGE: 377

The raven sitting in the windowsill squawked at me as it ruffled its feathers, blinking its beady eyes.

"What could you possibly want?" I snapped, narrowing my eyes at it in the hopes it recognized the vertical slits as those of a predator.

It did no such thing.

The bird squawked again as if it actually answered my question, its head tilting to the side.

"The world may whisper all the variations of powers I have, but I hate to inform you that speaking to animals is not one of them." I turned back to the pestle and mortar on the counter, grinding the comfrey leaf, plantain leaf, and calendula flowers to a powder.

I started researching a way to help Sirians hide the damning Marks on their foreheads other than elaborate headdresses or hats. When outside of Riddling or during warmer weather, they would need something to help hide them. The mortals were also getting suspicious of people wearing such things, guards stopping people to reveal whether or not they had the Mark hidden beneath.

Just as I was about to dump the powder into the olive oil, the raven screeched an awful sound, and I stiffened with my eyes shut tight.

"Gods above, animal," I cried over its continuous call. "What in the Heavens—"

"Karasi!" A familiar voice called from somewhere outside my plot. "Karasi! Help!"

I immediately dropped the mortar onto the counter with a clatter, lunging across the small kitchen to the door. Swinging it open, I was greeted by a blood-coated Clark and Petro, the latter holding a limp female in his arms that was covered in far more blood than either of them.

"What the fuck is—" I choked on my words when Petro angled the female's body so he didn't smack her head on the doorframe.

A Sirian Mark on the middle of her forehead.

"We were out by the woods and there was this murder of crows flapping between the trees around this one shadowed area," Clark explained as he swiped everything off my small wooden table.

Petro moved to lay her down, but I stop him with a hand up. "She won't fit on that table. Grab that quilt off the chaise and lay it here."

Clark wasted no time snatching the fabric and haphazardly unfolding it onto the ground. Petro knelt, gently laying the woman down. I followed suit, trying to find the source of the bleeding.

"She was stumbling through the trees, and the ravens

were following her," Petro said, shaking his head as he panted. "All she got out was *please* before she quite literally fell into my arms."

Placing my fingers against her throat, I counted the pulses as I listened for the pocket watch somewhere within the house. "Her pulse is far weaker than I would like it to be."

A claw shot out from my nail bed, and I swiped its sharp tip down the edge of the woman's tunic. It was then I realized she was wearing a male's slacks, as well. If I had to guess, she was trying to pass herself as a male to avoid any attention.

I ripped at the cotton and, sure enough, she had tightly wrapped strips of cloth around her chest to flatten her breasts underneath.

One long, *deep* gash sliced across her stomach from the bottom of her right rib to her left hip. The worst of it was directly in the middle where I believed I could see more of her internal organs than I ever wished to.

"You should be grateful you carried her the way you did," I grumbled as I rose from my crouch and jumped toward the cabinet filled with various healing potions and tinctures. I gathered all the ones I knew to help, along with a curved, thin hook and the hemp thread. "If you had thrown her over your shoulder like a sack, you undoubtedly would've killed her."

"She's going to live?" Clark asked, peering over my shoulder as I kneeled back on the ground and dumped all the contents from my arms onto the floor.

"We shall hope so—"

The woman's eyes shot open frantically as she gasped for air, trying to sit upright. Clark and Petro were no strangers to injuries, and they both grabbed a shoulder and pinned her back down to the floor. She whimpered, shaking her head. Strands of copper hair clung to her face despite the movement…

Not copper—blond, just darkened by blood.

"Hush," I cooed, bending over her so I was in her line of vision. She connected with my eyes and stilled, her own widening. They were a bright, pale gray that speared me through my chest from their eerie beauty. "You have to be still. I'm going to help you."

"Please," she whispered, her voice hoarse and the sound barely audible. I couldn't place her accent because of it. "Help."

"Yes," I assured her, cupping her cheek with my hand. She shut her eyes to my embrace, a tear slipping down her temple. "I have to add some things to your wound that may sting and burn. But that won't be the worst of it, I'm afraid. I'll need to stitch you up, and that may send you back into rest.

"When you're resting, hang on, though." I nodded, trying to get her to show me she understood what I was saying. "Understand?"

She nodded once, dipping her chin.

I didn't waste any more time. As I poured the first tonic into the wound, she screamed, nearly bucking off the floor.

To my dismay, Clark began to unlatch his belt, and I gawked at him until he folded it in half and put it in front of the woman's mouth. "Bite down on this."

She didn't even hesitate. She opened her mouth around a sob and Clark carefully placed it between her quivering lips. The woman turned her gaze to me, blinking once.

"We're with you," I promised, grabbing the second tonic. "We'll be here with you every step of it."

Even as I continued to torture her for the next hour, she didn't pass out until I was nearly done with her stitches. The boys stayed through the whole thing and late into the night, until I finally ushered them out by reminding Clark he did have to return to The Red Raven. They agreed, but not without letting me know they would come the next day to check on the woman and see if she made it through the first night.

I was changing her dressing as dawn broke through the sky when the Sirian woman stirred in the bed. Her eyes fluttered open, remaining heavy-lidded as they flickered around the room. When they landed on me, I caught her pupils dilating.

"Do you remember me?" I asked, covering her stomach with the blanket as I sat beside her.

She mouthed *yes* but then grimaced. She cleared her throat and answered in that hoarse tone, "Yes."

"Give it a few more hours and I'll grab you some water." I laid my hand on her chest, giving it two gentle pats. "After that, we'll try and get you to drink a healing tonic. You've lost a lot of blood, and it will be a few rough nights. Something tells me you're a fighter, though."

She blinked her glassy eyes as they roamed around my face and up and down my body. She cleared her throat again and lifted her hand to lay on top of mine. "*Eden.*"

I frowned, unfamiliar with the term, and I desperately wanted her to speak more so I could place where she was from.

She either read my face or felt the need to elaborate because she took a deep, steady breath and said, "My name… Eden."

"Well, it's nice to meet you, Eden." I clasped her fingers and brought her hand to my chest. "Although, I would've preferred different circumstances. I'm the Great Karasi."

Recognition flared briefly in her eyes, tears glistening in the light. I offered a grim smile as I brushed my thumb across the back of her hand.

"You… I tried…" She winced, shutting her eyes, but it appeared to be out of frustration rather than pain.

"Take your time," I whispered, letting our hands fall to my lap. "I would actually prefer it if you didn't strain yourself to speak."

She shook her head back and forth once, swallowing. "I tried to find you."

Pizian.

That was her accent.

She had traveled all the way from The Northern Pizi to get here, which meant hiding or disguising herself on a ship. "Did you stow away on a ship?"

The corner of her lip twitched, and she turned her head fully toward me. "Stole it."

I couldn't help the breath of laughter that fell from my lips. "You stole a ship?"

Her lips lifted more, and it actually looked like she was smirking at me. Her eyelids were drooping lower, though.

"Get your rest." I patted back her copper-tinged hair. It was lighter in hue after we tried to wash her up as best as we could without affecting the wound. I didn't doubt she had nearly white-blond hair. "You're going to need it, and we're about to spend a lot of time together if you keep fighting for your life."

Eden Beaumont was a fierce fighter if I'd ever met one, and I was nearly four hundred years old.

She was also a long descendant of Taranis, a demi-god descendant of Danica, which meant Eden could wield not only the Light, but lightning.

Over the *months* she stayed with me healing, I particularly enjoyed it when she had enough strength to wield her lightning god-power any time it stormed outside. She explained she could call it to her with or without a storm, but she preferred to draw less attention to herself and made a vow to only use it during storms.

I had no complaints. It'd been so long since I'd seen

Sirians willingly wield their powers. Many chose to just learn to control them and leave it be, but Eden was one with her power, a part of her just as much as her blond hair or beautiful gray eyes were.

And she was beautiful.

Some days, it made being her caretaker difficult because that was all I could be. I refused to push the boundaries with Sirians who passed on my doorstep, if only because their lives were just as fleeting as mortals, even more dangerous because of what they were.

"Enjoy yourself?" I asked as she joined me in the protection of the porch. Her clothes clung snugly to her body, accenting every soft dip and curve.

"Quite much," she answered, and I chuckled to myself at her Etherean. It wasn't all that bad, but there were times she missed words or added some in.

"Well, let's get you warmed up inside. I lit the fire the minute you stepped outside." I handed her the wool quilt to wrap around herself, and she chuckled low.

"You know me well." She followed in after me, and I headed straight for the sofa. She paused in the kitchen after shutting the door behind her and hung the quilt on one of the chairs. "You avoided the question earlier."

I squinted at her from across the room, but my eyes went wide as she started to undress in the middle of the kitchen.

I don't know why it increasingly became a problem for me to see her undress. I had already seen her entirely nude many times between the first few weeks of her healing. As she was able to lift her arms above her head and bend over, I slowly allowed her to do more on her own until the scar was just a risen, bright pink slash across her abdomen.

The very scar that was now on full display beneath her brassiere.

She lowered quickly to take off the slacks she insisted I get for her, quickly jerking up and frowning at me. "Something wrong?"

I pursed my lips and shook my head, but I couldn't help my gaze dragging across the exposed expanse of her fair skin. It lingered on her breasts and where her legs were flexing tight together.

"You stare at me a lot like that lately." Eden grabbed the quilt again, wrapping it around her shoulders as she strolled across the kitchen and to the living space. She sank down beside me on the couch, tilting her head. "Something must be wrong."

"You think something's wrong because I'm staring at you?" I snorted, and she reached over and flicked the tip of my nose. I scrunched it, rubbing. "I'm just admiring… my work."

I gestured lazily to where her stomach was, but she didn't buy it.

Eden was so damn clever and blunt.

"You were only admiring," she amended, leaning back against the cushion with a smug grin. She shrugged. "I admire."

"When?" I snapped my gaze up to her, startled by the

mischievousness winking in her bright eyes.

"You leave your bedroom door cracked." She bit at her bottom lip as she sunk further in the sofa. "Especially after bathing."

"Eden!" I couldn't help the laugh that burst from me as I gawked at her, heat climbing up my neck and chest. She chortled under her breath, averting her gaze to the flames.

But she wasn't silent for long.

"You did not answer my question still." She peered at me from the corners of her eyes; a few strands of her blond hair stuck to her cheeks.

"I can't tell you how old I am," I said solemnly, shaking my head. I reached over and tucked the damp strand behind her ear. Her eyes darkened, and I was shocked at myself for the tenderness.

I really hadn't shown her any since she was more alert and could move about.

"Why?" Eden cocked her head, turning to fully face me on the couch. The quilt slipped off her shoulders as she clutched it at her chest. "Because of a prophecy?"

"It's a choice." I slowly breathed, staring at my hands in my lap. "To protect myself, just as Magics have always chosen to have only one name. The less others know about me, the quieter I can be, and the more I can help Sirians and Magics."

She blinked, but then she reached out and wrapped both of her hands around mine as she leaned forward. The blanket slowly slid down her back, bunching at her waist. "You do not protect from friends."

I offered her a sad smile, flipping my hands to hold onto hers. "I don't have friends."

"Are we not friends?" The question was innocent and genuine, like Eden sincerely wanted to know.

"Not for much longer." Her arms stilled briefly. I forced myself to look her in the eyes. They were dimmed slightly, a franticness about them. "I told you, Eden, you can't stay forever. Your wound is merely a scar now, so you should be on your way to a safe haven. You'll be with others like you."

She frowned, her brows pressing together. "So, I am a friend? For now?"

"For now." I agreed, because at least I could pretend to have someone that cared about me enough beyond my gifts and what I could do for them. Especially because Eden never once asked about her future. "Once you leave, I don't foresee us ever meeting again."

"I will age." She reached her hand up, her fingertips brushing along my jawline before resting beneath my chin. "You will not."

I nodded once, but her fingers stayed. She tilted her head again, a slight squint to her eyes as she studied me. "What are you looking for?"

"Nothing." She met my eyes as she said, "I looked for safety and acceptance when you found me. I found safety and acceptance."

My resolve snapped like a twig, and I don't know who moved first.

We both rose to our knees on the couch, our lips crashing together. I clung to her waist as she drew her hands on either side of my neck. We kissed in hungry caresses, like we had been starved in one another's presence for the last few months. I slid my tongue along her bottom lip, and it elicited a moan of relief from her chest.

That was when I knew I was utterly fucked.

I pulled away from her only to step down with a hand held between us. "Bedroom."

"Bedroom," she breathed, and I didn't waste time tugging her behind me.

The minute we passed under the threshold, she yanked me back into her with a renewed passion, her tongue curling around mine as she angled my head back. At the same time, she took a step forward, urging us closer to my bed with every drag of her lips on mine.

Living side by side each day had tuned us to the same rhythm. As I lowered down to the bed, she followed the lead and straddled over my lap. When Eden kept kissing me, I leaned back until my back was flat against the mattress and she had me caged between her arms and legs. My hands lightly trailed up the sides of her bare thighs and up the luscious curve of her ass, smiling against her mouth at her skin pebbling in response.

"You have too many clothes on," she muttered against my lips, rising to tug my tunic out from underneath my skirt and where she sat on my legs. I lifted off the bed to rip the cotton over my head.

Eden was there with her punishing, urgent kisses again. My hands were back on her hips in an instant, and I dug my fingers in as her hand painstakingly journeyed from my neck down to my breast. She gently cupped it, stroking her thumb over the peak once, twice, before continuing down my bare stomach.

"When I woke up from rest the first time," Eden whispered, her breath sweet from the honeyed tea she drinks during lunch, "I thought the Gods had taken me to the Heavens."

"Why?" My breath hitched when her fingers slipped beneath the band of my skirt.

"Because I woke—" her fingers circled once over my clit, and I arched into her touch—"and a Goddess was looking down at me."

I tried to huff a laugh, but it came out more like a breathy moan when she slid her fingers over my entrance, pressing against the swollen ache. I managed to get out, "I'm no Goddess."

"You brought me back to life." Eden brushed her nose against mine as her lips moved to my ear. "So, you are *my* Goddess."

She slipped two fingers into me, and I cried out in pure bliss as they pressed into where I ached the most. She rested her forehead against mine, and as our breaths mingled between us, she slowly but thoroughly pumped her fingers in and out of me.

Of their own accord, my hips rolled in tandem with her own smooth rhythm, inching me closer and closer to the edge. When she added her thumb to circle my clit, I shattered as wave after wave of release washed through me. I tightened my grip on her hips and willed the claws to stay back as she continued to curl her fingers.

She peppered kisses down the side of my face and neck before whispering into my ear, "I will never forget you."

Eden lifted her hand from my skirt, but I wasn't done with her. I rolled us so that I sat on top of her, smiling down as her eyes glittered.

"You think I will?" I slowly leaned down, planting an equally punishing kiss as the ones she had given me. I let my canine snag lightly on her bottom lip, and she gasped sinfully.

"You will," she whispered, clasping my head in her hands. "You live many lives, and I am just another in your vast existence."

I frowned, shaking my head. "That's not how it works with me. Not for my friends."

"For now."

After spending the better half of the evening in my bed, we took breakfast together and acted like it was any ordinary day between us. The storm let up outside, and we both fell asleep facing one another.

When I woke the next morning, Eden was gone. She left with nothing but the concealment salve we created to hide her Mark—hide *any* Sirian's Mark if applied to their skin.

There was a single strip of parchment left on the

middle of the table beneath a mug, a single lily sticking out of it. My mouth dropped open at the sight, and *his* voice snuck into my mind, rattling me.

Mi leiron.

My lily.

I swallowed the burn at the back of my throat as I picked it up and read over her choppy handwriting.

Karasi,

You once spoke of your great love and the name he gave you. I feel maybe you don't share with others often, and for that, I am forever grateful. Letting me hold your heart is worth more than you saving my life.

You say goodbye to many. So, to repay you, I refuse to say it to you.

When you see lightning, think of me.

Eden

HOUSE OF ARGO

1499 A.V. | AGE: 692

It had been almost three centuries since I stepped foot in Mariande, and I found myself in the heart of it just a few miles away from the castle where the angriest mortal king ruled. I questioned whether or not this was the best choice, but I knew the person I sought would be here.

I had foreseen it, after all.

I kept my head lowered as I walked through the malnourished neighborhood, frail folk reaching out to grab my jacket as I passed. Most appeared mortal, but they could easily have been Magic if I dared look into their eyes or sniffed them out.

These days, it was rare to find Magics who had any of the qualities of their House. They had maybe one trait—the bright eyes or sharp canines—but never more.

The male I sought, though, had plenty of characteristics based on the vision of him I saw.

I approached one of the dozens of homes haphazardly thrown together. Rows upon rows stretched for blocks, a strange sequence of mismatched brick, wood, and other materials supporting the structures.

I felt eyes peering through windows, watching me as I strolled through their settlement. I caught movement within a small square pane, the curtains swaying shut.

I sighed, glancing down the road I came from, hoping the royal military or guard didn't follow me. I threw my hood back, widening my eyes so they could see I was a Magic.

I knocked my knuckles against the piece of wood functioning as a door. There was a commotion on the other side as I waited, staring at the window in case they decided to look at me again. I tapped my foot as the hushed whispers grew, rubbing my arms against the chill wind.

"For the Gods' sake, Jorah." The door cracked open, revealing half the profile of a young male. A dark brown, monolid eye stared at me, a black braid hanging over his shoulder. "We don't take visitors."

"I'm sure you don't," I chided, sensing the other male behind the door. The one peeking at me confirmed that hunch when his eye flickered to his left. "I come with a peace offering if you care to let me in."

"Peace offering?" The male narrowed his eye. "What sort of peace offering, and why do you wish to be let in?"

I produced a jar of ointment from my cloak, wiggling it in front of him. "You've heard of the Great Karasi, have you not?"

"How do I know it's you?" he asked after there was an indiscernible mumble from the other side.

"This is a concealment salve," I explained, eyeing the

jar in the hazy daylight before peering back at him. Sure enough, his eye had blown wide. "I foresaw us meeting. If I am correct, the male you live with is Magic with scales on his neck and fascinating blue eyes. Yes?"

"It's definitely her, Jorah," the male said without tearing his gaze from me. Instead, in a quick flurry of movements, his hand shot out and grabbed my wrist, yanking me into their home and shutting the door behind me.

I stumbled into the small hut, roughly the same size as the residence I built on the edge of Orion's Lake, except this was far dingier. It subtly smelled of mildew, and the air was damp and chilled. I brushed off my cloak as I scanned the dim interior, thrusting out the jar toward the male.

The other half of his face matched the side that had watched me from behind the door, an identical brown eye and another black braid over his other shoulder. The only thing different now was the nearly-white Mark on the middle of his forehead.

He cautiously accepted the salve, inspecting it before scrutinizing me. "Did your vision give you our names?"

"I'm assuming the male hovering behind you is Jorah," I guessed, tilting my head toward the Magic standing by the door, still as a statue.

He, too, had black hair, but that was the only similarity between them. Instead of a Mark, iridescent scales glistened by the light of the candlewick he held, stretching from the base of his jaw and down his neck, vanishing beneath his stained tunic. He glared at me with eyes that nearly glowed on their own, pure blue irises swirling like the ocean, white strings blinking in and out of existence.

"You're probably the most beautiful Magic I've seen in quite some time," I whispered in awe, shaking my head as I gently shoved the Sirian male away. I'd seen enough of those in my life. "I don't think there were even many from the House of Argo when I was young."

Jorah backed away but couldn't go far with the wall behind him. He visibly swallowed, opening his mouth to speak, but nothing came out. I relented, giving him some space.

This man was different from the version of him I saw in my vision, but I ventured he was *far* older in it.

"What's your name?" I asked the Sirian, backing up to look at both of them.

The Sirian male wiped his free hand on his patched slacks before extending it between us. "Maurice, but you can call me Mo."

"Pleasure," I said, nodding once. I couldn't tear my gaze from Jorah, particularly interested in how he kept the hand not holding the candle bunched in a fist by his sternum.

"I don't mean to be rude, and I greatly appreciate the salve," Mo began, his gaze bouncing between Jorah and I, "but why have you come? What has your vision shown you that led you to us?"

I pressed my lips into a thin line. I didn't want to

offend this Sirian male. The visions I saw of Jorah only brought Mo into it one time. In the far future, I only saw Jorah when he would be the most useful to me. "Do you have somewhere we can sit?"

"The floor," Jorah blurted, his voice almost regal like the kings and queens I'd encountered. It threw off my composure as I blinked at him, seeing too many faces of those long gone.

"I'm okay with that," I said quietly.

I followed them into what could've been a bedroom, a single mattress shoved against the wall. Mo handed Jorah and me a pillow, tucking his own beneath him as he sat. I waited for Jorah to do the same before I mimicked their movements.

Jorah placed the candle in the middle of the circle we created, then quickly snatched his hand back. He tucked them both in the space between his legs.

"You've inherited more than the physicality of your House, correct?" I asked, scanning Jorah's face. Mo's eyes were wide as he bounced his attention from me to Jorah.

He looked to Mo for support, his eyes wary, but the Sirian nodded encouragingly. "The water speaks to me."

I dipped my head, folding my hands in front of me. "The House of Argo used to be able to speak the water language. The waters can tell you what has occurred in the past and what secrets lie within that water. By the way you keep your hands into your body, I venture you've learned there is water in the blood, and you can read people's stories."

"By the touch of their skin, I can glimpse some of who they are," he explained, blinking up at me. "I've never touched their blood directly."

"The reading is far stronger if you do." I shrugged nonchalantly. "If you wish to, that is."

"So, what use do you have of his power?" Mo asked suspiciously, narrowing his eyes as he angled his body protectively. I couldn't decipher whether these two were lovers or simply companions. "You risk exposing us by coming here."

"Indeed." I laid my hands flat on the dirt ground, staring intently at Jorah. "Listen to me carefully. Your life is about to change dramatically, but only if you wish." I lowered my chin, looking up through my lashes. "I encourage you to accept what I'm offering.

"Over the last few centuries, I've been collecting Sirians across the globe that are in hiding." My gaze flickered to Mo, and he fidgeted. "When a Sirian requires safety, I have them come to a post and use a special phrase. I introduce the Sirians to one another, teaching them how to create the concealment salve. What they do next is up to them, whether they live close to one another or decide to relocate somewhere safer. I do so to ensure they do not wield the Darkness, but the Light."

Mo's shoulders rose and fell quickly; his eyes latched onto the side of Jorah's face. He clenched his jaw, the muscle twitching.

"You wield the Darkness," I whispered, leaning back. His silence was answer enough. "It's arguably more dangerous than wielding the Light."

"Don't you think I know that?" Mo snapped, and those dark brown eyes turned black, even consuming the whites as his Mark darkened to match. Jorah rested his hands on Mo's sleeve, and the male relaxed. "I had no choice in the matter. It manifested this way. I didn't wish it—"

"I know," I assured, raising my hands. "It develops as a result of how you were raised. Your parents made you fear what you were."

Mo nodded solemnly, his eyes returning to normal.

"Regardless, I want to prevent it as much as possible," I continued. "By connecting other Sirians, I hope to share the knowledge of teaching their children to control their powers, not fear them. We don't want the Abyss to return. Too many Sirians wielding the Darkness will ensure it does. Balance must remain."

Jorah bit his lip as he glanced from Mo to me, shaking his head. "I still don't understand where I come in."

"I can't continue jumping from country to country at the word of Sirians being present within a village." It wasn't entirely true, but it was the best explanation I had to set up an outpost for Magics and Sirians in Mariande. "I want to establish a place here in Mariande where someone can direct them to the right people."

"You're asking for us to risk our identities to help other Sirians?" Mo stared at me as if I had a third eye in the middle of my forehead.

"And Magics." I offered an encouraging grin. "I

know what it's like to be alone and solitary but wish you didn't have to be. I know this is a big ask, but Fate brought me here because it believes you will play a mighty important role in returning Magics and Sirians to the world, to rise back to an equal place as the humans."

Jorah seemed to consider what I was offering as his attention pinned on Mo. The Sirian kept his eyes on me until he noticed Jorah's penetrating gaze. He slowly turned his head to his companion, frowning with confusion.

"What do we get in return?" Jorah snapped his head to me, his tone serious and assertive. He sounded like a prince. "Outside of doing the good work, what else?"

"I'll give you the funds you need to build a store. It'll be where you conduct your business." I sat straighter, locking with those churning eyes, the blue swirling like waves as the colors crashed together. "You'll hire a few mortals to run the store, but you will have an enchanted room where you can meet secretly. These mortals must be trustworthy and willing to accept what you're doing. They'll pose as the owners and workers of your store until the time is right to reveal yourself as the true owner."

"We'll have money?" Mo startled as though the idea was preposterous.

"I'll support you here in Mariande until you're in a good place," I explained, talking to both of them. "You can live in the space above the store. As long as you wear your salve and learn to control the Darkness, you can pass as any regular mortal. I will teach you both how to make it, so you never run out.

"Something tells me you're a collector?" I jerked my head toward a pile of tomes, and Jorah pursed his lips. "You collect old books."

"I do," he drawled, tilting his head. "I'm afraid they're no use to most, though. I collect them because I find them in strange places when scavenging, and I know no one else will read them."

"Why will no one read them?" I asked only because I believed I knew the answer if I read that part of the vision correctly.

I never read them wrong.

"They're in the old Etherean language…" Jorah trailed off, the swirling blue halting as he narrowed his eyes. "Wait. You said *over the last few centuries*… I know tales of the Great Karasi, but your age is unknown."

"And it will stay that way." I winked, a half-smile peeking out as awe slackened Jorah's face.

"You know the old Etherean language," he whispered, excitement churning those blues again. "You will teach me?"

"I *must* teach you," I assured, chuckling darkly. "I have much to teach you, but we will manage. We have time… We have plenty of time."

Jorah's eyebrows twitched in the middle, and I wonder if he caught the hidden meaning behind my words. He exchanged another glance with Mo, who seemed not to want to respond. They appeared to have a silent way of communicating with one another, and my chest twinged with envy at the proximity and frequency required to develop such a talent.

"I agree, but only if you let me read your blood," Jorah said suddenly, which startled me. I hadn't seen that coming. "You said it reveals people's pasts and secrets. I want to know if you're tricking me or hiding something. I don't trust easily and want to, but it has to be my way."

I extended my hand across the space, holding it palm up. I knew this put me at risk of revealing the fact that I was the child of a demi-god, words that were just a myth these days, not to mention my age.

I also knew I needed Jorah, as did Fate.

These were small sacrifices I would make to ensure this prophecy came true.

"Here," I said, slicing a sharp nail across my palm. I squeezed it in a fist. "Do you have a bowl?"

Mo lurched from his seat, lunging toward a pile of cracked dishes in the corner of the room. He thrust a bowl toward me, and I carefully accepted.

I spit into it, followed by a few drops of my blood. I swirled it before handing it to Jorah. "I hope this was clean because you have to drink that."

"For the love of the Gods," Mo grumbled, covering his eyes. "I'll simply vomit."

Jorah curled his lip at the bowl, his gaze bouncing from it to me a few times before he took a heavy sigh of resolve. He shut his eyes tight and whispered something to himself before downing the little bit of liquid.

He immediately gasped, the sound a croak, as the

bowl clattered to the ground and his eyes shot wide open. I smirked from where I sat, watching the wound on my hand seal closed into an angry mark. Jorah's eyes emitted a soft glow as the blue ran circles around his pupils, the ocean in a raging storm. Mo went to grab him, but I shook my head slowly.

"You're—" Jorah inhaled deeply, trying to catch his breath around the overwhelming amount of information he was undoubtedly receiving. "You're the child of Sybil."

"What?" Mo shouted, snapping his gaze at me. "The demi-god?"

"The one and only."

But Jorah wasn't done.

At nearly seven hundred years old, I thought surprises in my life were over. I thought the world would be predictable from here on out, but what Jorah said next changed very little, yet enough.

"You reign from two Houses," Jorah whispered, his eyes dimming. "You inherited the gifts of two Houses."

"What?" I bit out, stiffening. "What do you mean by that?"

"Sybil created the House of Echidna," Jorah explained, blinking as he tried to collect himself. "So, your father must have been the one to reign from the House of Nemea."

"He did..." I trailed off as I eyed him with suspicion. "You can read my gifts in my blood?"

"The prophecy from your mother." Jorah nodded as

if he were listening to someone tell him the answers just as I did. "The mind walking from your father."

"The mind walking?" I couldn't believe what I'd heard. I was stunned into silence, unable to wrap my head around this. I searched my memory for any time I walked into someone's mind or dream, but then again, I never trained to do so.

The visions came, forced upon me when I least wanted them. I learned to interpret and control some aspects from instinct, maybe the voice itself. Sybil tried her best to explain how it worked, but no one ever taught me to tap into mind walking.

That was something you had to practice, similar to how Magics trained to tap into their enhanced strength. Mind walking was moving from one place to another, placing a mental image somewhere else.

"You didn't know." Jorah frowned, but when his face slackened, I knew he had come to the correct conclusion on why I didn't know about this ability. "I didn't think it was possible to inherit gifts from two different Houses."

"It's extremely uncommon." I cleared my throat, wrapping my arms around my stomach. "Sybil mentioned she'd only met a handful of Magics who had two gifts in all her years."

Jorah and Mo shared a pitied expression, and I fidgeted, uncurling my arms from around me.

"Well," I asked, "am I telling the truth?"

"Well, yes," Jorah said, shaking himself out of his stupor. "Your blood had much to say, but I caught that much.”

"Good." I nodded sternly as I rose from my seat, trying to shake the strange disconnect I felt from my body. "How about we get you boys out of this wretched place?"

HOUSE OF NEMEA

1639 A.V. | AGE: 832

After centuries in Eldamain, I grew to hate Teslin.

While the weather patterns were similar, Eldamain had a clarity about it you didn't recognize until you stepped into Teslin, particularly in the spring and summer. It was humid and thick, the air clinging to my skin and weighing down my limbs. The further toward The Red River I traveled, the heavier the air got. It was lighter toward The Raven's Wood, away from the ocean, though still damp.

That was always where I ended up: directly beside The Red River in Rian.

I strolled through the tightly packed brick buildings and apartments, keeping my enhanced hearing and sight alert. It'd been some time since I'd traveled to Teslin, especially near the home of the royal family, and I wasn't entirely sure of its state when it came to how they viewed Magics.

When I first met Jorah nearly two hundred years ago, I was lucky to find Magics outside of Eldamain. If they lived in another country, it was in hiding because they had no means to travel. It'd been that way roughly two hundred years after the fall of Eldamain and the Sirians, the prejudice and hate gradually growing every fifty years.

Except I knew the day was coming when Magics would slowly start peeking their heads out of their hiding places. I just didn't have a specific date, and I didn't know which country would be the first to allow Magics to live openly within their borders.

It appeared that Teslin would be the first to start warily accepting Magics.

I kept my head held high, and while some paused when they caught my eyes, they tucked their heads and kept walking.

It was an odd feeling to be walking overtly in public.

I finally reached the end of the main square within Rian, hitting the first row of single-story homes on the most northern edge of the border. I stopped in the middle of a cobblestone pathway, peering down an alley as I searched for the home Jorah had described.

Working with Jorah proved far more beneficial than I realized when I first set out for him. Not only had he helped connect Sirians to me to send them safely on their way with salve and safe havens, but he formed strong connections with Sirians and Magics alike, particularly those with rare gifts like him and me.

While most Magics carried hints of the Houses they reigned from, some would occasionally inherit *something* substantial. I inherited prophecy and mind-walking, my father had that and wings, and Jorah had his water language. These were the extent of our gifts outside of physical appearance.

Jorah said this was the first Magic he'd ever encountered that had an actual shifting ability, a gift even Sybil lost entirely over the centuries.

The male couldn't shift to his full primal form like Magics once could, but he manifested wings, and that alone was something worth investigating.

I knocked my hand against the thick mahogany door, tucking my hood back and patting the plaited braids coiled across my head. Despite the bearable temperature, the dampness in the air clung to my skin. I was damn-near ready to scream from the irritation when the door swung open.

I had to use my sheer willpower to school my face into indifferent neutrality. I acknowledged how beautiful Jorah was, but in an intriguing way due to his scales and eyes.

This man, however, was beautiful in a way that stirred something low in my stomach I rarely felt these days. It was enough for goosebumps to ripple across my damp skin.

Like Jorah, he towered over me—but where Jorah was lean, this man was carved. His white tunic hugged tightly to sculpted arms, a defined chest stretching the fabric across his body. It contrasted magnificently against his cool brown skin and matched the white dreadlocks pinned away from his face and flowing down his back. There was a spattering of black stubble above his full lips and down their corners, and his dark, stone-gray eyes studied me just as thoroughly as I admired him.

"Miraculous, really," the man said, tilting his head as he crossed his arms over that chest and leaned against the doorframe. "Here you stand in my doorway, examining me like some wonder while you are one of the few I've ever met with *drakon* eyes."

"You know your mythological Beings," I said, the corner of my lip twitching. "Here I thought I would find yet another Magic entirely unaware of their heritage, whom I would have to educate."

"Is that what you've come here to do?" He smirked, revealing a canine tooth that glistened in the glare of the sun. His eyes dragged from mine, down to my shoes, then back up, lingering on places tightening and heating under his gaze. He sighed heavily, shrugging. "Pity. If you've carved out time from your day, I'm sure there are other things we can occupy our time with."

Of course, the male was arrogant. Who wouldn't be when you were the first of your kind to produce wings in only the Gods knew how long?

I hummed, playing his game. This wasn't my first interaction with an arrogant man who had a way with words. "I'm sure we could. Luckily for us, that's not all I've come here for."

"Does a beautiful creature such as yourself need my services?" He leaned closer into my space, his eyes dancing with intrigue. "Jilted by a former lover? Wish to see them dead?"

"So you use your gifts for assassinations?" It was my turn to tilt my head, blinking at him.

He frowned, those dark brows pressing together. "You're not here for that?"

I scoffed, placing a hand on his chest and shoving him into his own home. I stepped under the threshold and into the entryway, throwing a crooked grin over my shoulder. "I can't say whether it's fortunate or unfortunate, but no. That's not why I'm here."

"By all means, come in," he grumbled, shutting and locking the door behind him as I stepped further into his home.

There was a living area with a single sofa before a fireplace with a table on either end. I narrowed in on the bookcase tucked into the far corner of the wall, jammed with various tomes and books.

"Tea?" he asked as he poured himself a cup, glancing up at me through his lashes.

"No liquor?" I raised an eyebrow.

"It harms the senses, which doesn't bode well for someone who relies on them for his profession and survival." He curled his lip momentarily, then poured me a cup of tea. "I never got your name, my lady."

"Something tells me if you thought hard enough, you would know." I inched closer to the bookcase, catching the title on some of the spines. There were various books on the creatures we could shift to long ago. "I have a few names, but they've always begun with *The Great*."

"Karasi," he whispered, his head jerking up from where he'd placed the kettle onto the silver tray. He grabbed both teacups in his hand and met me by the bookcase. "Well, if I've been personally graced by the presence of the Great Karasi, something tells me you already know my name. For the sake of being a gentleman, though…" He extended the teacup to me with a coy grin. "Voss."

I accepted the tea, my fingers brushing against his, their warmth startling. "Something tells me you're not much of a gentleman."

Voss laughed, throwing his head back with a single hack. "Well, if you've lived as long as the rumors say, I expect you can read people rather well." He ventured to the sofa, ushering me to join him. "No, most who have met me wouldn't use the word *gentleman* to describe me."

I snorted under my breath, clutching the tea between my hands as I lowered beside him on the couch. I sipped the earthy brew, watching him over the rim as he drank his own.

"So," he placed his cup to the side table, "if you don't need someone killed, what have you come for?"

I rolled my eyes a little at that, setting my cup aside. "I have many questions, some of which have come to me since the moment you opened your mouth."

He smiled broadly, rousing two very conflicting emotions within me: agitation and arousal. "By all means." He extended his hand out between us.

"How old were you when your wings came to you?" I asked, leaning back into the cushion. "And how old are you now?"

His eyebrows arched, amusement flickering across his face. "I was eighteen when they came to me, rather abruptly, I do have to say. I'm nearly fifty now."

"You look quite young for fifty, even for a Magic," I observed, scanning his face for any signs of age. Other than deep shadows within his eyes, he looked to be in his late twenties. "As you may know, I also inherited a gift beyond our enhanced capabilities, and I'm far older than I look. There's a friend of mine who is similar, and he has lived almost two hundred years."

His smile faltered, barely perceptible. The idea of his potential lifespan was news to him. "You have prophecy. Can you not tell me what age you see me living to?"

"It doesn't always work like that," I muttered, squinting at him, even as the voices began to whisper numbers and incoherent words. "I take it you learned to fly, then?"

"I have learned to do quite a bit as a Magic." He rose from the couch, slowly walking towards the fireplace with his hands clasped behind his back. "The moment the wings came to me, I taught myself to reach in and call them forward or place them back at will. Once I did that, I made it my mission to gather as much information on our people and my House as possible, especially regarding the ability to shift. I have spent thirty years educating myself, and the last ten years I've slowly perfected flight to my advantage."

"You haven't come across any others with wings?" He shook his head, maintaining eye contact. "Have you come across others with *any* rare gifts?"

"Outside of what I've heard about you and this friend you speak of, no." Something dark passed quickly over his eyes again, raising the hairs on my neck. "I'm quite fascinated by the prospect of more, but even more curious why gifts appear sporadically without correlation between them. For example, you reign from the House of Echidna while I am from the House of Nemea."

"Well, if it's a research project you seek, I have one more drop of information for you." I wasn't about to tell him my mother was Sybil the demi-god, which explained my gifts. I also wasn't about to tell him my father was also from the House of Nemea. "My friend is from the House of Argo and speaks the water language."

"Fascinating," Voss whispered, his eyes alight with awe and the ghost of a smile. "There must be *something* to it."

"Possibly." I shrugged, crossing one leg over the other. I let my gaze wander momentarily, my next question coming forward. "So, you make your income by killing people?"

Voss rested an elbow on the fireplace mantel, narrowing his eyes. "I detect a tone of judgment."

"It's neither here nor there." I rose from the sofa then, observing the various trinkets and decorations on his wall. They appeared to be from different places around our world, one for each country and culture. "How do you conduct your business?"

He sighed as he saddled up beside me, our shoulders brushing as we observed a mask from the southern colonies of Riddling. "People come to me from far and wide, as I've heard they do for you. Instead of seeking a prophecy, they ask for my assistance in someone's demise. It's not always murder. Sometimes they wish to threaten, typically a beating with a message from the one who contracts me."

"I suppose murder requires more coin?" I peered at him from the corner of my eyes, his penetrating gaze burning me from the inside out.

He smirked, no doubt having that enhanced sense of smell. If he did, he likely smelled the arousal. The House of Nemea was known to be quite *feral* regarding mating. Something to do with the creatures they hailed from. "It's also more coin depending on an individual's importance in the world."

My body locked up then, and I stared at him. "Lords and ladies? Kings and queens?"

"I have only killed one lord thus far," he explained, wagging his head. "I wouldn't be opposed to a king or queen. None of them have done much for me thus far."

"Is Teslin not accepting of Magics?" I turned to face him then, pursing my lips.

His eyes fell to my lips, darkening with something far more sensual. "The Magics of Rian have fought their way to the top against the desires of the king and queen.

Eldamain may be no man's land, Karasi, but Rian is where the devils live."

I understood exactly what he meant.

The Magics of Rian were angry and resentful. They climbed to where they are by doing exactly as Voss did: killed. If a Magic community was being built on those pillars, Rian wouldn't be much safer for a Magic than living under the nose of the royals in any other country.

"Is that what you are?" I stepped into him, shortening the distance between us. "A devil?"

He smirked, hunching over until our noses touched. "Are you frightened, dear?"

I narrowed my eyes, fighting the warring urge to slap or kiss him. Lucky or not so lucky for me, he quickly lurched back with a deep inhale, waving his hand toward another room in his grand home.

"Are you hungry?" He started walking away, calling over his shoulder. "We can continue to discuss all your questions over dinner."

Voss answered my questions well enough, describing his upbringing in a small, unmarked village near The Raven's Wood in Teslin with his Magic parents, both Nemea immigrants from Riddling. He discussed how his business endeavors worked in detail, some of the precise clientele or tasks he'd achieved, and how he desired to relocate out of Teslin. Despite his form of unrighteous employment, he strongly disliked the reckless way Magics were making their place in Rian.

He asked me about my life and what I do, how a Magic of an unknown age had entertained herself over the years. I found myself discussing the Sirians, except I didn't reveal exactly where the posts were or who was involved across Aveesh.

He may have been beautiful and exuded an air of haughty grandeur, but his beliefs and what he did rubbed me the wrong way. There was no limit to what he did or didn't do for coin—mortal or Magic alike.

I didn't trust him with such a precious secret as my Sirians.

"Final question before I take my leave to my inn for the evening," I said, glancing over my shoulder as I approached the foyer. I paused at the threshold of the living area. "I want to see them."

"Oh?" Voss stood in the space beside the sofa, an eyebrow raised. "Do you not believe I have them?"

"I have full faith you have them," I corrected, slowly twisting on my heel. "Regardless of how old I may or may not be, I've never seen wings from either House, and I did travel all the way from Eldamain to simply meet you. I think the least you could do is show them to me."

"You seem to believe you are owed things, especially for a decision you made of your own accord," Voss said, not unkindly, hands folded in front of him. "Alas, you have offered me some rather entertaining company, and I enjoy talking about myself."

"I caught that." My lips betrayed me with a coy smirk, which his eyes latched onto again. My stomach dipped and heated.

I watched in fascination as, within a blink, his wings gracefully unfurled from behind his back, the sound like hitting a rug with a wooden staff.

And Gods did they make him even more alluring.

Spreading broadly, farther than the width of his shoulders, were feathered, beige wings that reminded me of a dove. They twitched here and there in response to their release, some of the feathers swaying with the movement. He fought his smile, and I knew then I had relinquished all control over my facial features.

"I feel like astonishing the Great Karasi may be an accomplishment I must cherish." He chuckled, tracking me with glittering eyes as I drew nearer, placing my right hand against his left bicep.

That was a mistake because I held his firm, thick muscle in my hand.

I blinked at him, gently swallowing as I lifted my left hand and wiggled my fingers. "May I?"

Something unfamiliar flashed across his face, but he nodded in encouragement or permission, possibly both. Bracing myself against his arm, I reached my fingers out and carefully caressed a few of the feathers dangling from the concealed cartilage.

Each feather was like silk.

The wing quivered in response, Voss's bicep flexing under my hand. I peered out of the corner of my eye, biting my lower lip at his shut eyes.

I lifted my hand higher to where the feathers stretched across the entire wing, clustered to protect what I believed was skin beneath. I didn't change the strength of my touch, unsure what response it would elicit.

I learned rather quickly, though.

His bicep flexed once more, but this time he gripped my extended arm, his large hand wrapping around my wrist. He moved swiftly, so much so that my enhanced senses barely picked up on it enough for me to respond. I expected anger or agitation in his gaze, but it was quite the opposite.

The lust oozed from him. My sense of smell told me as much, and while I should've been appalled by his audacity to grab me so firmly, I was molten.

"They are…" He attempted to gather himself, his throat bobbing. "They tend to be rather sensitive to touch. Being hidden away will do that to them, as does my own inability to touch them."

"Pleasantly sensitive?" I whispered hoarsely, realizing I'd unintentionally drifted closer to him. Heat radiated from his body, and something stiff barely brushed against my pelvis.

"Depends," he answered, his jaw clenched in apparent restraint. His other hand gently embraced my waist, slowly snaking around my back. He urged me closer, my breasts pressing against that impossibly firm chest beneath. "Pleasantly… If the other party has an enticing motive. Not as pleasant if I'm left alone afterwards."

I hummed at the insinuation, my eyelids heavy as he inched closer to my lips, our noses brushing. I slightly ground my hips against him, and his chest rumbled in a true growl. "Is this the hospitality you offer all your guests?"

"Only the ones who ask to touch my wings." His lips quirked, and I glided my hand up his arm and across his chest, marveling at the strength beneath the tunic. "I should elaborate, few have the brazenness to do so."

"Well," I sighed, my hand lifting to cup the side of his neck, my thumb resting against his pulse. "Best get to it then—"

That feral male wasted no time the moment the words left my lips, silencing me with his own. We moved quickly, my back hitting the nearest wall as he pinned me there. He parted my lips, tongue sweeping into my mouth, and I ached on the most primal level.

I tugged at his tunic, yanking the hem out of his pants as I lifted it up and over his head. His arms followed my movement, helping pull it off, and I took the opportunity to admire the body that was hidden beneath.

Sculpted was the only word for it, like a statue within Etherea's castle. His skin was smooth, stretching across the swell of muscle on his chest. His stomach held various quadrants, trailing down to a defined "V" complemented by dark, coarse hair that disappeared beneath his slacks.

He worked on the strings at the front of my dress as I maneuvered around his hands to untie his slacks, concealing what I most wanted. Once my dress was loose enough, we switched and shimmied out of the only garments separating us.

Once the flimsy fabric slid down my curves, Voss's full attention gazed over every inch of my body, leaving a heated trail behind. I peeked at his impressive length.

"We won't need a bed," Voss grumbled, bending before me and gripping my legs. He easily hoisted me up his body, adjusting his grip so he cupped my ass as he moved to the sofa. My senses focused only on the feel of his unnaturally warm body against mine, every shift like lightning through each point of contact.

I gasped as Voss lowered to the sofa behind him, precariously placing me on his lap with my entrance poised on the underside of his cock. He groaned as I rolled my hips, throwing his head back with his eyes shut, tension pulsing at his temple. His grip tightened around my waist, digging into my soft flesh.

"A marvelous creature," he grumbled as I continued to coat him, throbbing as I clenched around nothing. He looked down at where we touched, his eyes darkening as he ground his hips in time with mine. My head lolled back as I braced my hands on his shoulders. "Have you ever ridden a birdman before?"

I chuckled low and dark. "Naughty—"

My words morphed into a deep moan as Voss used his grip on my waist to lift me onto his cock at the same time he thrust his hips up into me, effortlessly gliding in. I braced my shins on either side of his legs as I continued to slide down over his thick member, the stretch hitting exactly where I'd hoped.

"*Godsdamnit,*" he growled again, grinding his hips up to hit a deep place within me that sent a spark of pleasure through my body.

That sound unleashed both of us.

I lifted myself and plunged back down, and Voss met me with rough thrusts that hit precisely the perfect place that coiled with blissful tension low in my stomach. He angled my body closer to him, dipping his head to roll my nipple into his mouth, sucking and carefully nipping at it to avoid his canine.

Wild and untamed. That's what we were.

"Grab the back of the couch," he said as he removed his mouth, slipping his hands over the curve of my ass to brace me.

I reached behind his shoulders, leaning forward so his head nearly rested on my shoulder, his breath tickling my neck. I could barely move in this position with his hands on me, but it didn't matter because Voss began pounding, and this angle hit a place within that most men didn't bother trying to find.

"Oh, Gods," I moaned, the words trembling.

That coil within me only wound tighter, and Voss kept me just at the edge, slowly inching me closer and closer to the release I craved without granting it. My panting became frantic as I tried to grasp onto that moment of ecstasy, but Voss only teased.

"How badly do you seek it?" He whispered roughly against my ears, my legs starting to tremble from the intensity. "Will you beg?"

I snarled as I pulled my head back to meet those gray eyes, my lip curled. I brought my claws forward, dragging one carefully down the side of his face, and he faltered in his rhythm. "I beg for no man alive."

"If I knew you had claws…"

I squeaked as Voss flipped us, laying me down on the couch and hoisting my leg over his shoulder as my other braced on the floor. Stars flashed across my vision as my hands sought purchase on his back, claws concealed.

"Use them," he commanded, although it was half a plea. "Make your mark."

He snapped his hips down and up, and release shattered me, rippling like waves of sweet, sensuous relief. I clawed at his back, and he hissed, thrusting hard one final time before slowing his pace into a slow, languid twitch.

When he finally stilled, he pulled himself out and lay back on the opposite end of the sofa, our legs tangled together as we tried to catch our breath. He lifted his head, peering down his nose as he threw me a lazy smirk.

"What else are you hiding?" he asked, breathlessly. "I have to admit, I haven't had a partner who can keep up entirely with my desires."

I laughed, not quite a full caliber one, but pretty close. I dug my foot into his rib, narrowing my eyes. "How quickly will you go again?"

"Gifted Magic, remember?" He prowled toward me like a predator. "Enhanced stamina."

We continued to pleasure one another long into the night, eventually retiring to the bedroom where we fell back in exhaustion. While his breaths quickly turned shallow, I was not one to stay the night.

I wasn't the one to linger.

And when it came down to it, I didn't trust Voss.

So I didn't see him again for a long while.

WHEEL OF TIME

1775 A.V. | Age: 968

I slipped through the houses gathered on the southern edge of Saros—the same ones I traipsed through in search of a boy from the House of Argo. They were more developed this time with sturdy brick walls and thick-plated roofs but still built too close together for comfort.

"This way, Great Karasi," the man who fetched me from Eldamain said, guiding me to a row of houses down the far edge of the street. I pulled my hood tighter toward my face, glaring at the back of his head.

Maximus appeared after using the code I'd dictated for mortals and Magics to find me, different from the one I used for Sirians. He requested my assistance back in Mariande because his friend's wife was having a difficult pregnancy, and they worried about the baby.

"You use discretion to come retrieve me and yet utter my name out in the open in a hostile country," I chastised, clinging to the strap of my satchel. "I find it rather cumbersome."

Maximus huffed heavily, shaking his head. "This side

of the village isn't necessarily for or against Magics. We're far enough from the town square that no knights patrol here."

"How badly are they patrolling Saros?" I scurried closer, trying to match his steps.

He shrugged, emerald-green eyes glistening in the dimming daylight. "No different than the past few decades. I think since the birth of King Pallas's son, he's grown even more obsessive about eradicating Magics."

"Marvelous," I grumbled, but the words came out weak as my vision wavered.

This wasn't the time.

[Claims a King.] The voice hissed, although it bordered on a snarl. I tried to swat it away, but it shot an image of a mop of blond hair with a crown through my mind.

"What's the baby prince's name?" I asked, fingernails digging into my palms as I fought the urge to claw at my skin.

"Prince Darius Hesper."

I stumbled as the voice echoed the name repeatedly, except it said *King* Darius Hesper rather than *Prince*.

This child would be important to my prophecy after he became king.

"This is their home," Maximus explained, waving his hand to the small brick structure before me. It was narrow but had two stories and an incredibly slim alleyway between the houses neighboring it.

"How are you related to them again?" I side-eyed

him, squinting.

"I live down the street," he explained, tilting his head. "Walter and I've worked at the butcher's together for the last decade, and he told me about his wife's condition. I finally convinced him to let me fetch you."

"Well, thank you." I nodded once, holding out my hand. "Maximus…"

"Wardson." His grip was firm, those eyes shining with his soft grin. "Maximus Wardson."

My vision wavered again, and I saw a different version of him, except his features were softer compared to his pointed angles.

I watched him leave with an uneasiness in my chest.

My heartbeat echoed in my ears, a rhythmic thumping as I turned and rapped against the wooden door. Heavy footsteps shuffled on the other side, and the voice cackled in my head, a grating sound that churned my stomach with bile burning in my chest.

I wasn't prepared as much as I should've been for this introduction. I nearly called the claws forward to counter the nausea and tunneling vision, but the door opened, and I immediately knew who this was.

Not because of the voice in my head, but because he looked *just like him*.

"You must be the Great Karasi," the man said, his voice very similar to one from my past.

I swallowed the sharp pain in my throat. "I take it you're Walter?"

Walter confirmed with a slow nod, his eyes the only

thing he didn't inherit from *him*. They were a pure golden hazel, bright in the shine of the lamp beside him on the wall.

Other than that, everything else about him looked just like Brand.

"Walter Carraphim," he said, the second surprise of the day. "My wife needs your help."

I moved like a ghost through the motions as he brought me into the house and explained the progression of his wife's condition over the last few months of pregnancy. I absorbed it, but I was transfixed by how time worked.

Korbin's were the sole reason the significance of the Carraphim name was lost to history. Yet, this Korbin line would be the single reason the importance of the Carraphim name would be remembered.

Walter may not have known a lick of his heritage, but I knew it all. He was a descendant of Brand Korbin, but the Carraphim name bled into it somewhere down the line.

Mrs. Carraphim went into labor not long after I arrived—painful but expected. I had the herbs I needed to treat her condition, and Walter helped me maneuver the infant so she birthed it headfirst rather than feet–first. She screamed at the pain, but eventually, her cries faded when the baby took its first breath and took over the screaming.

"It's a boy," I announced, cleaning him off before handing him to his mother and father. Mrs. Carraphim smiled down at the child, but Walter's smile never quite reached his eyes. "Do you have a name for him?"

"Jedrek," Mrs. Carraphim answered softly and breathlessly. "Jedrek Carraphim."

I sucked in a harsh breath of air at the name, and Walter's eyes snapped to me, frowning. I lost my balance, stumbling, but Walter caught me just as my vision vanished entirely.

"Jedrek Carraphim," the deep voice said, a smirk curling beneath golden eyes. "You're Bryn, right?"

"Bryna…" The scene morphed and revealed the woman's face but alternated between two versions with subtle differences. Instead of gray-blue eyes, one of the faces had golden eyes like the male's. "It's Bryna Paddock, not Bryn."

"Maybe I'll call you Bryn." The smirk only widened.

"Great Karasi?" Another voice cut in, snapping me from the vision. I gasped, yanking my arms from Walter. I turned toward the worktable, steadying the shiver crawling over my skin. "Are you okay?"

"Fine," I snapped, shutting my eyes. "Just a vision."

"What did you see?" Walter sounded concerned, a frantic undercurrent. "Was it our son?"

"His future," I answered, waiting for the voice to stop me. "I saw a piece of his future. I think it may be his future wife."

I peeked over my shoulder, gauging Walter's reaction. He seemed visibly relieved, and the longer I looked, the clearer it became how different this male was compared to Brand. He may have looked like him, but he was nothing like him.

If anything, he reminded me of Brand's older, crueler brothers.

"I can't thank you enough," Mrs. Carraphim said from the bed, her finger trailing down her son's face. "I greatly appreciate you risking your safety to come here."

I nodded.

There was nothing more to say. I saw what I needed.

This baby—Jedrek—and his future wife would usher in the child I had waited centuries for. It pained me to know this boy would die in early adulthood, losing his wife too soon. They would never see their daughter grow.

The world may have forgotten the historical significance of the Carraphim name, but it would be their daughter who ensured the world remembered it.

BLOOD OF MAGICS

1785 A.V. | AGE: 978

I didn't expect a guest when I stepped out of my bedroom that evening.

I also didn't plan on seeing this particular Magic lounging on my sofa, staring out the window as though someone out there caused him some great offense.

Especially considering it'd been over a century since I'd seen him last.

"Either someone has put a bounty on my head or you're incredibly rude," I chided, hitching my hand on my hip.

"If there were a bounty on your head, you would've known." Voss dragged his flat, dark gray eyes toward me. "I thought since you left me in the dead of night over one hundred and fifty years ago, I would appear in your home in the dead of night."

I rolled my eyes to the back of my head, starting toward the kitchen. He watched me as I shuffled through the cabinets for two mugs and tea leaves. I lit the fire under the burner and placed the kettle on top before twisting to face him, bracing my hands on the counter.

"Why are you here?" I asked, tilting my head. He stared at me, blinking. "I heard you abandoned the bounty life, but I find that rather unbelievable since that's the only way you knew how to make a living."

"I slowed my bounties over the last century, year by year." He dragged his gaze back to the window, his jaw ticking. "I formed relationships with different kingdoms and only had to do an occasional bounty for the money and protection they offered."

"Protection," I said, deadpan, my shoulders slackening. "Really? A kingdom offering you protection? It's a little early for that."

"Oh, is it?" Voss snapped, his tone mocking, and I snorted at how childish he sounded.

My experience with Voss only went as far as that single encounter we had, but the man had a personality as big as his ego, so it wasn't hard to tell what kind of man he was.

The kettle squealed on the stove, and I turned around to pour the hot water into our mugs. "I won't ask again, Voss. What are you doing here?"

A few beats of silence passed before I grabbed the mugs and approached him. I handed him one with an eyebrow raised. He accepted, and I made my way to the chair at my kitchen table.

"I was working in Riddling when I heard rumors of a male who had grown wings," he said, and I stopped mid-sip.

"Another with wings?" I lowered my mug, frowning.

"Is it—"

"He was House of Nemea." Voss nodded slowly, inspecting the leaves in his tea. "Not that I knew anything about taking an apprentice, but who better to teach him than the only other person in this world with wings? Lucky for him, I was of his House, too. I took him as my apprentice about five years ago."

I huffed in disbelief. Not only had I met a Magic with wings, but Voss was saying there was a *second* one.

Except he looked far too thoughtful for this to be the only thing he wanted to tell me.

"You know what was even more fascinating?" He chuckled darkly, shaking his head and raising his eyes to me. "Only two years after that, I received a letter from the son of an old friend in The Clips saying that *his* son had *also* sprouted wings. This time, he was from the House of Echidna."

I nearly dropped my mug.

Not two, but now *three* Magics had wings in Aveesh.

I didn't understand how this was possible. I knew why I had my gifts, but I never understood why Jorah or Voss inherited theirs. I thought maybe every few hundred years or so, a Magic would gain some sort of gift from their shifting heritage.

But that theory was now squashed since two men had wings only a few years apart from two different Houses, two different corners of the world.

"The only hypothesis I have come up with over the years is Magic blood versus mortal blood." Voss tightened his grip around the mug, shaking his head. "Our kind continues to cluster in large communities, so we are mating with each other once again. The mix of Magic blood from both sides is bringing back these powerful gifts and shifting abilities we have not seen in years."

"*Centuries*, Voss." I winced at the heat of my tea, setting it on the table. "You forget, even in my youth, I never saw wings. Not until you."

"And did Magics live amongst one another in your time?"

"Yes!" I laughed, although the sound was hollow. "That's all I'm saying about my time. I think the reason these Magic gifts are returning is far more complicated than you believe it to be."

"As though what we pass down through our blood is not complicated enough." Voss curled his lip and redirected his attention to the crackling fireplace.

Voss had changed, but not in the ways I was used to. He was already a haughty male when I first met him with a few unsavory morals, but there was an added edge to him that led me to believe there was no moving him. His beliefs weren't just inquiries anymore—he held them as truth.

I didn't fault him for wanting to understand why these gifts were popping up; I was just as curious, but his explanation bothered me.

Long before Magics spread across the world in small pockets, they mated with mortals *and* Sirians, and this never inhibited their gifts. Sybil told me plenty of stories of royal Magics and Sirians marrying mortals and producing some of the most powerful of their time.

My own hypothesis was that it had something to do with the True Prophecy.

"If I told you it may have to do with the Gods, would you believe me?" I leaned my body sideways to try and meet his gaze, but I only caught an incredulous smirk.

"Sure." Voss's eyes flickered to mine, and he shrugged, adding, "Does it really matter in the end?"

Maybe it didn't for Voss, but for me, it did. Sybil once said the Gods were either locked or hidden away from the world, and with apparent reason. If by some chance Magics' powers were tied to the Gods—maybe to Morana's own powers as the Goddess of Death and Magics—it could mean they were coming back or getting out of wherever they were trapped.

"I know why you left," Voss said suddenly, still not looking at me. The flames reflected in his light eyes, dancing and flickering. "When I told you my choice of profession, you shut yourself off, or whatever you came to speak to me about."

"You were working with kingdoms, Voss. I couldn't trust you." I sighed, folding my arms. "You understand that, don't you? I was working with Sirians, and the last thing they needed was someone who could be paid to kill them."

"You're still working with them, aren't you?" He finally faced me then, and something about his expression looked hurt.

"Not like I was back then." I shook my head. "I met a man and woman about twenty years ago who I knew would take over for me in corralling them to safety."

"Good." He cleared his throat, blinking. "You know, I did try to do good by taking these two boys in. I taught them everything I know about accessing those extra powers and fighting. In the end, though, they left. Doing good got me nowhere."

"Did you truly do good to help the world?" I studied his face, squinting. "Or did you do it to make yourself feel better for the harm you've done to your own kind?"

"You don't know anything about what I've done to survive!" Voss lurched from his seat, advancing on me. I quickly stood, narrowing my eyes further as he shoved his finger in my face. "Just because we are gifted doesn't mean we're destined to sacrifice ourselves to save the world, and for what? At least what I was doing, I was getting coin for it. What is the difference between murdering for *the greater good* and murdering for coin?

"You're killing innocents either way, in war or sport." He scoffed, taking a step away from me. "Might as well get paid for it, knowing they wronged someone somehow, even if it was petty reasoning."

"You're the worst sort." I chuckled harshly, walking toward my door. I flung it open, staring him down. "Do you know why?"

"Enlighten me, Karasi," Voss said, strutting to the door leisurely. "Heavens know you're a Goddess of our own on this plane."

I ignored his comment, counting to four before speaking again. "At least those you do evil bidding for know what they're doing is wrong, otherwise they wouldn't hire an assassin to do it. You act like it's only business and see nothing wrong with your actions."

Voss's jaw ticked in aggravation as he stared me down, his eyes boring into me. After a moment of searching, his face fell. Whether he found what he was looking for, I couldn't say.

"You all leave in the dead of night." Voss sighed, shaking his head as he walked onto my porch. He threw his head over his shoulder. "At least I can acknowledge I'm alone in this world. You sit here hiding, pretending you have true friends who care about who you are, not just what you can do."

With that, Voss launched into the sky, the night swallowing those beige wings.

I knew he intended for his final words to hurt, but they had no effect. I couldn't pretend I had friends. I knew those I connected with were nothing near that, and I was aware that my powers or what I could do for them were what drew people in.

It had been quite some time since someone cared for who I was within my soul.

COLLECTOR OF MAGICS

1789 A.V. | AGE: 982

Rol and I sat silently in one of the booths at The Red Raven. He counted the coins from the previous night, scribbling onto his parchment. I sipped the mulled wine, its warmth spreading through my limbs.

"How long will you wait?" Rol asked, his cigar bobbing against his bottom lip with every word. He raised a bushy eyebrow as he momentarily stopped writing.

I shrugged, my eyes lingering at the door. "Until I must. It's not like I'm given dates and times for these things."

"But you knew it would be today?" He went back to his bookkeeping, plopping his cigar onto a tray.

"When I woke this morning, yes." I swallowed two mouthfuls of the wine, wincing at the burn. "Just knew I needed to be here for someone's arrival."

"How many people come in here daily?" Rol shook his head, chuckling. "Will your little gift tell you—"

The bells above the door jingled over the low chatter of the current patrons. Rol and I snapped our heads toward it as two figures shuffled in haggardly.

[Them.]

At the same time, Rol grumbled, "I hate this pub."

I smirked over the rim of my wine as I took a final sip and winked at him. I left the table, patting his shoulder on the way. "I'll handle them."

"Of course you will."

I slipped behind the bar just as the two strangers sat at the stools. They were both worse for wear, not because they were filthy, but because the defeated looks on their faces reflected how they carried themselves.

The female had sharp features, which were further accented by the deep shadows under her brick-red eyes. Her skin was pale and dull, lacking any inner glow that naturally showed with one's personality. Her black hair was braided back away from her face, and her frame appeared rather muscular for someone her height, shorter than me.

I knew beneath the hopelessness, she was beautiful.

The male looked even worse. His blond hair was ashen, lacking any deeper hues, knotted into a bun at the base of his skull. Where the female had dark circles, his face seemed sunken, with deep shadows around his entire eye socket and below his square cheekbones. An ungroomed, patchy beard matched his hair color.

I'd say he looked like he didn't want to be here, but it was far grimmer.

He looked like he didn't want to be alive.

"What can I get for you?" I asked, directing it to the

female.

She sighed heavily, throwing her hand up and letting it fall back to the bar top. "Anything strong."

"Clear or dark liquor?" I let my eyes bounce to the male briefly.

"Dark," he grumbled in a hoarse tone.

I went to work immediately, grabbing the whiskey off the shelf while focusing on the woman.

"Clear," she answered quietly, studying me intently. Something flashed imperceptibly in the depths of those transfixing eyes, gone in a blink.

I handed them their glasses, then leaned back, resting my hips on the counter and crossing my arms over my chest. "Where do you come from?"

The male stiffened, his fingers flexing on the glass as his eyes pulsed once. In one swig, he downed the entire glass of whiskey. The female peered at him with a shared despair, sipping her own before returning her attention to me.

"Etherea," she said, the word like a crack of a whip.

I startled, unable to hide the shocked horror from my face. Even some of the regulars paused their conversations to inspect.

I knew nothing about these two. I didn't see their faces in my vision, let alone one with them. When I woke up that morning, the voice said *strangers*, and I had this sense that I needed to be at The Red Raven—no knowledge of who they were, where they came from, or why they were there.

"Magics in Etherea?" I raised my eyebrow, searching the woman's face. "That sounds like a dream."

"It was a nightmare," the man snapped, his lip curled. He shoved the glass across the wood and tapped harshly on the bar top. "Another."

"Willem," the woman said softly, shaking her head. She sighed when he shot her a menacing glare. "I'm sorry. We've just come from Lolis. We were trying to establish a Magic community like the one that was once in Ghita and what you have here in Main Town."

"I suppose it didn't go as planned?" I uncorked the whiskey with a wince, filling his glass nearly to the brim.

"Etherea came and… did what Etherea does best." She shook her head slowly, tears brimming those red eyes. "We lost a lot of important people…"

My heart ached for them because I knew exactly what they meant. In the last handful of centuries, the world only treated Magics more cruelly, nearly as much as they had treated Sirians. Etherea was the worst of them.

It appeared there was a curse they couldn't break out of since Alrik Korbin sat on the throne.

"I'm sorry, but I know that doesn't heal the wounds left behind." My gaze bounced between the two, my eyes catching on a golden band around the male's finger. I glanced at the female's hands wrapped around her glass, but she didn't have a matching band.

Gods, did that realization hurt.

"We figured the only safe place was here." She shrugged as she sipped her liquor, hissing at the bite.

"Nothing good can come of trying to expand our reach, I guess."

I wanted to tell them the world would change soon. I felt it in my bones, even without the voice. It wasn't the right time to offer them words of encouragement when their loved ones had just been massacred.

I wasn't sure when it would be safe again in Etherea, not that I knew much of an Etherea that had ever been truly safe.

"What are you two good for?" I leaned forward on the counter before the woman. She raised a tired but amused eyebrow, but the Willem fellow didn't seem to care in the slightest. If we were attacked right now, I had a feeling he would let them take him. "If you want to live in Eldamain, you'll need a job."

"Oh." She frowned, but she shook her head. "Willem was something like a butcher. I have a long history working in pubs if…"

"Rol is looking for a bartender." I smiled gently, jerking my head to where the grump glared at me over his shoulder. "Don't give me that, Rol. You could use the help."

"She's pretty enough," was all Rol said as he resumed his bookkeeping.

I deadpanned at the back of his head as the woman snorted.

"Seems like we'll fit right in, Willem," she muttered to him, but her eyes were on me as she lifted the glass to her lips. She kept them pinned on me over the rim. "I'm

Dahlia, by the way. Something tells me you're the Great Karasi."

Months after they arrived, I still didn't understand how Dahlia and Willem fit into my life or the True Prophecy. I found it fascinating that I'd collected Magics and Sirians since meeting Jorah, some of whom I rarely saw or never saw again.

There was something different about Willem and Dahlia, though. I wasn't sure if it was because Willem was an absolute ass of a man, one I undoubtedly believed was the product of his circumstances, but Dahlia appeared to be pushing through *despite* her circumstances. She was a bubbly, sarcastic barkeep, not to mention entirely flirty with anyone and everyone.

Including me.

"Does this look right?" Dahlia stood over my kitchen table, angling her head at the jars she was prepping for me. "I feel like there shouldn't be particles floating in this."

"Because there shouldn't be." I chuckled as I shuffled over from the sink, picking up the jar and holding it to the light. Sure enough, small particles were floating in what was supposed to be a clear elixir. "You'll have to do it again."

"Godsdamnit," she growled, rubbing her forehead. "I swear, I'm hopeless when it comes to making potions and shit."

"Hopeless is a strong word considering you've only been practicing some of these for a week." I shot her a bored glance before heading back to the window above the counter. I cranked it open, tossing the contents and resting the jar on the counter. I braced my hands on it behind me. "These are some of the more advanced elixirs that require patience, especially as you learn them. You must pay attention to what you're doing, or it's ineffective or even dangerous."

"And if there are particles in elixirs that shouldn't be?" Dahlia folded her arms across her chest, and I couldn't help but linger on the way it pushed her cleavage up.

I cleared my throat, shrugging. "It means it would be too potent, and most of the time, that means too strong. Too strong is too dangerous. The herbs we're working with for these elixirs could be lethal in high dosages."

"Fantastic." She sighed, running both of her hands through her black hair.

I chuckled again, the sound low in my chest as I shook my head. "Give yourself some credit. You've come from an entirely different background than most Magics."

"You mean an entertainer?" Dahlia smirked, and I rolled my eyes. "You can say the word. It's not going to set me off. I did what I had to survive in Teslin. I have a friend to thank for finally getting me out."

"Willem?" I held her gaze as I approached the table, helping her clean up some of the mess she'd left behind.

"No, someone else." She frowned at the stems of the

plants she used, a wistful glisten in her eyes. "We met in Teslin when he was working for Hugo. The kingpin found him useful once he learned he had wings."

The jar tumbled from my hands, rolling off the table and shattering onto the floor. Dahlia swore as she jumped away from the shards, her eyes frantic. She and Willem were accustomed to my episodes and knew what it looked like when I had one, but this wasn't that.

No, Voss's words rang in my head like a bell.

"What House?" I studied her face as we crouched to the ground and carefully collected the broken pieces.

"Well, my friend is from the House of Echidna," she explained, and her eyes downturned. "His lover also had wings and was from the House of Nemea."

"Was." It wasn't a question, but more of a reminder. They had lost him in the attack on Lolis. "I'm sorry. Where is your friend now?"

"Who the hell knows?" She snorted, a bitter tone to her words as she dropped the glass pieces into another empty jar on the table. "He took off shortly after we cleaned up what we could and helped set up survivors... He hasn't been dealt the best cards in life, but I thought he'd want to stay with us because we all had something in common."

"*He will come around,*" I said, rising from the crouch, although my voice went monotone. I frowned as I emptied my hands of the glass, wiping them on my skirt. "I understand his need for seclusion, is what I mean. It can happen."

She offered a tight-lipped grin that didn't reach her eyes.

We continued cleaning up in silence, and it wasn't until I filed away the final clean dish that Dahlia spoke again, but with reverence.

"How many people have you loved in your existence?" She shuffled toward my couch, examining some items hanging on my walls, hands clasped behind her back.

I tilted my head, following her to the living space. I sat down on the cushion with a heavy sigh. "Do you mean *lovers* or people I've loved, no matter the type of love?"

"Either." She fell back into the sofa beside me, hitching up her leg and tucking her knee under her chin with arms wrapped around her shin.

I gnawed at my lower lip, studying her face. There was a glisten in those red eyes.

I had to admit, despite the various colors I'd seen my entire existence, I always found mine unsettling. Dahlia's may have been even more so.

"I've loved very few people in my life." I turned my body toward her, throwing my arm over the back of the couch. "I had my one great love, and he died of age a long time ago. I loved my mother, I think, and I never knew my father. A Sirian lived with me a while back, but I only think it was a friendly love. There is another Magic I consider a friend I love, although we rarely see each other. Maybe once every decade or so."

"Rol?" She raised an eyebrow, although her lips

twitched playfully at the corners.

"Absolutely not." I laughed, shaking my head. "He's such a bastard. He's just a simple acquaintance. A means to an eventual end, I suppose."

Dahlia offered an incredulous smile, lowering her leg between us. Her knee pressed against my thigh, interest sparking through me. "You seem to live a lonely existence. I've never seen you talking with anyone other than Rol, Willem, and me."

"I suppose…" I stared out the window behind her. The Black Avalanches loomed in the distance, their snowy peaks reaching into the bright blue sky. "When you've lived as long as I have, you become friends with isolation. It happens in waves, and you have to get used to it at some point."

"Is this one of those waves you're taking in friends?" She rested her elbow on the back of the couch but placed it a breath away from my fingertips.

I wiggled them to see if I would brush her pale skin. When I did, she leaned closer, and I brushed my fingers up her arm. "I have a predetermined future. These next few decades are going to be some of my most influential. I guess I wanted a little company amidst it all."

Dahlia hummed, nodding her head slowly as she leaned in further. I was drawn to that gesture, excitement bubbling in my chest at its insinuation.

It'd been a long time since I'd pushed the boundaries of friendship.

"I appreciate you showing me all you know about

being a healer," Dahlia said softly, her voice smooth and even. Her eyes briefly dropped to my lips. "I wonder if I can repay you."

My heart twinged at where I considered this was going, but I forced a smile. "And how do you plan to do that?"

"I could always show you what I've learned in my profession." She rested her hands on my thighs, inching closer until our noses were nearly touching. "I'm sure there are plenty of things I can teach you as an entertainer."

I couldn't decide if she was doing it as a true form of payment or because she was interested and didn't know how to approach this.

My eyelids dropped as she rose to her knees, and I had to crane my head to maintain eye contact. "Is that what *you* would want to do?"

"I'm offering, aren't I?" Her lips brushed against mine, just a whisper, and I resisted the urge to lean into it.

"Are you offering because it's the only thing you know how to offer?"

She stiffened, her head lurching back as if I'd slapped her, mortified.

I gripped her face, pinching her cheeks between my thumb and forefinger, ripping a gasp from her lips as I brought her back.

"You may have been an entertainer," I whispered, my voice only slightly hoarser than I would've liked, "but I have centuries more experience than you."

I yanked her lips to mine, something primal within me satisfied at the startled moan that rumbled against my lips. I dragged my hand down to wrap around the front of her throat, squeezing enough to urge her back onto the couch so I draped over her small frame.

Dahlia's lips fought mine, trying to gain the upper hand, arching her back to grind her hips into me. Her body was so Godsdamn warm, I wanted to lose myself in it.

It only heated further as I trailed my hand down the front of her blouse, her breath hitching when I brushed over her breast, pausing to knead it on my way down.

She stopped trying to take the lead, her hands slipping behind my neck as I dragged my lips across her cheek and down her neck. My canines pinched at the skin beneath her jaw, and I smirked at the breathy moan it coaxed from her.

I slipped my hand beneath the waistband of her skirt, almost chuckling against her soft skin when I found she wasn't wearing undergarments.

Dahlia had a plan for today.

My fingers roamed down her pelvis and through her, marveling at how smooth and wet she was. It'd been so long since I was intimate with a female, but Gods, I forgot how much I actually preferred it.

Mainly when I circled her clit and her breath quivered across my cheek with a sensuous whimper, fanning my jaw and ear.

I continued to sweep my fingers over her,

occasionally dipping my two fingers into her opening, but just a tease. Her hips rolled with my hand, chasing my movements. I smirked, huffing a laugh against her shoulder as I pressed against her leg, rubbing against the throbbing heat between my thighs.

"Please," she breathlessly begged, her fingers digging into my arms.

"This?" I slowly eased my fingers into her, and I couldn't hold back my moan that echoed hers at her soft, wet, and warm cunt.

I stroked along her inner walls, finding the sensitive, tender spot I knew sent me into a frenzy. She gasped when I passed over it, pulsing around my fingers. I brought my lips back to hers, plunging my tongue into her mouth and swiping it over hers in time with the curl of my fingers. Her breaths increased as she climbed higher toward her climax, clenching tighter around me, quiet, teeming sounds mixed with her kisses.

I scraped a fang across her lip, nicking it at the exact moment I rolled my thumb over her clit. Dahlia fell, her body naturally riding my fingers as she shuddered around me. I drank in every moan, every whimper as I dragged it out as long as I could, grinning as she swore under her breath.

Once she came down, her movements slowly ceasing, I drew my fingers out as I looked down at her flushed cheeks. Her fingers toyed with my skirt, but I wrapped a hand around her wrist. "You don't need to reciprocate… At least not yet."

She frowned at me in mute shock, tilting her head as she narrowed her eyes. "What?"

"You were going to offer yourself as payment," I whispered, boosting myself up with my hands braced on the arm of the sofa behind her head. "If you wanted to fool around, you didn't have to offer it in exchange for me teaching you how to be a Healer."

She blinked rapidly at that, her mouth dropping open. Her eyes flickered wildly as a deeper flush rose to her cheeks.

"Something tells me as an *entertainer*, you were rarely ever pleased for your own enjoyment. I figured I would show you I won't accept it as payment, but I'll accept the interest." I shook my head slowly, a small smile on my face.

Unexpectedly, tears sprang to her eyes, adding a bit of a glow to the red depths. She cleared her throat as she averted her gaze, her voice broken when she said, "She said the same thing."

She was referring to her lover, who was murdered in Lolis—Maddie, Willem's oldest daughter.

I softly smiled as I leaned back down, placing a tender kiss against her lips. A tear mixed between us, the saltiness foreign, bringing back old memories I rarely thought of.

I pulled away far enough to speak again. "I can promise fun as long as I'm able."

"I can't imagine ever offering more," Dahlia admitted, her hands caressing my hips. "I don't think I'll ever be able to."

You won't, I wanted to say, but she was still so very young. I was young once and thought maybe there would be someone else.

No one could ever measure up to that first, great love. But sometimes, someone could help you forget for a while.

I still had my path and couldn't let existing relationships get in the way.

Call of Night

1795 A.V. | Age: 988

The last time Sybil and I left Eldamain to journey to Etherea, the Black Avalanches looked as they always had, looming between The Clips and my home country. After we witnessed Tyra Korbin wield the Darkness, we returned home, and the Abyss was suddenly there like black ink splattered across the peaks.

Eldamain had been frightened, rightfully so. As far as anyone knew, the Abyss didn't exist at any point in history before then. Maybe that was correct, but Sybil knew what it was before we returned to Eldamain. The world echoed the same name she used, yet we claimed we never knew what it was or where it came from.

After Tyra Korbin, the Abyss was merely a tale told to Magics, an omen. If the Abyss lived, something terrible was about to happen. Something evil was coming, because the first time it appeared, that is exactly what happened.

The Sirians were massacred and Magics became the scum of the world.

When my vision foretold the Abyss returning, I

anticipated a phenomenon similar to what happened nearly nine-hundred-and-fifty years previously. With my work to ensure more Sirians were wielding the Light versus the Darkness, I thought it would take a great Sirian coming to their power to bring it back. I believed it to be the other girl I saw in my vision within the guarded tower.

Except when the Abyss finally returned, it was slow and gradual.

The day I knew it had come back, I didn't see it. Instead, I *felt* it.

All the Magics of Eldamain did.

"Something's in the air," the storekeeper said to one of the other patrons, shuffling through their payment. "It's like when you get a feeling in your bones it's going to rain—it's not right."

"Someone I know who runs the shops closest to the base said they can't live above their business anymore," the patron explained. "It's like they can feel something outside their window. When they look, there isn't anything there."

I grabbed the cloths I needed off the shelf and walked up behind the patron, balancing the bundle in the crook of my arm as I hitched my hand on my hip.

"What are you talking about?" I asked, my eyes bouncing between the two males. They exchanged wary glances, the patron gnawing at his bottom lip. "Don't be shy. You had no problem discussing it mere seconds ago before you realized I was here."

"The Black Avalanches," the storekeeper answered quietly, shaking his head slowly. "It's probably nothing. I bet some animals have taken up space and are spooking everyone."

I narrowed my eyes, placing my items on the counter and fishing some coins from my purse. "Enlighten me."

The storekeeper sighed, counting my change. "Like I said, it's something in the air. It's hard to explain, but I only know a few others who have had this experience. It's not like many go to the Black Avalanches."

"Indeed." I hummed as I shuffled the herbs and trinkets into my satchel, wagging my head back and forth. "Well, good day, gentlemen."

I turned on my heel, a tight-lipped grin slowly slipping off my face as I walked under the threshold. Instead of heading south to my home, I cut through town and west toward the Black Avalanches, while the voice repeatedly whispered one of the lines in the prophecy.

[When Darkness comes again…]

I knew immediately what the men in town were referring to when I hit the base of the Black Avalanches.

It was like wearing an old wool cloak that itched at your skin. The weight on my chest was oppressive, filling my lungs with a heaviness. It reminded me of Teslin in the summer, humidity thickening the air and making it difficult to breathe. It burned the back of my throat, too, as though a wildfire raged nearby, smoke tainting the air.

Except the day was clear, not a cloud in the sky, no smoke from The Overgrowns.

I rested my hand against the closest wall of rock, its cool surface sending a jolt through my body. It was like iron against my palm, a sharper cold biting my fingers. I frowned at the peaks towering over me, searching the sky for the source.

There was no Darkness like there had been when Tyra wielded her power.

I wasn't familiar with the *feeling* of the Abyss. Sybil ventured to the Black Avalanches after our visit with Tyra. I stayed home because I couldn't bear the visions that came from watching Tyra wield the Darkness, and I wanted nothing to do with the mountains at the time.

It was clear the Abyss was back or was coming back. I may not have known what it felt like before, but my sixth sense told me this was exactly what it was.

I stepped onto the nearby path, hiking my skirt up as I stepped onto boulders to navigate between one opening and the next, one hand still resting against the gritted surface of the mountain. When I finally hit a level floor, my vision began to waver, and the voice started to whisper incoherent words as it magnified into multiple voices.

My knees locked in preparation for the coming vision, but a shove at my sternum had me stumbling against a nearby rock structure.

A girl with golden locks screamed as black vines erupted

around her, her body hovering off the ground. Her veins pulsed between black and white light like the moon's glow in the night sky. Another female's scream joined hers, and beneath their tones, a male chuckled darkly, the sound circling in the room but unheard by either woman.

Black smoke engulfed the scene, morphing into another with the blond child, except she was older. She snuck around corners, walls covered in dark red velvet, like blood dripping from the ceilings. She gently pushed open a red door, a shade lighter than the walls, slipping into the room as her body weaved through the opening. A man with fire-red hair grinned at her, but his grin morphed into shock before the scene faded once again.

The chuckle from the start reached a crescendo, a rumble as something snapped like lightning cracking through the sky. A fathomless black rip flashed intermittently, blue and gold sparks flickering around the edges—

I fell back into my body, all my senses returning at once. The burn sitting at the back of my throat coaxed a dry heave, and my hand immediately slapped over my mouth.

I couldn't tell if the vision affected me because of how quickly I returned or if it had to do with everything I'd seen and felt within it. I made sense of the child and knew within my bones that while the girl's power had yet to manifest, it appeared Fate had made its decision with her. This unfamiliar girl would wield the Darkness, strengthening the Abyss, which was just a hint of what it could be.

[For balance to remain…] The voice hissed quietly, reminding me of the phrase that grounded this entire world.

Again, that foreboding crawled across my skin, and I knew if this child's fate was sealed, it meant another powerful being was dead so she could come into her power. My heart pounded in my chest because I hadn't seen who.

The Great One will fall.

I wondered if this line didn't just apply to me because of my titles, but if it meant different Great *Ones* would fall—those like me.

Magics like me.

No. The first who came to mind was Jorah. Possibly the most powerful being after me, the most skilled in his gift, considering he was the only Magic I'd met in centuries who spoke the water language.

His future was secured; he would still be of use to me in roughly thirty years, so it was not him, although I wondered who would be born that would take him out.

It couldn't be Dahlia or Willem, for while they had small characteristics of their houses, they weren't nearly powerful enough to match a Sirian. I knew it had to be someone who had crossed my path. All those vital to the Path of Aveesh crossed me in some way—

It hit me with a gust of wind carrying a sharp, tangy scent that tickled my nose. Under any circumstance, I would've recoiled, but I was too caught up in my thoughts and revelation to react physically.

Voss.

The voice instantly answered clearly. *[Yes.]*

Despite my detestation of the male, my initial reaction was anger. Why would Fate execute Magics so Sirians could rise? It was always the Magics who had to atone because of the Sirians.

Their extinction led to the hatred of Magics.

Every time a new, powerful Sirian came back, a Magic had to die or would die.

What was it about Magics that we had to suffer?

[Consequences.] I tilted my head curiously at the voice's answer to my rhetorical question. *[The consequences of those before you.]*

I ground my teeth together, inhaling through my nose and wincing at the smell that stung again. I shook my head fiercely, trying to clear the intensifying whispering.

It irked me to no end how I could see a future so influenced by events that I believed had been lost to history. I yearned to see what had happened before…

And I immediately knew how I could.

I secured my horse and found myself galloping through the streets of Mariande in the dead of night.

I was surprised to find the lack of a patrol as I dismounted my horse at the edge of Jorah's street. From my memory, the last time I'd been here—which wasn't that long ago at all in the grand scheme of things—King Pallas Hesper had scores of knights traipsing through the streets at night to try and nab any Magics living in their city walls.

Not tonight, though, which was rather startling and more than unnerving.

Despite that observation, I kept to the shadows as I quickly navigated to Jorah's storefront. I snuck through the alley beside it, counting the bricks along the wall until I reached the loose one. I listened, tapping into my enhanced hearing, and pushed when I confirmed no one was following me or lurking around.

The mechanism clicked within the wall, and a small gap opened into a narrow stairwell leading to the back apartment on top of the building. I shut the hidden door behind me and padded up the stairs, careful not to wake whoever Jorah was renting the front apartment to as I stood before his door.

The soft bells were already tinkling somewhere within his home, more than likely into his bedroom, and I heard shuffling on the other side and a grunt before the door swung open.

Jorah's black hair was disheveled, sticking out in various directions. Those swirling eyes were bright in the dark as he narrowed them on me with his lips pressed into a thin line.

"If I were a normal Magic, I would consider matters urgent with the time of night you've arrived at my doorstep," Jorah grumbled low, his voice rumbling in the small space. "But you're also prone to appear in the dead of night simply because you require a rare gem or plant. I'm unsure which scenario I hope it may be."

I pursed my lips, narrowing my eyes right back at him. "Where are the knights who patrol the streets?"

Jorah deadpanned, blinking rapidly. "What?"

"There were no knights on the streets." I crossed my arms over my chest. "Why?"

"You haven't heard?" Jorah blew out a breath of disbelief, shaking his head slowly. "King Pallas died last year. He and his wife's carriage were ambushed. Rumor has it the thieves were hired by Etherea."

Something told me I knew *exactly* who was hired by Etherea.

My face slackened, as the voices whispered incessantly at this knowledge. "That means…"

"Mariande has a new king." Jorah smirked, his eyes twinkling. "A twenty-year-old king, nonetheless, the youngest in Mariande's history."

"Prince Darius?" The voices grew louder. "He is now King Darius?"

[The Truth will be revealed.] The voice grew louder. *[Abyss claims a King.]*

This wasn't the time.

"The Abyss is back," I blurted, searching his face.

His back straightened, a frown pressing his dark brows together. "It's happening."

I squeezed between him and the door, shoving his arm out of my way as I entered his home. I felt his eyes on my back as I went straight for the small table in the middle of the kitchen and fell heavily into the seat.

"It's nothing like I've explained," I began, shaking my head as he lowered slowly on the opposite side, drawing his robe tighter around him. "There is no Darkness swarming the mountains, but it's *there*. You can feel it when you stand before it."

"It's not as sudden as you anticipated," Jorah clarified, tilting his head. "What have you interpreted that to mean?"

"One of the children has been born, that much is certain," I elaborated, unfurling my hand over the table. "Fate has sealed their future, and she's the one to wield the Darkness. I believe she's far too young to have developed her powers, but something in her life has set her Path to Dark in motion."

"Okay," Jorah drawled, nodding slowly. "Are you here to tell me I'm the one to die for her to come to her power?"

I shook my head, keeping my eyes on him. "I told you centuries ago that you would be vital for what will come. The other child has yet to be born, and I saw you with her when she's an adult."

"So, who has left or who will leave?" Jorah clenched his jaw to quell the rising agitation in his eyes.

"Voss is gone already," I whispered softly, and Jorah flinched in shock.

"But that child hasn't wielded her powers?" Jorah rubbed at the scales along his neck. "I thought once the power came—"

"It's not always exact." I sighed, shaking my head. "Sybil left this world well after I developed my gifts. I don't know when I'll pass once the child who chooses Light develops that power. But I'm confident that Voss is gone because of this child."

Jorah drummed his long fingers on the table, his groomed nails clicking with the low beat. The cloudy white within those blue depths winked in and out as he stared at me, his face void of emotion.

"Why are you here?" Jorah finally asked, his head cocking predatorily. "You didn't travel all the way to Saros simply because you wanted to tell me about Voss and the Abyss. You could have at least waited until the morning."

I reached into my satchel, producing the glass jar marked with red wax and the one with black wax. The jar with red wax contained water from one of the waterfalls within the Black Avalanches, while the other contained water from Orion's Lake.

"I need to know what the water says," I said gently, pushing the jars toward him across the table. His eyes instantly flashed as they widened, staring at the jars with his hands in his lap beneath the table. "These waters might be able to speak the past to you. You'll see things from Tyra Korbin's time, but I wonder if you can see far enough back to when my mother and the other demi-gods roamed Aveesh. I believe something happened long ago that affects—"

"Everything?" Jorah finished, raising an eyebrow as he dragged his gaze back to me. "Are these from where I think they are?"

I could only nod, and Jorah's shoulders slacked as he ran a shaky hand through his hair.

"Karasi," Jorah muttered, his eyes still wide. "I've never read the water of something so old, so embedded in the entire *nature* of our world. The *ketea* shifters were far more primal than I am. They could sift through the noise of history to speak to one another and read only what they needed. I'm not *nearly* that skilled, nor do I know how to scrape through the noise."

"Try," I begged, which startled Jorah further. "It's a burden to see a future and not know why it will exist or what happened before me led to this Path. I always feel like I'm missing something vital, something crucial. My mother…"

Jorah sighed heavily, lifting himself from his seat to make his way to one of his cabinets.

"After we met Tyra, Sybil looked terrified when the girl wielded the Darkness, like she'd seen a ghost." I waited as he unscrewed both jars and poured a bit of each into the glass he'd fetched, his eyes on me the whole time. "In all my life, Sybil was never scared of anything. Apprehension maybe but never fear.

"She left me two years after that, but during those years she fell into hysteria." I hadn't thought of the final day with her in such a long time, and my heart clenched. "She said so many things, and none of them made sense.

She used unfamiliar words, referred to people we've only heard legends about… She told me never to believe the history I've been taught; that it wasn't true."

"You think something catastrophic happened." Jorah paused with the rim of his glass poised beneath his bottom lip. "Do you have any idea of what it could be so I can at least attempt to concentrate on it?"

I racked my memory for a historical event Sybil mentioned that could help Jorah find answers. Her words sprang to memory, and my head snapped up to him. "A battle. She mentioned a battle when talking about Asteria, possibly around two or three thousand years ago."

"I once found a text that listed Asteria as a General for Eldamain." Jorah shut his eyes as he took a deep breath, his forehead furrowing. "Anything else?"

"A lock." My voice wavered with uncertainty. "She mentioned she had to keep the Gods secure."

"Like Morana and Danica?" He peeked out of one eye, the other still tightly closed. "Karasi… I don't know if this is enough information."

"Please, Jorah." I reached across the table, placing my hand over the one that wasn't nearly crushing the glass. "I'll be here to help you out of it again. I'll make sure you don't fall into Madness."

He sat silently for a few heartbeats before closing his eyes and tossing back the liquid he'd mixed in his cup.

Jorah started screaming as his eyes lit up nearly as bright as the sun.

I lunged for where he sat, curling myself behind

him and slapping my hand over his mouth to muffle his screams. His hands gripped the edge of the table, and I realized how much enhanced strength he had inherited when the wood splintered beneath his fingers.

I pressed my forehead to the back of his head, shutting my eyes against the agonizing screams muted by my hand, tears prickling my eyes with guilt. I breathed carefully, allowing enough time for him to find something—see *anything*—that could help us.

After what felt like a whole other lifetime, I finally shot my claws from my nail beds and sliced down Jorah's arm.

I released my hand from over his mouth at the same time he doubled over, bracing himself on the table as he emptied whatever had been in his stomach onto the floor of his kitchen. I went over to the bucket on his countertop, dipping a loose rag and grabbing a new cup.

I whirled on my heel, my heart aching at the hunch of his shoulders and damp black hair hanging with his head. "Has this water been previously boiled with a cleansing herb?"

Jorah's head twitched up and down just barely in confirmation, his eyes still shut as he slowly breathed through what I assumed was another wave of nausea. I dipped the fresh cup into the water bucket and kneeled before him, resting the rag on his neck.

"I can't..." Jorah's voice was hoarse, and he tried to clear it. I held the glass beneath his head, and he glared at it before raising that penetrating gaze to me.

I don't think I ever faced a genuine threat in my life until that moment. If looks could kill, something inside me screamed to run from him.

"Don't you—" Jorah winced at the sound of his voice again. Finally, he accepted the water and slowly uncurled from his hunch to take delicate sips.

Then he stunned me by throwing the remaining contents in my face. His hand shot out, gripping my throat, and fear sat heavy in my stomach. "Don't you ever ask me to do something like that again, do you understand?"

Gods, this was no longer the terrified boy I'd found in the slums of Saros almost three hundred years ago.

"If you force me to do something like that again, I will burn this Godsforsaken store to the ground." Jorah's voice was *menacing*, and he was so damn strong. Air struggled to reach my head. "You might think yourself all powerful, that you *have* to do these things, but I draw my line with you where Fate is no longer concerned. You didn't need me to do that to help in saving this world—or whatever the fuck it is we're doing."

I tucked my bottom lip under my teeth, suppressing the urge to ask him what he saw. He released me forcefully, and I fell back onto my ass at his feet. He stared down at me with contempt, and I realized I may have very well soiled this relationship with my actions.

My actions.

For once, I couldn't blame it on Fate.

"You want to know what I saw?" Jorah laughed

harshly, shaking his head as he used the damp cloth to pat the sweat off his forehead. "I don't know. Everything, too much, and yet not enough. I tried to grasp onto events based on the two criteria you gave me."

"Were you able to?" I asked carefully, leaning away from him just a little more.

He scoffed, rolling his eyes. "I managed to grab a single image that made sense." His eyes grew distant as his body stiffened. "So much death, destruction, devastation—"

"Jorah," I said, rising to my knees, placing both hands on his legs, and gazing up at him. "Stay with me. Tell me what you saw, and we can let this go, and you can stay here in this era again."

Jorah blinked, clearing his vision. He swallowed before saying, "You know how the brick outside acts as a sort of home for the lock to my door?"

I nodded eagerly, my eyes flickering across his face.

"The Black Avalanches serve a similar purpose now." His brows pressed together, his irises swirling restlessly. "It's a home for the lock you mentioned."

I frowned, searching my memory, but my mind was far too silent. "What sort of lock?"

"A magical one." Jorah met my gaze then, the blue swirls ceasing entirely. "A lock concealing our world."

HOUSE OF ECHIDNA

1799 A.V. | AGE: 992

The din of The Red Raven was rather boisterous for a weekday, but there seemed to be a celebration of sorts at one of the far tables. I shook my head with an exaggerated eyeroll when I caught Willem standing on one of the tables, screaming nonsense at those who were listening.

"You chose quite the time to come to the pub," Dahlia shouted over the noise, setting down a glass on the rack behind her. I curled my lip at one of the stained, worn-out wooden stools. "What are you doing here?"

I sighed, smoothing out my skirt as I sat before leaning my elbows on the bar. "I need you."

Her red eyes twinkled as a lopsided smirk climbed up her cheek, but I glowered and shook my head.

"Not like that, you heathen," I grumbled, tucking a stray dread behind my ear. "I have… questions and a request."

Dahlia's brows twitched in the middle as she slowly mimicked my stance, mere inches separating our faces as she tilted her head to the side and drawled out, "Okay."

"You said you knew men with wings in Lolis." I watched her face, studying her reaction to this question.

My heart pinched when her playfulness dimmed with sudden sorrow, the smirk on her face falling entirely.

She cleared her throat, blinking. "I did."

The memory of him landing in the middle of my lawn flashed in my mind. "One was from the House of Echidna?"

She nodded with her lips pressed together. "Did you see him—" she paused, lifting an eyebrow, "or did you *see* him?"

"I *saw* him." I sat straight on the stool. "What's his name?"

"Remiel," she admitted, backing against the counter behind her. "I haven't seen him since we all left Lolis. As far as I know, he's been traveling aimlessly for the last decade."

"I had two visions of him." I tapped my nail on the counter, waiting to see if Fate stopped me. "One was him on my lawn. The other was him walking through the Black Avalanches. Do you know why he would do the latter?"

"I thought you said you only see what's to come." Dahlia crossed her arms over her chest, narrowing her eyes at me. I snarled, but she sighed. "Remiel and the other winged male were Voss's apprentices many years ago. From my knowledge, it's how they met. They trained with him and lived in the Black Avalanches for a few years before they realized *exactly* what Voss stood for. That's when they went to Lolis."

For the life of me, I couldn't begin to guess why Voss chose the Black Avalanches to live and train men in.

I hummed, considering what I needed to say to get Dahlia's help in summoning Remiel here. I didn't quite understand why, but I would need him just as I needed Jorah. "I suspect you've heard about the strange goings-on within the Black Avalanches."

She wiggled her head back and forth. "I've heard the rumors."

"I would like his expertise on the matter," I explained, folding my hands in front of me. "For someone who lived and most likely learned to fly around those mountains, it would benefit to have him look. If anything, to quell Main Town's concern."

Dahlia frowned, pursing her lips as she blinked at me. "I don't know if Remiel will come for something as trivial as concerns about a mountain range."

[The drakon will come.]

I'm well aware, I shot back. The corner of my lips twitched as I slid off the stool. I shrugged at Dahlia. "Send him a letter anyway."

I turned on my heel and started for the door, catching Willem from where he still stood on top of the table.

"Karasi!" I stopped at the door, an eyebrow raised as I threw my head over my shoulder at Dahlia. "How the hell am I supposed to send him a letter when I don't know where he is?"

[Crows answer the call...]

"Something tells me a raven may be able to find him."

I let the boy journey up the mountain path, hanging far enough back so that he wouldn't catch my steps above his own. I didn't need to do much hiding, though. He appeared overwhelmed by whatever he was looking for.

I hid behind a wall of rock, smirking at the swears and whispers of confusion falling from his lips. I didn't know much about Remiel, but from Dahlia and Willem's warning, he had a sharp tongue and an attitude that could rile even the most patient individual.

I was ready for the challenge because it'd been quite some time since someone kept me on my toes.

My lower back twinged, and I knew something was about to reveal itself to him. I stepped out from behind the rock wall just in time for one of those black masses of the Abyss to flutter before him. The smell tickled at the back of my throat, ears faintly ringing.

[Darkness comes again.] The voice whispered frantically at the same time wide, leathery wings suddenly shot out from Remiel's back. He fell to his knees with a sharp inhale, growling another curse under his breath.

But I was captivated by his wings. I'd seen Voss's wings so long ago, feathered and beige, but something about the wings on Remiel called to a primal instinct within me, urging me to reach out and caress them.

"Fascinating," I mumbled as I continued to study the

membrane stretched across the bone, almost a deep red where the sun's rays pierced through them.

Remiel spun around, still hunched on the ground, his eyes narrowed in suspicion.

He was raggedy and gangly, a true wild man if I'd ever met one.

Shabby, dark brown hair hung around his face, brushing past his shoulders in wild curls. An unkempt beard hugged his sharp features and angular jaw, bringing attention to a slight button nose. His bright purple eyes were absolutely magnificent, glittering in the light like a gemstone from Jorah's shop.

I let him study me right back as I admitted, "I have known very few from the House of Echidna to be marked by the Gods, and yet here you are, baring the wings of a *drakon*."

I was almost envious of him. They stretched open behind him and twitched like limbs that had been catatonic. Sybil once told me she could shift into a full *drakon* long ago, and I wondered how much of his wings resembled her form.

"You know the old Etherean language." Remiel sighed, shaking his head. "And you know the animal we reign from."

"We?" I tilted my head to the side, but I wasn't surprised he knew we shared the same house, what with being an apprentice of Voss. I wanted to know how much the bastard really taught him, what gaps I would need to fill in. "And you suppose I hail from Echidna?"

He exhaled as though he were releasing a weight, waving his hand. "The eyes. Reptilian, no?"

Reptilian. I tried to control the involuntary muscle movement in my cheek. It was safe to bet he knew more than just *drakon.* "You've been educated in the Houses quite thoroughly, I suppose."

"You suppose?" A small roll of his shoulders and the wings vanished into nothing. He lost his balance from the force, stumbling, and I raised an eyebrow at that.

I wondered how long it'd been since he used his wings if he acted like they were a foreign burden.

"You are Remiel, are you not?" I motioned for him to follow me back down the path he'd come from, staring straight ahead.

"It's Remy, thanks." The sound of his feet close behind me, crunching over gravel, brought a smile to my face. I knew Voss had to have said something about me if my reputation wasn't enough, and I waited for him to utter the next words, "You're the Great Karasi, aren't you?"

"It's Karasi." I threw my head over my shoulder, catching his own smile underneath his beard. "Thanks."

I heard his scoff in response, but it sounded choked as he cut himself off. "The Black Avalanches… What's going on with them?"

[If the Abyss lives, Darkness has risen again.] The voice scratched at my temples, clawing to get out.

I looked back over my shoulder again. "I take it you brought a horse?" He nodded. "We shall ride back to my home together. Some things are better discussed in private, away from prying ears and eyes."

I watched Remy observe my home with a peculiar expression that alternated between confusion and nostalgia. He shifted back and forth from one foot to the other as he unabashedly perused.

I felt stripped bare by the way he looked at my things.

"I don't spend much time in this home," I explained, ushering him to the kitchen table. "I travel quite often, and it is just myself who lives here."

[*For now.*] I ground my teeth together as I slowly lowered to one of the chairs.

"So I've heard," Remy mumbled as he took the chair opposite me. "You asked Dahlia to summon me. Why not summon Voss? The old man has lived in those mountains for Gods know how long."

I found it strange Remy didn't seem to know what happened to his mentor, but then again, Voss himself and Dahlia hinted at a falling out between Remy, this other apprentice, and their mentor. She'd also said he'd been traveling around the world for the last decade.

"Voss died four years ago, Remy," I admitted, waiting for his reaction. "I apologize that I'm the one to break the news to you."

He simply blinked at me, but then his hand flew to his sternum, and his face morphed into a frown. "How did he die? Was it age?"

[Confess.]

"*Long ago, the Gods decided that our world required balance.*" The words were pulled from my lips. I could only stare at the young *drakon*. "*Another being fated with a great power emerged, another of equal caliber had to leave this world.*"

Remy shivered, shaking his head and arms before leaning back in the chair almost imperceptibly. "Well, if that isn't ominous. Do you always talk like this? In jilted, vague sentences?"

My entire life I spoke this way when Fate used me as a messenger, but none had outright asked in such a blunt way. Then again, the gift of prophecy was even more rare now than it was in my adolescence. As far as I knew, I was the only one in this world left who had any form of foretelling.

"Some have found it a nuisance. Another version of myself would have probably found it a nuisance many, many years ago. But alas, that is how the clock goes round." Something dark swirled behind his eyes, and I thought about the version of Remy I saw in my vision. He was different, possibly more mature than he is now, yet I knew that version was not far away. "You know a thing or two about being different people, do you not?"

He seemed to consider my words, his eyes flickering over my face as he rolled his lips together in contemplation. Again, his face alternated between nostalgia and another emotion that reminded me of grief—downturned eyes and a cavernous depth in his eyes.

Dahlia's words came back to my mind then, and I nearly kicked myself at not thinking about it sooner.

Dahlia mentioned years ago the two winged men she knew were lovers, one of which being Remy. She used past tense to talk about the other male, which meant this boy was running from the grief of loss.

Remy folded his arms over the table, leaning closer as he asked, "So, what's going on with the mountains?"

"Did your mentor ever tell you about the Abyss?" I countered, waiting for his reaction. Some Magics knew about it at a young age, a threat whispered around campfires. With Voss as a mentor to teach Remy the history of Magic Houses, I didn't doubt he would've told him about the Abyss.

"He didn't need to," he whispered, which meant his parents had told him when he was young.

My vision wavered, and I clenched my fists as the voice whispered nonsensical words in my head, many overlapping with one another.

"*If the Abyss lives, Darkness has risen again.*" My words were once again not my own. Almost instantly, I regained control of my vision and my body, and Remy stared at me in shock.

"What's that supposed to mean?"

I sighed, wondering how many more times I would have to educate the world on what the Abyss truly was. "Long ago, the Abyss would rise when the power of the

Dark Sirians would. It has returned, which means Sirians are wielding the Dark power in our world."

"The Sirians can't actually be completely gone." Remy rubbed his arm absentmindedly. "How do they develop Light or Dark?"

"If they grow to fear themselves and the power they wield, they will bring forth the Darkness." I reached for the hematite in the middle of the table as the voices started up again with their nonsense. Clasped in my hand, they muted almost instantly.

"Wouldn't every Sirian child that's been shunned since the Korbins nearly wiped them out wield Darkness, then?" He studied my reaction, but I rolled the stone as I thought about one Korbin that had nothing to do with the extermination of the Sirians. "The whole world fears them."

"Not always." The voices fought to come through and utter the True Prophecy, the hematite searing in my palm. I let it roll out of my hand. "But now there are enough of them, or one powerful enough, to summon the Abyss back."

He straightened slowly, piecing together what I hadn't said. "It was a Sirian, wasn't it? Who Voss had to die for?"

I waited for the voices to stop me, staring at the table. I thought about the True Prophecy, the child screaming and sobbing in a tower, the Darkness like a cloak around her.

"The Sirian should be in their early childhood. Their

power should form within the next decade, and for now, the child's fate will lead them into the Darkness. But by the Abyss in the mountains, I would say others are wielding the Darkness already."

I was never sure why I neglected Teslin in my warnings. I had a post in nearly every country, a trusted individual to help guide Sirians in the right direction. Even more so now that Osiris and Megara had established their little community, manipulating the old code I once had in place to lead Sirians safely to them.

Maybe Fate allowed me to ignore Teslin because they needed to harbor the Darkness, building their little slave trade of Dark Sirians. I may not know all of Fate, but I had one of those strange feelings that the blonde girl I kept seeing would find herself among those Dark Sirians, and she would be the one to lead them to retribution.

And the girl with the raven hair—*aster*—would be her counter.

"Well," Remy grunted as he rose from the chair, his hand splayed across the table, "this has been an interesting history lesson, and it was great meeting you. But Dahlia summoned me to figure out what was going on, and based on this entire conversation, you only needed me to confirm a suspicion you already had. So, I will take my leave and be on my merry way."

I knew the resolve with which Remy walked in. The closer he got to my door, the louder the voices whispered amongst themselves. I couldn't make out their words, but I saw the vision of him once again on my lawn.

[The sun and the moon.] The voice was clear and strong, for once sounding like a gender.

My soul, the manly voice whispered.

This had never happened before. The voices never spoke of the past, and they never had a gender.

"You run from the memory of him." Remy froze with his back to me; his shoulders hunched into his ears. "What would your *soul* say if he knew that you refuse to think of him in life?"

"No!" He whirled at me with a finger raised. "You do not get to speak of him. You did not know him. No one knew him as I knew him. He was my heart, and he took it with him when he left me."

He was a boy cut from the same cloth as me, haunted by the pain of his loss, of someone who was everything to him. I could see he, too, was angry with Fate for taking them away from him.

Do not feed loneliness, mi leiron.

"The dead never leave us willingly," I said, watching him. "It is okay to believe that a part of you went with him when he died. But a part of him also *stayed* with you."

Tears dripped down his face, disappearing into his beard as he clenched his jaw.

"Do not forget what existed between the beginning and the end." I rose from my seat as another vision of Remy standing in my kitchen, decades older, flashed in my mind. "For while he may be gone, you have much to live yet before you are reunited with your other half. You will do well to spend your time doing anything other than running."

"So, what do I do until then?" He blinked to clear his tears, his lower lip quivering as he said softly, "Where do I go? I have no one. I have nothing."

[For now.] The voices whispered in unison, but this time those words were not for me.

"There is a place for those who have lost and do not know who they are anymore, who do not know where to go." I swept my hand toward Main Town, where I knew his friends waited for him to join them in their discovery, to find meaning in their lives again.

While I may not have known what Remy's ambitions once were in his younger years, I knew with certainty he would find his purpose in life, and it all came back to the child who would appear on my doorstep in just a few short years.

MOTHER OF SIRIANS

1801 A.V. | AGE: 994

I thought Time and I knew each other well.

We'd agreed; Fate would show me what I needed to know, what moves to make for Time to go on as desired, and I would let Time pass unfazed. Each step of my life had always been to usher the world toward an inevitable outcome, one that was still hazy to me, but I understood what it meant.

Until Time and Fate conspired against me, because while I'd lived such a long existence, people of all walks of life coming and going in my life, I realized one day with a sudden shock that I had acquired more people around me than ever before.

At some point, I'd not only collected a network of Magics and Sirians, but I'd collected a small group here in Eldamain.

The morning I concluded I had created a *family* was the same morning I woke up and knew exactly what day it was. The voice hummed in my head, and if I were a betting woman, I would have believed that voice was laughing.

Nothing about my day was different. Remy delivered the extra supplies I was stocking up on in preparation for this day, and I sent him on his way as I always did after I bought the herbs and ingredients I needed.

I methodically made my lunch before sorting the extra ingredients into the cupboards, reorganizing to make room for everything. After the kitchen was arranged, I prepared the spare room and fetched fresh pails of water from Orion's Lake to heat.

While the water boiled above the fireplace, I sipped on the soup at my table, my elbows poised with the mug just beneath my nose. I inhaled slowly, letting the warm aroma wrap around me and calm the anxiousness from the inevitable.

I had roughly nine hundred and fifty years to brace for this moment, and somehow, that still hadn't been enough.

As I waited for the beginning of the True Prophecy, I thought of Brand's daughter, Annabelle, and I wondered what it would've been like if she knew what would become of her bloodline. I was grateful that I could tell Brand before he passed, but all I saw in my head was that young girl gazing up at me as though I were the most fascinating thing she'd ever seen.

My enhanced hearing locked onto the shuffling on my porch. I sat still, hoping not to alert the man I knew to be outside. What he had to do wouldn't be easy, and he deserved the chance to take his time with it.

After only a few moments, I frowned when he spoke quietly. "Papa loves you, *aster*. You be a good girl, and don't cause too much trouble. You have a journey ahead of you but never forget that you are loved. If not by those on this plane, then by the two waiting for you on the other side."

His words brought tears to my eyes, latching onto my heart and digging their claws in. My grip tightened on my mug, and I pressed my lips together as a tear tracked down my cheek.

It was that moment the weight of everything—my entire existence—hit me in the chest.

After all I'd done, I had to listen to the fate of this child be sealed with no say in any of it?

I closed my eyes, and all I saw was a young me staring back.

I changed my mind.

I delivered that baby who was now a man outside on my porch, and I couldn't let him leave his child behind. I had all the resources to protect *both* of them. Remy, Willem, and Dahlia all knew combat. I could recruit them to help protect my home. I could cast enchantments, and no one knew where I lived without uttering the code, and I had the say if I accepted anyone. The child could be raised on my land, and she would have her father.

But when I tried to move from the chair to stop him, Fate grumbled low in my ear. *[The Father must leave.]*

Why? Another tear tracked down my other cheek as I carefully set my mug down. I willed my legs to move—no, internally screamed at them to move—but it was like my brain no longer communicated with my body except to keep it still and breathe.

[Many Paths, but one True Path must prevail.]

Fuck your Paths. My face dampened as Fate even silenced my sobs.

I hoped Fate could hear me. I dreamed it heard the snarl I would've added to my words.

The dead silence in my head was enough to tell me it did.

The father's fading footsteps had my heartbeat racing, but I still couldn't move. I didn't feel my limbs again until I could no longer hear his footsteps.

I nearly tumbled to the floor when I finally regained control over my body, silently cursing Fate. I rose from the chair with shaky knees, walking the short distance from my kitchen table to my front door.

I opened my door and found a small infant on the doorstep, bundled in layers thick enough to withstand a blizzard. Lying on top of her small body was a necklace of sorts, and there were three different letters tucked into the side between her body and the braided wicker.

She was no more than a few months old, not even half a year. She was fast asleep, unperturbed by the crisp winter wind picking up around us. I tilted my head, studying the baby and the winter cap covering her head.

With a heavy sigh, I pulled the cap back, confirming what I already knew.

The child was Sirian.

[Many Paths.] Fate answered, and I scowled at the child. *[She must choose the Light.]*

"Let's get you out of the cold," I said to the sleeping baby, picking up the basket and carefully carrying it into the house.

It was small enough that I could place it in the middle of the dinner table, and I didn't want to wake the child. She seemed comfortable and content, and I wanted to enjoy the solace before my life continued to alter drastically.

I plucked the letters from the basket, and scanned the names scrawled across each one. There was a letter addressed to me, and the second was addressed to a Reva.

[The child, aster.]

I thought for a long time the child's name was *aster*, but Reva made more sense. It had a similar meaning to the old language: star. How her father had known that was beyond me, but I considered both titles important.

When I read the third name on the final letter, my home fell away from me. The room spun as I collapsed into the chair at the table, gawking at the scribbled letters.

Darius.

I peeked at Reva, hoping I hadn't woken her, but she was still sound asleep. I let my gaze fall back on the last letter hesitantly, shaking my head.

I was all too familiar with this name. Why in the Gods this child's father wanted to deliver a letter to a king was beyond me.

"What are you planning..." I set the two letters aside

and opened the one addressed to me, carefully unfurling it.

The Great Karasi,

By now, I expect you've discovered the precious valuable I left on your doorstep. I don't doubt you knew I was coming, or that my daughter would be yours someday. I was plagued with strange dreams after her mother's passing, but all I kept thinking was that I needed to bring her to you. I anticipate you'll treat her as your own. Well, at least, I hope you do.

You know how to handle both of your paths and futures, but I have a few ~~instructions~~ requests that I only hope you can trust me, as her father, to follow.

I was fortunate in my life to be given the amazing friends and family that I had. While I love Reva more than life itself, she's a gift I can't risk losing. A gift I never deserved. I wasn't able to give her the life she or her mother deserved.

The letter continued to explain the circumstances of Reva's birth and her mother's death. He explained that the necklace with Reva was her mother's, a family heirloom passed down to the females in her line for centuries. He also gave me instructions for the other two letters.

Whether you read the letters before you give them to their recipients or not is up to you. They are both clearly labeled. I can't tell you when to give them to these people, but I have a feeling you'll know when the time is right.

I scowled, rolling my eyes.

I fear death may be near. I've protected my daughter fiercely in the last four months and made more enemies than I already had. Please care for her and, above all, remind her that she is and always will be loved, especially by no one more than her mother and me.

"Sincerely, Jedrek Carraphim," I whispered to myself, still amazed at the funny games Fate played. All the events in my life flashed before my eyes.

"I've never met a Magic with eyes like yours before… It's nice to meet you, Great Child."

Korbin's were the sole reason the significance of the Carraphim name was lost to history. Yet, this Korbin line would be the single reason the importance of the Carraphim name would be remembered.

"Walter Carraphim… My wife needs your help."

I resisted the urge to throw the nearest item across the room in frustration. Instead, I resorted to a coping tactic I hadn't practiced in hundreds of years.

I stuck a claw out and ran a scratch along the inside of my forearm, relishing the silence of the voices and the memories that were assaulting my mind. Every single moment that led me to this child, to this Destiny, to this outcome.

I consider the many *Paths* that Fate spoke of.

What if I'd been there to deliver this child? Her mother would've never died, and they would've both been able to protect her.

What if I had run after Jedrek or stopped him from leaving? He could be here for his daughter like he wanted.

What if I had stayed with Brand, traveling the world until his dying day? He would have never married Clarissa Bronte, and Annabelle would've never been born, which meant this child right here wouldn't be alive.

What if I'd never been born? Sybil would still be alive and carrying this weight.

What if I ended it all right now?

Would Fate stop me?

Would Aveesh be doomed?

Reva squeaked in her basket, yanking me out of the spiral in my mind, and I realized what nearly happened.

The Madness.

I looked down at where she was wriggling beneath her many layers, but she wasn't crying. She gazed up at me with big, beautiful eyes that glistened gold in the faint light of my home, small lips shaped like a bow.

"Oh, of course you're beautiful," I whispered to her, carefully plucking the necklace off her body and setting it aside.

But when the gem glistened in the light, I recognized the stone immediately.

This was no ordinary family heirloom.

Jedrek claimed it was a family heirloom of Bryna's, Reva's mother, but I didn't believe he or Bryna understood the significance of this necklace.

Otherwise, they wouldn't have been so shocked when someone within their family birthed a Sirian.

The hematite necklace hummed in my hand, a strange sensation tugging on a cord within me, drawing it tight. I dropped it, curling my lip when it hit the table with a clatter.

Fire danced across a line of trees, burning any that stood in its raging path…

She was a descendant of the demi-god Dionne.

For the first time in centuries, I found myself wishing Sybil was still around. I knew Reva had to wear this necklace at all times until she could control and wield her powers.

Until she crossed paths with someone who could teach her.

Reva let out a strange sound again, staring up at me.

I sighed, peeling back some of the layers Jedrek covered her with. I slid my hands beneath her arms and carefully lifted her from the basket. When I drew her to my chest, she placed her tanned hands onto my collarbones, her eyes wide and her little mouth popped open as she gawked at me.

"What are you looking at?" I frowned, shifting her more to one side of my body as I made my way to the couch. "In these parts, folks are going to be looking at you like that if we don't get you some salve made to hide that pretty little Mark of yours."

I couldn't help the smile that tugged at the corner of my lips when she let out another squeak, a smile brightening her face and lifting her plump cheeks.

"Let's set the record straight, young one." I groaned as I plopped down on the couch, positioning her on my lap so she was poised on my knees. I gripped her hands in mine, and something tightened in my chest when her fingers wrapped around two of mine. "There will be many rules set in this home. You see, I have a gift that lets me see the future, but sometimes I can't speak it or do certain things that would affect the future. It'll be pretty annoying for you as you start asking me why all the time, but be patient with me.

"And don't try to use my powers against me," I lectured, pointing my finger at her even as her grip tightened around it. A small giggle fluttered off her lips. "Like that. I won't have it, but more importantly, Fate won't have it. I can't do anything about it."

She gummed my finger with great determination in response. I sighed, shaking my head.

"I know nothing about children," I admitted aloud. "I don't know much about love either, if I'm being honest. I've loved very few in my life, but they're long gone now. One of them is actually your many, *many* great-grandfathers. He would probably melt on the floor if he could see me talking to and holding a baby. A Sirian, nonetheless!"

Reva frowned, and she screeched once around my finger in her mouth. I startled slightly, but she went back to her task.

"My apologies." I tilted my head to the side. "Where are my manners? We've just begun one of the greatest journeys, and you don't even know my name. I am the Great Karasi, but you can call me Karasi. I prefer that name, anyway. I'll be your mentor and guardian. I'll teach you all I know to prepare you for your future.

"And from what I know…" I leaned into her, pressing my forehead to hers. She stopped sucking on my finger to look at me, and I smirked. "You have *quite* the future ahead of you, *aster*."

THE CRONE

The past, the present, the unwritten—she held them all.

Soul & Stars

1806 A.V. | Age: 999

"Gods, child," I blurted as Reva appeared out of nowhere. She blinked up at me with those bright golden eyes. "Where have you—What in the world have you done?"

Reva glanced down at her body as if she didn't realize she was covered in soot, her curls sticking out in different directions. "I was playing in the fireplace."

I deadpanned. "What do you mean you were playing in the fireplace?"

"Well, when you went to bathe, I was cold from my hair being wet," she explained in her high-pitched, melodic voice. "So I tried to light the fire, but it didn't work."

"Okay…" I sighed heavily, rubbing my temples. "Next time you're cold, why don't we try to grab a blanket?"

I went back to the cabinet to continue sorting through my supplies, but once again, Reva appeared at my side. I slowly dragged my gaze to her, an eyebrow raised. I cursed internally.

She needed another bath now.

The child often required two.

"Can I go play outside?" she asked, tilting her head to the side. "It snowed last night."

"I'm well aware," I chided, resting a hand on my hip. "Do you require my assistance, or can you manage to stay right out there on the front lawn?"

Her eyes lit up, probably just excited to be out from under my watchful eye. "I'll be good!"

"Alright, then." I grabbed her coat off the hook and bundled her into it, foregoing a hat knowing her curly hair would rebel. "Remember, don't go past this house on either side, and don't go anywhere near Orion's Lake."

She answered with a smile, then she ran down the porch and into the snow. I caught her bouncing form from the window, rolling my eyes when she began to throw handfuls of snow into the air above her.

I set to work counting the remaining herbs we had and cleaning out the cabinet for anything that expired. Every time I had to throw old supplies away, I cursed myself for overstocking before she had arrived on my doorstep five years ago.

I peeked out the front window overlooking the lawn and Orion's Lake, letting out a breath of a chuckle when I spotted Reva packing snow atop another mound.

The girl was building a snowman.

I shook my head as I sorted through the herbs and dried meat that I bought off a foreign traveler in exchange for a particular elixir he asked for.

When Reva was an infant, it was easy to wrap her in a papoose against my body, burying her head so none could see her Mark. I refused to let the people of Eldamain know I was at my residence, fearing they would come unannounced and discover the girl. Instead, I would venture with her just beyond the borders of The Clips to a nearby farmer whom I knew preferred solitude. We had an agreement for food I would gather from him before the snow fell.

As Reva grew too big to be swaddled, I renegotiated the arrangement with the farmer to send one of his stable boys with food. When I saw him approaching from the horizon, I'd slip Reva her sedative for naptime and meet the boy outside.

She was smart enough to associate the potion with sleep, now. She recently started referring to it as her *sleep juice*. Just the other day, she fought me about it because she insisted she didn't need rest and then bartered with me to go to the Black Avalanches to feel the *funny tickle,* as she called the sensation caused by the Abyss.

I lifted my gaze again to the window, my heart increasing when I didn't immediately spot her. It calmed once I laid eyes on her dark jacket standing out against the snow. She must've given up on the snowman, resorting to simply lying on her back with her arms and legs flung out around her.

I chuckled under my breath, making note of the additional ingredients I needed to buy. I'd have to start requiring Reva to wear the concealment salve over her

Mark, so I made sure there was enough for trial and error. I anticipated her rubbing it off haphazardly until she remembered she had to leave it on.

I filed the various tins and jars into my cabinet, but a ripple of warning ran up my spine. I threw my head over my shoulder, searching for something within the house, but it dawned on me that the strange alert could be something outside.

I lunged for the door and yanked it open, my eyes snagging on not just Reva, but a rather tall, lanky individual huddled close to the ground in what appeared to be an attempt at mimicking her size.

"That son of a bitch," I grumbled under my breath, stomping onto the porch as my hands trembled with fear. My heart fluttered in my chest, realizing I saw this exact moment over seven years ago. "What in the Gods' names are you doing here?"

Both Remy and Reva jumped to their feet, and I stiffened when she wrapped her hands around his leg, her eyes noticeably wide from this distance.

"What am I doing here?" Remy dared to laugh. He pointed both of his hands at Reva. "What the fuck is this, Karasi?"

I narrowed my gaze at him, pressing my lips together as my clenched fists shook at my side. I was enraged that he would come unannounced, particularly after I'd gone quiet to involve as few as possible with this damned prophecy.

"You're gone for five years, and you expect all of us

not to come looking for you?" He was about to move forward, but then his gaze found Reva.

She returned his stare, and Remy relaxed his tense shoulders. I glimpsed a tenderness within his face I hadn't experienced before. My own body loosened as he picked her up, and Reva flung her arms around his neck, their faces nearly pressing together from the proximity.

Maybe she needs a father. I shook the thought from my head, remembering his accusation.

"I'm honored it took you all so long to check up on me." I crossed my arms over my chest, my nerves still on edge as he walked to the porch.

"You're prone to travels, and we all have our own shit to deal with." He winced when his eyes flickered to Reva. "In fact, I thought you'd be dead before I ever saw you with a child."

"Karasi is dying?" Reva lifted her head off where she was resting it against Remy, staring at him in horror.

Remy glared at her. "No, nobody is dying—"

"I wouldn't count on that yet." I leveled Remy with a curled lip, but he just scoffed at me.

"You think I'm going to tell people about the kid? Do I seem like someone who is going to turn you and a child over because of what she is?"

At the time, I really didn't know. I barely trusted anyone I formed connections with. I could name those I did, and I only knew Remy a few years before I went into hiding with Reva.

"The less people that know about her, the better." I

turned my back and went into our home, praying Remy followed.

His sigh echoed behind me along with his footsteps. "You can't possibly think you can handle her on your own. You have entrusted me, Dahlia, and Willem with quite a lot over the years, and you didn't consider trusting us with this? For fuck's sake, Willem actually knows what it's like to raise kids, especially girls—"

"Formerly a father or not, I wouldn't trust the cynic with a child," I interrupted, gesturing toward Reva, still clinging to him. "Besides, none of you know the first thing about raising a Sirian child. This is my burden to carry."

I almost corrected myself when Reva's little eyebrows pressed together, her confusion evident. My shoulders hunched because she could very well remember this conversation, and I just referred to her being in my care as a burden.

I didn't mean it in that sense, but it was already out there.

"Do you think it's healthy to hide a child away from existence?" Remy tried to remove Reva from his neck, but she only tightened her grip. He shot me a glare as he fell into one of the chairs at the table. "First of all, she is clinging to a stranger. She is desperate for contact, Karasi. Second of all, why is she so damn filthy? Are you bathing her?"

I pursed my lips at the unfortunate timing, because it did look like this child was—for lack of a better term—a wild heathen. I never considered what the lack of socialization would do for her because she wasn't quite at an age where I thought it mattered.

When I was young, we ventured into town two or three times a year until I grew older than Reva, and I didn't think it was necessarily detrimental to me.

Remy threw a vial that was on the table toward the sink, the glass clanking. "How 'bout we don't play with the poison, huh?"

Reva pouted at Remy, and I smirked briefly because the child knew better. More than likely, she was reaching for it to hand to him.

"What did you plan on doing once her Light manifests?" Remy continued his interrogation. "I get you have prophetic gifts and some other things, but you don't have any Magic abilities that manifest into a physical element. I'm the only one amongst our crew with an animate gift. If anything, you should've told *me* about her. I'll have to be the one to teach her control one day."

"I have helped hundreds of Sirians in my lifetime." I joined them at the table, slowly lowering myself into the chair. I grabbed a stick that Reva had found the night before the snowfall and passed it to her. "I have the means necessary to access any educational material she will need."

"Okay, but you'll have to teach her how to read first," Remy chastised, and my patience vanished as I simmered, all the while Reva began to tie her pieces of fabric to the stick. "I have a feeling you haven't taught her that yet."

"Oh, Gods, Remy," I grumbled, sinking further into the chair as I rubbed my forehead. "I'm not completely incapable of raising a child."

"Well, at least you're doing that!" Remy glowered at Reva, swiping a smear of dirt off her cheek. "Daily baths must be where your knowledge—"

I was over his criticism.

"Do not come to my home uninvited and patronize me, boy. You don't know the first thing about this child. She loves playing outside from the moment the sun rises over the horizon until it sets again. She is fed, monitored, bathed, lo—" I choked on the word, not because Fate prevented me from uttering it, but because I had told no one I loved them for over nine hundred years.

"Loved?" Remy said for me, drawing Reva closer to him. "Is she, Karasi? Are you capable of that?"

A sharp pain speared my chest, my eyes burning as my vision blurred.

Of course, I loved Reva. I loved her like my own, even if I never planned on it. The thought of losing her sent me into a raging fit, and imagining my world without her resurfaced an old ache. I blinked the tears away and averted my gaze to the wall over the couch.

I couldn't utter the word to Reva because I didn't want her to know what loss was. I knew she would lose me one day, that I would die so she could be great, and I knew what losing someone you loved was like.

I also feared that if I told her how much I loved her, the prophecy might change, and I would outlive her, too.

I turned my head back to Remy at the same time his gaze dragged from the wall to me, his mouth propped slightly in shock. I looked at Reva in his lap, my heart clenching as he toyed with a strand of her hair.

"What are you to her?" Remy asked quietly.

"Her guardian." I shrugged, meeting his bright purple eyes as I added, "Her mentor."

I hoped he could hear my silent admission hanging in the air. *Her mother.*

He looked back down at her, his eyes softening the longer he held her. I knew long ago Remy had a great love he lost, and I wondered if he ever wished to have a family with him. The way he observed Reva, I wasn't sure if he saw that future in her or if he saw the past, but I couldn't deny how right it felt for him to be here.

"And what do you suppose you'll be to her?" I folded my hands on the table, tilting my head. "*If* you were to be part of her life."

He swallowed down a powerful emotion that flickered across his face. I would never forget this moment as long as I lived.

Tears brimmed in Remy's eyes as he gazed down at her, and I witnessed the moment he fell absolutely in love with her. An invisible weight lifted from my shoulders at the idea that I wouldn't have to do this entirely alone, that I'd have some help, and that Reva would have someone who could tell her he loved her.

Remy cleared his throat, tapped Reva on the head with the stick she had decorated and gifted him, and bounced the leg she sat on. She turned heavy-lidded eyes on him, the ghost of a smile on her lips.

"I didn't get your name, kid." He poked her, and she giggled as she squirmed on his lap. "Who are you, stranger?"

"Reva," she squeaked, smiling widely as she nuzzled her face into his chest, curling up in his lap.

Remy didn't hesitate then, adjusting her closer to him. I knew that if she ever needed him, he would go down protecting her.

The voice chuckled in the back of my mind, and I pushed it away, breathing slowly as I crossed my arms over my chest.

"If you'll let me," Remy said as he raised his gaze back to me, a glimmer there, "I want to help you with her. Whatever that looks like, however you need me."

I nodded in agreement as we both watched her fall asleep in his arms, her face serene.

It was the first time in years that Reva fell asleep for a nap without the aid of her sleep juice.

Father & King

1810 A.V. | Age: 1003

I entered the throne room unannounced, much to the dismay of the knights standing guard outside. One kept sputtering nonsense as the young king's head snapped up with narrowed eyes.

"You might want to consider new guards," I announced, strolling across the dome-shaped room.

Despite everything King Darius endured since ascending the throne, he still looked his age. Golden blond hair curled away from his face and at the nape of his neck, with a short beard framing his jaw. Amber-hued eyes glowed by the light of the sconces on the walls, but they still appeared dimmed by sleepless worry.

"What do I owe you for your time?" The king sighed, rubbing his forehead.

"I don't accept payments," I explained, curling my lip.

"I find that hard to believe," he scoffed, shaking his head. "No coin? No requests? No favors?"

I crossed my arms over my chest, letting my gaze travel the length of the room. It had been centuries since I stepped foot in the Castle of Andromeda, and I was surprised to find the murals on the walls still intact. It was the story of the creation of Magics and Sirians, and they still proudly displayed them. Maybe they found the stories simply that—mythologies to tell that had different meanings and lessons rather than facts.

"Well," he paused and leaned back in his throne, "my wife?"

I snapped my head to him, sighing. "Your wife's condition is permanent, I'm afraid. She suffered unfortunate damage to her spine during delivery due to the child's misalignment. She'll be confined to a wheelchair for the rest of her life, but other than that, she is healthy, well, and healing. If you'd summoned me sooner, I may have been able to stop the damage before it was permanent."

"It would've taken us two days to get there and back, and that's by horseback with no carriages." King Darius thrummed his fingers against the arm of the chair. "Unless you have faster means of getting here?"

"I could've ridden a horse if you sent one man to retrieve me," I explained, shrugging. That gesture seemed to agitate him more. "I could've made it."

[Never.] I kept my face a neutral mask, even if I wanted to growl at the voice. *[The boy is the Marked Soul.]*

I blinked at that, but King Darius didn't seem to notice when he asked with a quieter voice, "And Clint?"

"The baby is complicated." I paced before the dais, the words that spoke to me while I treated him echoing through my mind. "You see, what he needs goes far beyond a Magic's capabilities. He will need something I can't provide, nor any other Magic that you may summon to your doorstep. He needs an old, forbidden, lost power that will be much harder to find."

"Please, no riddles." King Darius pinched the bridge of his nose.

"Patience, Darius," I grumbled, and he lifted an eyebrow at the omission of his title. "My powers don't allow me to say things outright, even if I want to, so I have to work around what Fate will allow.

"Magic medicine will be able to treat him until he becomes immune to it. You will know when that time comes, and you will summon me again. I will not answer the call, though. Someone who is more equipped to treat him will come in my place. You must accept her."

"It's another female Magic?" Darius asked, leaning forward.

I studied him as I slipped my hands into the pockets of my cloak, my fingers brushing the stiff parchment. I waited for the voice to answer, hoping it would tell me to stop and that this wasn't the time, but for once, it lay in silence.

I slowly pulled the parchment out, and Darius tracked the movement with a heavy gaze. All I could think about was Reva's smiling face as the letter trembled in my hand.

I knew she was more than likely fast asleep in her bed, buried under layers of blankets. She probably suckered Remy into telling her a bedtime story until she fell asleep, and the helpless man would be sleeping beside her by the time he finished.

She was safe and happy, and this could put that in danger. I wanted Fate to say something—*anything*—to reassure me, and yet when I needed it most, it was quiet.

"There is a child that was put into my care ten years ago," I whispered, cautiously stepping toward Darius, gripping the parchment tight—the one addressed to him. "This child is very important to your future."

"Are you telling me this child will save my son one day?"

"Your son..." I took one step up the dais. "Your kingdom." I took another step and extended the letter toward him. "The world... If you let her."

Darius side-eyed the parchment as if it carried an incurable disease, but he accepted it, nonetheless. He tilted it, and when he beheld the handwriting, his grip loosened and face went slack.

"How did you..." His eyes set ablaze, and he lurched from the throne to full height. "Who gave this to you?"

"You should read it," I said, holding my hand up between us, my palm inches from his swelling chest.

"Have you read it?" he asked, his voice quiet.

I shook my head. "It didn't seem right. I suspect there are personal things within that letter that aren't for my eyes. I had my own letter, as does the girl."

Darius stared at the letter with wide eyes, carefully handling it as if it were going to disintegrate between his fingers. His eyes flickered over the top of the page, and he looked like he might be sick.

I waited in silence as he read, and when he got to about the halfway point, tears rimmed his eyes as he raised them to mine.

"You said ten years ago," Darius whispered, his voice hoarse. He swallowed back the emotions. "You mean to tell me the child… The girl…"

I nodded once, keeping my girl close to my chest. I wasn't ready to reveal anything to him until he finished that letter. I would let Jedrek decide how I moved forward with her.

A few more beats of silence passed while Darius finished, many different emotions warring on his face: grief, guilt, pain, nostalgia, and confusion. One after the other, the muscles in his face twitched imperceptibly, and even if a tear didn't streak down his cheek, I spent a millennium learning how to read people.

"Sincerely, Jed," King Darius said when he finished the letter. He lowered his voice, "Reva is her name?"

Again, I only nodded.

Darius moved closer, mere inches between us. "Where is the chi—Reva, now?"

"Safe," I assured him, and his shoulders relaxed. There was so much guilt radiating from him, I wondered if it overshadowed his grief. "She's healthy, intelligent, talented, and a force of nature."

Darius chuckled around what I believed was a sob, his voice catching in his throat. "Does she know who her father and mother are…were?"

"She knows he saved her by making the decision he

did, and that they both loved her. Unfortunately, that's all she can know right now. She doesn't know her last name."

"Jedrek capitalized the word *Light*," Darius admitted, and my heart broke because this meant he wanted Darius to know. "I truly don't know what your powers can do, but if I'm guessing right… Is there some way you can show her to me or let me see her?"

I sighed, contemplating. I wished I had the chance to speak with Jedrek, and I wished he revealed his and his wife's motivations for not entrusting their friend. I knew I could use the mind-walking I'd inherited from my father, but I warred with whether or not I wanted the king to see what she looked like.

His father had been a terrible man, especially toward Magics. I couldn't imagine what he'd been like if faced with a Sirian. The image curdled my stomach, and I reluctantly drew my gaze to Darius's face.

I searched for the cruelty of his father. Instead, the way he worried about his youngest son and wife, his reaction to a friend I supposed he thought dead—it had to be enough for me.

I placed my palm against the side of his cheek, closing my eyes and recalling the memory forward to place into his mind.

Reva ran across the lawn toward Remy, who was sauntering up the grass with a sack slung over his shoulder. When he found her form bouncing toward him, he dropped the sack and crouched so she could launch herself into his arms. He picked her up with ease, twisting in a circle as her arms locked around his neck.

"Who is that?" Darius asked beside me, voice echoing as he watched the memory.

"For all intents and purposes?" I inhaled heavily, shrugging. "He's her father, now."

"So, he is dead, then." Darius's voice cracked, and I turned my gaze to him at the same time Remy set Reva down. "Jedrek?"

"He never came back for her." Reva slipped her hand into Remy's, and even from the porch, I could hear her voice carrying on the wind as she told him what he missed in the week he'd been gone. "I suspect your Jedrek is a man who would've come back for her if he lived."

Darius said nothing, only gawking at Reva the closer she got. "This is a memory, yes?"

I nodded, my heart picking up and reverberating around us as Reva and Remy neared the porch. "This past summer, shortly before she turned ten."

She finally turned her head to where I stood on the porch, granting us a full view of her face. I already knew what would come next: Reva asking if Remy could stay for a sleepover because she'd missed him so much.

Instead, I watched Darius, waiting for him to see what lay on the middle of her forehead—for him to confirm what Jedrek tried to tell him in the letter.

His face dropped in shock, but tears glistened in his eyes. I frowned just as I pulled us out of the memory—

My hand slowly slid from his face, and I took a few

steps back to the edge of the dais. His face mimicked the same expression he had in the memory recall, but another tear slipped free. This time, he let it get lost in his beard.

"She looks so much like her mother," is what the King of Mariande said, and my hand flew to my chest.

The first thing this man said had nothing to do with the Mark on her forehead, the one thing that would damn her in a world that shunned her kind for the last one thousand years.

No. His first thought was that she looked like her mother.

Darius cleared his throat, shaking his head, and what he said next also stunned me. "How do you expect to hide what she is from the world? She advertises it before they can glimpse her powers."

My mouth dropped open of its own accord. Again, I was dumbfounded to find the next thought was concern for her.

I didn't understand why Reva's parents hadn't trusted him with this. He only glimpsed her in a memory, read the letter of his dead friend, and it felt like my competency to care for her was in question.

Again.

I wanted to know what was in the letter, but it wasn't my business.

"There is a salve I created many centuries ago to help her people hide themselves amongst mortals," I explained, shaking the surprise from my mind. "As for her powers, we're going to do our best to ensure she has control over them."

Darius sighed, plopping back down onto his throne. "So, I have to wait until she is older and wiser? Why can't I meet her now? From my understanding, you've never been tied down in this way, and yet you're just okay with having a child around?"

"I've raised her for the last ten years." I scoffed in disbelief, frowning. "She has a home."

"She could be here, though," Darius argued, his hand flexing around the arm of the throne. "Jedrek was a brother to me. We grew up beside one another. That makes Reva like family to me, not to mention I have children who are only two years older than her. Our friend, Eamon, has a son who is her age. She could be here with people who knew her parents, who can care for her—"

"I care for her!" I snarled, my claws poking into my palms. I took a steadying breath before continuing, "Besides, even if I didn't want her, I wouldn't be able to give her up. Fate forbids it. She must be in my care until the time is right."

And if Fate didn't care who she was raised by, I still wouldn't give her up. I was her mentor and guardian, but she was the second person in my life that I'd ever *chosen* to love.

"So, when she comes to me, what do I do?" Darius asked, a harsh laugh bursting from him. "Hello, Reva. I'm your dead father's best friend. Welcome to the kingdom! Why even bother with fetching you if I know I'm to receive her?"

[She cannot know.] I clenched my jaw, rolling my eyes at the voice that assaulted my mind. *[She must remain orphaned until the Great One falls.]*

"You have to be oblivious to this," I explained, turning my back to walk down the dais as I laced my fingers together in front of me. "There's a prophecy that she's connected to, and she must not learn who she is until one of those lines comes to pass."

"A prophecy?" Darius frowned, straightening his back. "What will happen?"

"*The powerful must be few for balance to remain,*" I recited, my voice taking on an echoed quality. "*The Great One will fall.*"

Darius's attention latched onto me, those fiery eyes burning as I stood frozen in place, unable to move. "Are you saying you are to die? For her to come into her power?"

I swallowed around the lump in my throat, but I nodded once, shutting my eyes.

I wasn't afraid of death. I never had been.

I was afraid for my *aster*, because if I wasn't here, how could I ensure she was safe?

"She has yet to manifest her main power," I said quietly. "She may have another gift as well. It's possible she is a descendant of a demi-god."

"Something big is coming, isn't it?" Darius asked, reclining into his throne.

"It will change the world," was all I could say on that.

I cleared my throat, tightening my hands. "Darius, might I speak candidly?"

"I fear you've been doing so the entire time." He laughed without mirth, a hand running through his hair. "I won't stop you now."

"Many believe Fate is linear," I began, studying his face. "There is but one Path the world will hurtle down, no matter what you may do to stop it. Of course, there are outcomes favored by Fate, and that is where people like me come into play. Fate can use us and influence us to make sure the outcome it desires unfolds. For those like you, though—"

A cough broke off my sentence, and it felt like my chest might collapse in on itself. King Darius moved quickly, coming to catch me as I doubled forward, gasping for air.

[You speak too much.] The voice growled.

You meddle too much, I snapped back, and I took a giant breath past the harshness there as I whispered into the young king's ear, "You have more free will than I ever have. Just know there are many Paths you can take moving forward, and many decisions—" I gasped through Fate's clutches tightening, "Many decisions can still lead to the same outcome, so don't linger. Choose what feels best for you."

I finally took a big breath of free air. Darius studied me as I righted myself, hitching my hands on my lower back as I tried to restore the air in my lungs.

"Are you saying I could tell her?" he asked, searching

my face. "I could tell her I know who she is and what she is?"

[*NO!]* Fate screamed in many voices, but I just shrugged.

"One thing is for certain, Your Highness." I rubbed my chest, panting. "What you throw out into the world is like a boomerang. The clock goes round, and it comes right back. Will you be ready to catch the consequences of your decisions when they do?"

Fire & Light

1813 A.V. | Age: 1006

Reva was ten years old when the Light manifested, and I didn't think I'd ever felt such relief when it did. The True Prophecy remained, although many details of it became quite clear to me the closer we approached when my orphaned Star would return *home*.

I wasn't sure when it would be time for her to leave. I assumed she would be an adult since that's what the visions showed me, but at what stage of her adulthood was unclear.

Instead of worrying, I tried my best to remain in this era with her, never lingering in the past or wavering too far into the future. The last time I had a reason to truly live was Brand, but Reva gave me a reason to do so again.

"I'm not asking for much, kid," Remy chastised from their place on the front lawn. I rested my chin in my hand as he attempted to instruct Reva on how to use the Light. "I just want you to play around with it. I promise you won't hurt me."

"I didn't like playing with it last time," Reva whined, mimicking Remy's stance by hitching her hands on her hips. I tried to stifle the chuckle bubbling up my throat when she stepped closer to him, only an inch of space between them, and inclined her head with narrowed eyes. "I don't want to play with the Light right now. Are you going to make me?"

I had to give Remy credit because he never got angry with her. He presently raised his eyebrow as he peered down at her, meeting her gaze. "If I have to coax it out of you, I can think of a few things that will work."

"Try me," Reva snapped, clenching her fists at her side.

I pressed my lips together, sighing as I rubbed my temples.

Reva never feared what she was, but the moment her Light came, she did. I could never understand what the Light felt like in her little body, but she described it as a buzzing sensation. I tried to empathize with her, explaining that my prophecies made me feel uncomfortable sometimes. I told her how the more she used them, the more familiar they would be.

Over the last few years, we'd coaxed her into calling it to the surface, to feel it under her skin and get used to it, but she was still too hesitant wielding it in any way.

Her favorite phrase lately was *I don't want to.*

Remy slowly knelt before her, clasping her shoulders to keep her gaze on him. The ferocity in her golden eyes faltered as her brows twitched, and I knew she was about to lose this battle.

"Either you can practice your gifts with me, or—" he

leveled a finger in front of her face when she opened her mouth to speak, "I will get Willem to come teach you instead."

Reva stiffened at the threat, her eyes frantically searching Remy's face to call his bluff. "You wouldn't dare."

It wasn't that Reva was scared of Willem, at least she didn't tell me if she was. Anytime we would run into him at The Red Raven or in town—or the rare times he would come with Dahlia to visit—he completely ignored Reva as if she weren't there. He didn't speak, and he mostly lingered on my porch.

There was one time Reva snuck out during dinner and spoke with him. I'm not sure what words were exchanged, but he pointed to the tattoos on his neck and arm and uttered quiet words to her.

She came sprinting into the house and stuck by Remy for the remainder of the evening and begged him to stay the night.

Which, of course, he obliged, because the man was wrapped around her finger.

"Fine." Reva relented, albeit with the most dramatic sigh I ever heard. I was positive it was laced with a low growl. "But I'm not going to enjoy it."

"I don't need you to." Remy shrugged and took a couple of steps back, putting some distance between them. He held up his hand, palm up to the sky, and tilted his head toward it. "Follow my lead."

Reva mirrored Remy's stance, taking a deep breath.

Her arm was rigid, but the rest of her body appeared relaxed.

"Close your eyes and focus on your body," Remy explained, demonstrating with his own eyes closed. Reva reluctantly followed, a frown in the middle of her forehead. "What do you feel inside your body?"

"My heartbeat," Reva answered quietly, the line between her brow lessening. "My lungs moving."

"Good." He opened his eyes and lowered his hand to watch her. "Can you feel anything else beyond the normal things your body does?"

"My chest feels kind of tight." She pressed her bowed lips together, a faint glow beginning in the middle of her forehead. "The buzzing is there, too, right next to my heartbeat. My chest keeps getting tighter, and it feels like someone is sitting on me—"

"Focus on your lungs again, Reva."

I wanted to applaud the gentle, steady tone Remy maintained. Her panic had me on edge, especially with her Mark glowing.

"Feel the air coming and going, slowly."

She took deep breaths in and out, the air leaving her lips in a small gust that deflated her shoulders. "It's not so tight anymore."

"There's nothing to be afraid of," Remy encouraged, taking an imperceptible step toward her, but he caught himself. The corner of my lip twitched. "I know it feels funny, but it's not going to hurt you. Think of it like lying in the grass. The weeds might tickle your skin, but they're not going to hurt you."

Reva's entire body changed with that comparison. Any limbs that were locked relaxed, and the hand hanging by her side unclenched, going limp as her face softened.

"Better, huh?" Remy smirked, his sharp canine catching the sunlight. A slight grin tugged at her lips, and she nodded once. "Alright. Now, find where the buzzing was before, but don't tug at it yet. Just feel for it."

"It's still by my heart," she whispered, but the slight mania with which she spoke before was gone. "It's glowing."

"That's okay." Remy absentmindedly slipped his hands into his pockets, rocking back and forth from his heels to his toes. "Now, imagine you're reaching your hand into your body like scooping water from the lake, and pull out just a little bit at your fingertips."

Almost immediately, small bursts of white-gold Light flickered at her fingertips, her veins illuminated with the same hue. She peeked one eye open, then both snapped wide in excitement. The breath was knocked from my lungs when her eyes illuminated, casting a glow across her warm skin.

"You think my claws and my speed are cool," Remy said, pointing his finger at the glow of her hand. "I think that's pretty cool, kid."

"Can I do more?" Reva asked enthusiastically, the Light winking out as she broke her concentration. She frowned at her hand, blinking.

"As you learn to control it, you'll need to give it just a little more attention before it becomes as easy as breathing," Remy explained, but he nodded. "Let's see how much you can wield—"

"Remiel," I hissed, lurching from the steps. "We don't know—"

"She's only thirteen." Remy held his hand out toward her, and Reva's gaze bounced from me to Remy, waiting to see which one of us would win. "She can't be *that* powerful yet."

I hummed, shaking my head as I crossed my arms over my chest. "I don't care if she is. There is no reason for her to yank on all that power and wield it around like it's a toy."

"She needs to know what it feels like," Remy argued, his eyes flashing. His shoulders twitched, and I raised my eyebrow. Remy rarely used his wings, and because of that, he seemed to have lost the control over them that he once had. "This is why she's afraid of it. What she feels is scaring her, so she should understand her limits, or lack thereof."

"You can't *really* stop me," Reva interjected, glaring at me. I narrowed my eyes as I clicked my front teeth together. "If I want to wield the Light, you can't take it away from me."

"Reva," Remy warned, turning towards her at the same time she stuck her hands out in front of her. "Hold on, Reva—"

"Just stick my hand in, right?" Reva scrunched her

face together, concentrating.

"Right, but don't go too quickly." Remy held his hands out in front of him, rotating them in a circle to demonstrate the speed, though she wasn't watching. "Take your time, let yourself feel it out."

"Is it supposed to be hot?" Reva asked nervously, and her expression fell.

Remy looked at me, confusion furrowing his brow. "I'm not sure…"

"Hot?" I stood a few feet from them, shaking my head. "Reva, the Light shouldn't be hot."

"This is *really* hot," she muttered, and I caught her forehead glistening with sweat in the sun. "It's so hot and bright."

Remy and I took a step away from her at the same time the golden glow of her Mark morphed into a warmer, redder tone.

"Karasi," Remy whispered, but the anxiousness in his tone was so foreign that Reva latched onto it.

"I can't stop it!" Reva's eyes shot open, and they too were glowing the same color as the Mark. Even her veins were turning a molten color beneath her skin.

[Fate demands sacrifice.] The voice reminded me as if I'd forgotten I would one day fall for Reva to rise. The only reason that would happen was if her power was equal or greater to my own.

Dionne.

When that thought finally popped into my mind, it was too late. Fire burst from Reva's hands in a quick flare, but she shouted as Remy lurched out of the way of the stream. At the sight of the flames licking her fingers, Reva's concentration broke, and everything winked out like the fire had been snuffed.

I opened my mouth to tell her what this meant, but the voice closed its fist around my throat.

[You cannot teach her this.] The hiss echoed in my mind. [It is not your job.]

I frowned at that, but my heart lurched as Reva shouted Remy's name. She ran toward where he was sitting in the grass, cradling his arm.

"You said I couldn't hurt you!" Tears rimmed her eyes, but she stopped herself from getting any closer to him. "You're hurt!"

"I gotta say, that's before I knew you could wield Dio—"

[No!] The voice shouted, and when Remy and Reva gawked at me, I realized it was using my voice to stop him from saying whose god-power she inherited.

I cleared my throat, motioning to the charred skin of his arm. "Don't touch it. Come inside and we'll give you some salve to help it heal. With that and your enhanced abilities, you'll be fine."

"You hear that, kid," Remy said, side-eyeing me suspiciously. He held his good hand out to Reva, ushering her forward. She pouted, but she inched forward. "I'll be fine."

She let Remy take her arm as he rose, pulling her against his chest. She instantly wrapped her arms around his waist, burying her face into him as she sniffed.

"Hey, now," he cooed, nearly bending in half to kiss the top of her head. "Why don't you run inside and prepare clean cloths for us?"

Reva yanked her head back and nodded, eager to help him. She ran up the front porch steps and through the door, and I heard something crash in the kitchen.

"She has Dionne's god-power," Remy murmured through a wince as I took his arm and inspected it. "Why wouldn't you let me tell her?"

"It wasn't I who won't let you," I explained under my breath. "Fate said it's not my job to tell her, and I'm assuming that means it's not your job either."

"So, what are we going to tell her?" Remy studied my face, scoffing. "She's already an outcast who has to hide who she is. Now she has to live thinking she's a strange enigma amongst Sirians, too?"

I waited for the voice to guide me, hoping what I said next would suffice. "We can tell her that sometimes Sirians inherit a power from a demi-god. We just can't tell her who."

Remy scowled at me as if it were my fault we had to lie to her.

"I can't fight Fate, Remy." I shook my head, recalling what happened when I tried to defy it with King Darius. "I've already tested it enough, and I fear what it will do if I continue to do so."

I let the implication hang between us and that had him stopping before the door, his face gaunt.

"You think…" His eyes drifted to Reva rushing about the house for clean cloths, his eyes soft and sorrowful as he watched her. "She's important to the prophecy. They wouldn't take her away."

"I don't know what Fate would do," I whispered. "But I won't test it and risk *her*. I will do whatever it wants me to do, so long as she's safe. That means you must do so as well, no matter how much it hurts. No matter what the consequences may mean for her in the future. Just as long as she's alive."

Remy pressed his lips together, groaning at the clear battle he waged in his mind. I knew the feeling, and it hurt that I dragged him into this complacency.

When Reva met us at the table with cloths and the correct healing salve, I caught Remy's resolve when he met my eyes.

We agreed from then on that we would do whatever Fate asked of us, if only because it ensured that Reva would be okay.

Starfire & Night

After someone nearly stumbled upon my lot in the middle of Remy's instruction with Reva the previous week, she was reluctant to use her Light and Dionne's gift once more. She chose to lock doors with her fingers rather than the kinetic energy and opted to start a fire beneath a cauldron just as I or Remy would do.

While she chose the Light over the Darkness, I didn't want her fearing the power she did have. I just needed her to control it with her emotions. The hematite necklace from her mother helped control the god-power, but it would do nothing to tame the Light.

"But it's raining outside," Reva whined as I ushered her out the front door. "Remy isn't coming today either."

"You are more than capable of practicing your powers alone without Remy's guidance," I explained, laying my hand against her lower back as she planted her feet on the porch, her hands clenched at her sides. "Don't make me use my claws."

She gasped, whirling her head around, the ends of her hair whipping at her neck. "You can't do that."

I narrowed my eyes at her, lifting a single eyebrow. "Do you want to test that, child? You don't heal like a Magic, so a nice little prick would remind you of what happens when you disobey."

She snarled as she marched to the edge of the porch but stopped before walking out from the cover of the awning. "Why do you care so much about my powers? It's not like I can use them for anything other than home activities. Besides, I have the Light now, so it won't manifest as the Darkness."

"There's much about the Darkness even I don't know, *aster*." I shook my head at her, pointing toward the Black Avalanches through thick, rain-heavy clouds. "We don't know if the Light can turn into it. We don't know if suppressing your powers like you have been at such a young age can make you sick. We don't know enough, which is why it's better if you teach yourself to control them so that they don't respond to your emotions."

I leveled her with a glare, directing my finger at her hand where the Light had been gradually brightening the harder she glowered at me. She glanced down at her hands, startled as though she didn't know she was pulling the Light forward.

Which was precisely why I needed her to practice.

"Fine." Reva finally walked out onto the front lawn, the mist dampening her clothes. Her hair whipped around her in the storm, and I cursed myself for not having her bundle it in a cap to keep it from tangling.

She stopped a few dozen feet away from the front

porch, and I crossed my arms over my chest as I watched her dawdle, her attention drawn to the direction of the road, the mountains, or the lake.

"Reva," I drawled in warning, tapping my foot on the porch. I swore the minute she turned thirteen, she became insufferably challenging, pushing the boundaries every day on the things I thought I'd ingrained in that head of hers. "You're stalling."

"What if someone sees me?" she shouted over the wind howling like a beast.

I knew if she didn't hurry up, the mist would become a torrential downpour. Then she'd truly be insufferable and complain about being cold for the entire evening.

"You're safe here, child," I assured her, my heart clenching at the reminder that I let someone come onto our land and threaten her sense of security.

Lightning flashed in the sky, and thunder echoed off the nearby mountains. Chills rose on my skin, and I hesitated at the grimness of it all.

Something wasn't right.

I watched intently as Reva closed her eyes and tried to center herself despite the edges of her hair whipping across her cheeks. She spread her arms wide, and I frowned at the strange heat emanating from her. An invisible aura shimmered around her form, and it wasn't until I saw another streak of lightning shoot across the sky that I realized how silent it was.

Because no roll of thunder followed.

It was as if the entire world around us had silenced,

waiting to see what my *aster* would do.

Reva's body jerked, her shoulders stiffening, and she winced as though she were in pain, holding her breath.

"Control, *aster*," I warned her calmly, unable to hide my uncertainty. This wasn't how she normally conjured the Light. This was similar to how Remy taught her to wield her fire power, except there was no orange glow. "You don't need that much to conjure it."

Reva gasped, her eyes still closed, the sound chilling my bones. It morphed into a snarl as her veins pulsed *blue* beneath her skin, her face scrunched as she fought something inside of her.

Around Reva, a strange force shot out of her, hovering over her head like an umbrella to protect her from the rain. The shield responded to the rainfall with a tremble of blue light.

"*Aster*." My arms slid from their place in front of me, falling limp at my sides. "Open your eyes."

I watched her peek out of a small opening in her eyelids, only for both eyes to shoot wide as she studied the shield above her and the dry space around her compared to the waterfall of rain beyond.

I blinked rapidly as Reva's image shifted momentarily, an unfamiliar woman trading places with her. The image was so quick, though, that I questioned if I'd seen her.

This…

This couldn't be possible.

I had never heard of a Sirian having two god-powers

before, but especially this particular one.

In my entire existence, I met Sirians who wielded all variations of the demi-gods: Dionne, Taranis, and Phoebe. But I never met a Sirian who wielded Asteria's god-power.

In my one thousand years of existence, *I had never met a Sirian who wielded Asteria's god-power.*

Reva's arms trembled as she held the shield, gasping when it vanished into her body, sending her to the dirt. The rain immediately soaked into the ground, her hair, and her clothes.

But I didn't rush to her at first because the voices whispered in my head alongside Sybil's as the True Prophecy echoed over and over. New lines appeared, flashing blue like the power Reva just wielded.

Asteria never got the chance to be a mother.

I braced my hand on one of the porch beams as the voices uttered the new lines in the middle of the prophecy:

[A betrayal by Death…]

[Raises the new Gods.]

Then they spoke two more lines, placing them at the end of the prophecy:

[She'll wield the Light and Dark…]

[A Goddess reborn.]

I wasn't sure at the time how this was possible, but I knew this was the cold terror Sybil felt when she beheld Tyra and her Darkness.

If what Sybil said was true, Reva shouldn't be a

descendant of Asteria, because Asteria never had children.

"Did I do something wrong?" Reva asked hesitantly.

I dragged my gaze to where she stood directly before me, rain dripping down her face through her drenched hair. The water made her hair nearly black as night and pin-straight, and the image of a strange male flashed in my mind.

The voices hissed menacingly.

"I…" I paused, gently gripping her chin between my fingers. "How did you do that?"

"I slipped into the other well of power," she said innocently, her voice timid. "Remy always said I should have one for the Light and one for the fire, but this one is just… there, too."

I huffed in disbelief, shaking my head. "What did it feel like?"

"Very cold." Her eyes pinched at the corners as she shivered once. "But it burned, too. Different from firepower."

I deeply inhaled, nodding once. "Come inside, out of the rain. Use your firepower to heat the tub."

I listened to her shuffling feet and the door creaking open behind me before I brought a shaking hand to my temple, trying to quell the voices thrashing in my head from whatever vision or person I'd seen.

I flinched when a scream of frustration echoed in my head, but I relaxed when it silenced the voices. The chills returned to my body as they spread across my skin, and my hand fell to my chest, where something felt like a wound.

The powerful must be few for balance to remain.

I slowly turned on my heel to join Reva inside, but I froze in place when Reva drifted past the living room toward the washroom. A strange, glowing mist with the curvy shape of a feminine figure appeared over her shoulder. I rushed into the house just as Reva slammed the door shut behind her, my hand quivering.

Something was most definitely wrong, and a thought slithered its way into my mind. I questioned whether it was my own, the voices, or someone else entirely.

I had to discourage Reva from using that power at all costs, or those final lines of the prophecy would come true.

And something—or someone—didn't want that.

THE TRUE PROPHECY

The Gods mourn their children,
Buried in the Dark.
The Stars will come back home,
Orphaned by the past.
When Darkness comes again,
Marks will be revealed.
Fate demands sacrifice,
The Great One will fall.
A betrayal by Death,
Raises the new Gods.
Chaos will govern thrones,
Crows answer the call.
The Truth will be released,
Abyss claims a King.
She'll wield the Light and Dark,
A Goddess reborn.

Fate & Time

1823 A.V. | Age: 1016

Reva sat at the table with her back to me, sorting through her payments from Rol and the few townsfolk who paid her for healing. She'd been adamant about ignoring me since the male came to The Red Raven, shooting me glares when she didn't think I was looking.

It wasn't exactly how I wanted to spend our last few moments together, but I didn't chastise her for it. From her point of view, I was difficult, and I deserved her scorn.

Reva shot me a glance when a knock echoed at the door, and my heart stopped in my chest.

I knew this was it.

I jerked my head toward the cabinet for her to put her money away, and I waited while she grabbed the nearest hat and pulled it down over her Mark. She took a steadying breath with her hand on the door.

When she yanked it open, I caught those eyes Reva talked about, even from across the hut.

Once again, a Wardson had come for me.

There was no denying that this was the moment. By

tomorrow, Reva would be gone.

The male looked at Reva with a ghost of a smirk, outright starstruck by the sight of her. I rolled my eyes as they exchanged a few words back and forth, but my heart warmed at the idea of Reva finding others to accept her.

To love her.

"My apologies," the man said, bowing in front of Reva.

I got to my feet as she stepped out of the doorway and waved her hand into the house, revealing not just the man but two others with him.

"What do you need, boy?" I said, and everyone in our cramped home stopped moving.

"Madam," he finally spoke, dipping his head. I held back the curl of my lip, reminding myself that at some point, this was a custom in greeting any woman or man of power. "My name is Finley Wardson, and I come from the royal family of Mariande with—"

"From where?" Reva snapped, but I knew that name, and the only thought I had was how the clock went round and round.

I doubted Darius knew my first encounter with this family, but he was aware of his best friend.

That damned King sent the son of his other friend, officially connecting Reva with the Wardsons and Hespers. I suppressed my slight agitation, directing my glare and the words I wished I could speak to Darius at the boy. "Oh, no. You can get the hell out of my house.

I will not play any games with—"

"I promise, ma'am," the Wardson boy stuttered, holding out his hands in what appeared to be surrender. "Please. The family wouldn't send us on a childish game. If it weren't the King's son, I wouldn't be here."

The confirmation that this was about the young baby I saved a decade ago was like a nail to my coffin.

"I understand you assisted with his birth," Finley said, fidgeting. I tilted my head at that. "And that you were able to give a remedy for him. Unfortunately, those remedies are no longer helping him. We were hoping that if you were to come to the castle, you'd be able to help."

I wasn't sure what to say next or how to play this game with Fate. The voice seemed to catch my hesitation, taking control, "*In exchange for?*"

"A generous salary, of course." Finley could not keep his eyes off Reva, his gaze flickering to her even as he spoke to me. "The King and Queen of Mariande want to offer a permanent position as the Royal Healer. We don't know what sort of treatment the Prince needs. He may need round-the-clock care from a witch for the rest of his life, but we're not sure. Which is why the King wants to offer a position in good faith."

This was everything I'd been waiting for—everything I prepared for since the moment I received The True Prophecy. The last step would be convincing Reva that she was safe to go in my stead.

"Will I be shackled against my will as I work, hidden in a broom closet to be called only when my skills are needed? It may not seem like much here in Old Eldamain, but here, at least I'm free."

I needed the boy to confirm not just for Reva but for myself that she would be safe under King Darius, regardless of whether he chose to let her know his relation to her father—the heritage he knew about, even though she didn't.

"There are no consequences for performing magic underneath King Darius and within Mariande borders." The pink returned to Finley's cheeks, and I saw what intrigued Reva. Everything about him was welcoming and bright. "The King ensures your protection."

I needed *more* from him. I gripped my cane tightly as I asked, "How can King Darius ensure my protection? There is no protection for Magics."

He shook his head, piercing eyes peeking at Reva, who was utterly flabbergasted. "You will be protected in Mariande. Magics live free."

"Free?" Reva repeated breathlessly.

This was what I needed.

My chest fluttered as I pointed my cane at Finley, my knees quivering. "And what will the King do when other kingdoms find out they've employed a *witch* as their Royal Healer?"

"There will be no need to respond," one of the other knights said quietly.

Finley clenched his jaw, and I suppressed my amusement. "There are already witches working with the prince now."

Reva inhaled a sharp breath, her lips pressed together. I could see the wheels turning in her head, a small glimmer of hope hidden underneath those golden hues.

"Well, that sounds like a generous offer—" I couldn't withhold my shock as that same omniscient presence I'd seen around Reva over the last ten years wavered beside her. I choked around my breath, my chest scratching as it coaxed a coughing fit.

I didn't register what Reva said as I tried to inhale fresh breaths of air, fumbling in my pocket for a handkerchief. I wiped the spittle at the corner of my lips as I asked, "How long did your King give you to fetch me?"

"We have another night's rest before we head back to Mariande."

[Time.] The voice seethed in my head. I felt Reva's gaze on me, occasionally bouncing to Finley. I wondered whether she thought I would accept or not, and if she expected me to send her instead.

Because that is what I had to do. She needed to go in my place.

"Unfortunately, I won't be going," I finally uttered. Finley started, but I picked up my cane reluctantly and pointed it at Reva. "But she will."

They all looked at Reva now. The two other knights studied her with scrutiny while Finley appeared a tinge excited.

"What?" Reva squeaked, her face slack.

That sound broke my heart.

She didn't anticipate this in the slightest. I tried desperately to prepare her for this moment, getting her to control all variations of her power over the last ten years. I taught her everything I knew about potions and healing to give her a good point to work with, including knowledge the world had lost.

But I didn't teach her self-confidence, and that hurt nearly as much as knowing she would be leaving the next day.

"I mean no offense," Finley interrupted, chuckling anxiously. "The King requests someone of your skill level. Is she as good as you?"

I had to help her understand. Not just how good she was, but how much I cared. "She's better. I am ill. Frankly, I've seen much better days, and I can't endure a trip to Mariande. She's been my trained apprentice since birth—" Reva curled her lip at that, "and I have full confidence in her abilities."

Reva stared at me in shock, her eyes scrutinizing.

"We need the night to discuss this before we take someone back that is not you." Finley sighed, rubbing his forehead. "I don't want to bring a woman back just to send her home."

"Take your time." I waved my hand at the door. They needed to decide to take Reva, so I threw my arms up in feigned excitement. "If you wish, you could camp on my plot. There's room for you out there, I'm sure. You came prepared with tents for the cold, yes?"

One of the knights muttered something that earned

him a glare from Finley as they shuffled to the door. Reva followed after them, but before she could close it, Finley stopped and rested his hand against the doorframe.

I couldn't quite make out what he said, which was concerning. My enhanced hearing was failing me, which meant I truly didn't have much longer on Aveesh.

Especially once Reva became more powerful.

She shut the door, but she didn't immediately turn around.

I held my breath because I knew my girl. She was about to snap, and I braced as she whirled around. Her hands lit up a mix of gold and red as her powers rose.

"Are you out of your damn mind?" she hissed, her veins flashing a white gold that briefly illuminated the hut.

Such incredible power, and I prayed to the Gods she learned to use it properly. I swallowed, making my way to the couch as I bit back the tears.

I wouldn't be here to see if she would.

I leaned my cane against the wall behind the sofa, pausing as visions of her decorated sticks flickered in my head. I turned to look at her, seeing both who she was and who she would be.

"Truly, Karasi," Reva said quietly. "What have you done?"

I frowned, tilting my head to the side. "As I always do."

I wanted to be angry that she wasn't seeing all the clues I left for her, all the hints I tried to give her throughout her life. I was upset with myself, always yearning to tell her more, but never allowed.

[Careful.] The voice released its grip on my throat just enough.

"Before you were ever put on my doorstep, I knew it would be my responsibility to give you a chance at life. The Stars called you home, orphaned by parents who tried to fight for you instead of turning you over." *[Too close.]* I envisioned a rude gesture. "The Fates and your father gave you to me to guide you down the right Path. Thus, I have. And I continue to do so, even now."

It had to be enough. She needed to understand.

"By putting me under the roof of one of the most powerful royal families in all the kingdoms?" She ripped her hat off and slammed it to the ground, her Mark glowing faintly. "With *this*? This life in hiding was safer than being killed if someone saw this. They may be accepting of Magics, but that does not mean *my* kind. If they find out—"

"I've taught you how to control yourself and how to hide it." Another round of coughs followed the rise of my voice, my frustration irritating the tightness in my chest. I fell back onto the couch, relaxing further as the coughing stopped.

Reva walked across the kitchen and took up the space beside me, rubbing her hands on top of her thighs. I stared into her golden gaze, committing everything about her to memory. I ached to reach out to her, to brush my fingers across her skin, to remind myself she was alive, here and now.

To remind me just how much she was mine.

"I can't trust myself that much," she whispered, and I was knocked in the chest again at her lack of confidence. "And how am I supposed to leave you? You can barely keep a fire going when I'm gone for a few hours. What are you going to do when I'm not here?"

I sighed, wrapping my arm around her shoulder and pressing my face against her hair, inhaling. "I took care of myself for a long, long time before you came into my life. I will manage after you are gone. I know I don't have much longer left in this life, *aster*. The Fates demand it of me. You are meant for much more than this, Reva. So much more. And it starts with taking this position."

"Remy knew I was leaving," she muttered quietly, pulling her head back to look at me.

Fucking Remy. I nearly throttled him for how much he spoke on the porch. It created an argument between Reva and me, one I didn't want to have when I knew the days were so few.

"I can only reveal so much to you, *aster*." I sighed as I tested the waters with Fate. "There is a prophecy far greater than any other I have ever received in my life. It brought me to my knees the first time I saw it. The events were put into motion long ago, but it grows stronger now."

"You mean to tell me that accepting this position will fulfill a prophecy?" Her face scrunched with a mix of doubt and disgust. "Why me?"

Despite her not being my own flesh and blood, it was moments like this that I saw a younger version of myself in her.

"Oh, child." I patted her shoulder, squeezing. "You still have so much more to learn. You're going to need every last swell of knowledge that I and the others have taught you. Just know there are Dark things happening in those kingdoms that even I don't have the answers to."

"Dark things," she repeated, glancing away from me. "The Abyss. It has something to do with this?"

It had everything to do with this. "Use what resources you can. The Abyss is strong. I feel it deep in my bones. Something Dark is rising, Reva, but always remember your Light."

Reva placed her last chest of belongings by the door. She must have heard the men moving outside because she suddenly stiffened, panic flashing in her eyes.

I hobbled over to her as she peeked out the cracked door. I reached up and lightly dragged my hand down her tight braid, her shoulders relaxing, but her breaths quickening.

Tears threatened to fall as I gave her braid a light tug. "Time flew by much faster than I'm used to." So much faster. "You will be extraordinary, *aster*."

"I'm not worried about my success, Karasi," she whispered as she turned around. Her tears reflected mine as she choked on a sob, suppressing it with a press of her lips.

I didn't want her to hurt. I wanted her to be incredible, to have the life I always hoped she'd have. I wished for her to know love like I had and to know what friendship was.

I set my cane against the wall, then cupped her cheeks.

"I saw you, *aster*, before your parents even walked this earth," I whispered, swiping away one of her rogue tears. "I saw you as I see you now, and I saw you when I'm gone."

She shook her head in my hands fiercely, clenching her jaw.

"Fate will demand sacrifice, Reva," I urged, trying to warn her as much as I could about what was to come of me. "The Abyss does not lie, and you have a role to play."

She needed to move on, but more importantly, I wanted her to know that it wasn't her fault. When my time came, my death triggered by her power, I didn't want her to blame herself as she was so prone to do.

"How could I have a role to play in something I'm not entirely aware of?" She searched my face, her eyes flickering across it.

"Trust me," was all I could say, reaching for my cane again. "Whether you know enough now, you have a strong destiny. You will be glorious, and I will always be there with you."

A loud whistle echoed from outside, and Reva took

it as her signal as she reached for her hat, her face falling.

I wasn't ready. I didn't want to let her go. I needed her to know just how much I loved her, how she was my entire world. She gave me strength and purpose before she ever showed up on my doorstep.

"I've lived many years and many lives, *aster*," I whispered, wrapping a hand around her shoulder to stop her. "But, you have been my greatest journey. You'll always know where to find me if you need me."

She leaped into my arms, nuzzling her face into my neck. At first, I was startled, trying to remember the last time we'd hugged, but then I realized this would be the last time I could hold her, and I wrapped my arms around her.

I pressed my cheek against her head, committing every point of contact to memory and the way she still felt like the young child who'd build unfinished snowmen in the front of the house every single winter. The child who gifted those she trusted with sticks decorated in ribbons, the same one who bled for the pain of others and thought to heal with a hug or a cuddle.

She was *my* child, and she always would be.

Reluctantly, Reva pulled away, and I knew I had to be the one to urge her forward. I took two steps back, followed by two knocks on our front door. Finley peeked through the crack Reva had left.

"Do you need more time?" he asked, and Reva battled with that question.

"We're ready," I said, gesturing to the chests. "Those

two trunks are her things."

Reva stared at them as the knights picked them up, a revelation settling across her face. She whipped her head around, her mouth parted as if she would ask me more, but something softened her face.

I hoped to the Gods it was enough, from letting Remy come into our lives to every small thing I'd taught her about control. She needed strength for what lay ahead, and all I could do was stand there.

Her eyes pleaded as I nodded, whispering, "Go now. It's your time."

She slowly backed away, and I followed until we stood on opposite ends of the threshold. I kept my eyes on her as I clicked the door shut between us.

I don't know how long I stood there. I listened to her soft footsteps climb down the porch, and the male uttered something to her. My hearing wasn't as good as it used to be, but I dropped my forehead to the doorframe and waited until the sun moved across the horizon.

Reva's leaving felt right in the sense of the prophecy. That was undeniable.

But it was so wrong in my heart to let her walk away from me and the life we built together over the last twenty-two years.

There was also something strange I couldn't explain, at least not then.

The gold-tinted presence followed. It didn't linger or vanish.

It left with her.

And I didn't know if that meant safety or doom.

Past & Future

The flames overlapped one another, the ones where I was missing something, the ones that came from a girl's hands, and the ones that danced in a fireplace where the breath of a man caressed the back of my neck.

I rolled my head and shut my eyes, his voice soft and distant.

Mi leiron.

I startled as I blinked away the strange vision, except it wasn't a vision.

I scratched a nail across my skin.

It happened again when I looked down at the line on my arm. Sybil commanded me to stop while she hovered beside me.

"No," I said to her, to him, to the voices in my head. I rested my elbows on my thighs, laying my face in my hands.

I knew what was happening. I watched Sybil suffer, and I was still lucid enough to understand what was coming.

I questioned my remaining sanity when I started chuckling. It scratched at my raw lungs, but the giggles didn't stop.

How funny.

I lived to be a thousand years old, far longer than most I ever knew, and I wanted more time.

I wanted more time with my *aster*, one last chance to see her, to touch her, to see her smile.

I drew my eyes to the kitchen table where a brighter Reva kicked her feet in the chair as she tied ribbon after ribbon onto a stick. My lips turned up at the sight of her so young and wild.

Before the world got its hands on her.

"Karasi?" someone said, a voice that reminded me of the past but also the present, and maybe there was a future there, too. I blinked as I turned my head to the source, bright purple eyes blocking my vision. "Where did you go there, old woman?"

I chirped an unintelligible sound as I swatted at Remy, waving his hands away.

"Have you gotten up since the last time we were here?" Remy asked, but more sounds came from the kitchen.

I looked back, and Reva was there again, still in the chair, but grown. She looked wary and tired as she opened the box where I had hidden her father's letters. I struggled to get up, snatching my cane. "Don't open that!"

Remy gripped my shoulders, easing me back into a comfortable position as he hushed me. "Hey, it's just Dahlia. She's making you something to eat, okay?"

I frowned at him, tilting my head back as I peered over my nose. "When are you?"

His eyebrows rose, his lips pursed. "I don't think you've ever stumped me before."

"She's losing it, Remy," a chirpy voice said from the kitchen. I carefully dragged my gaze back to a different frame in the kitchen, meeting brick red eyes. "Try to keep her in the present."

"I think food might help," Remy grumbled as he took a bowl from Dahlia, shoving it into my hands.

I curled my lip, but then remembered Sybil once doing the same thing to a bowl of soup beside a window overlooking the Black Avalanches with a dark Abyss swirling in the peaks, just like they swirled now because the Darkness had come again—

"Eat," Remy ordered, his voice stern.

I glared at him, but I relented, forcing the food into my mouth.

The more I ate, the better I was, although I still felt like I was standing on a tightrope, wobbling between the past, present, and future. Remy and Dahlia talked quietly to themselves at the kitchen table as I finished off my soup, occasionally glancing over their shoulders at me.

"This will continue to happen until I die," I said as I set the bowl on the empty cushion beside me. I peered at the wall behind me, disappointed to find there were no sticks with ribbons hanging on it. "My sanity will alternate between the past, the present, and the future. The things I say may not make sense, but know they are true. Some things might be useful to you, while some may be completely useless."

"Why now?" Remy asked, folding his hands on the table. I studied his face, and the sadness there ached my heart because it reflected how I felt knowing Reva wasn't here. "Why is any of this happening now?"

"You know the prophecy," I told him, shrugging my shoulders as I adjusted the blanket. "I told you long ago this would come. You should've prepared yourself."

"We're cursed with old age, yet it's never enough time." Remy sighed as he shoved his hands through his hair, shaking his head. "I haven't felt like this in Gods' know how long."

"She isn't dead, *drakon*," I chided, glaring at him from the corners of my eyes. "She's learning, listening, growing, watching… Reva won't come back the same girl that left this forsaken place."

"Do you need one of us to stay here with you?" Dahlia asked, leaning against the table.

"I don't need to be cared for like a child." However, that is precisely what I did for Sybil in her final years. "I will just wait for Fate."

"If we all waited for Fate to take us, there'd be a lot of us sitting around doing jack shit," Remy grumbled, huffing out a breath of laughter. "You have to do *something*."

"I don't have to do anything!" I whipped my head at them, seething. "I'm so fucking old, do you understand? I have lived countless lifetimes and visited every country.

I watched every king rule, century after century. I have ushered in a prophecy to restore Magics and Sirians, and I have raised a child destined for greatness. I am done. I am ready."

I tasted the lie for what it was, and while Dahlia didn't seem to catch it, Remy did. His gaze softened because he said as much the day Reva left us.

It was never enough time.

"Well, we'll just continue to come check on you," Dahlia explained, rising from her seat. "Feeding and bathing you."

"I refuse to let the man bathe me," I mumbled, side-eyeing Remy.

He snorted, stretching out his legs and crossing his ankles. "Trust me, old woman. I have no intention of bathing you."

"I don't mind," Dahlia said, and I almost countered with *of course you don't,* but I held my tongue because that wouldn't be fair.

I sighed as I sank into the couch, tucking my chin into the blanket. I shut my eyes at the memory that tried to overtake the present, clenching my teeth.

It seemed my old methods of grounding would only bring more unwarranted memories.

"Will you see her?" Remy asked quietly, his eyes searing into the side of my head. "Will you go to her?"

"I plan on it." I nodded, trying to distinguish the voice from the urge to mind walk to Reva, but the voice just growled quietly at the back of my head. Interesting. "It seems like the voices won't stop me."

"Fucking Gods." Dahlia slammed her head onto her arms, groaning.

I stood by the porch as Reva lay in the snow. She seemed content with this memory, a blissful air about her. I stayed in the shadow, letting her memory play out from her point of view.

I was also interested to see what Remy said to her on the lawn all those years ago.

Watching their exchange in silence, I held back my chuckle as the younger version of Reva stared at Remy in horror and awe, trepidation pinching her shoulders closer to her ears.

I almost burst out laughing when she nearly slapped him after he asked how old she was.

I waited for the memory to continue, feeling my spirit within her dream, just as the ghost of me opened the door. I stepped into the shadowy form, taking over from here.

"Reva," I said softly.

The child form of Reva flickered from the five-year-old to what I presumed Reva was wearing now. A flash of light burst across the memory, and I frowned because that was neither of our doings. The sky morphed from the hazy gray to a beautiful sunrise, the colors merging from yellow to orange to pink.

I stepped across the lawn as Reva's current form held, her adult frame sitting on the ground in a nightgown. She stared up at the sky in confusion, tilting her head.

"Reva," I said again, standing beside her.

Her head snapped to me, and I almost lost my composure when tears immediately sprang to her eyes. "Am I dreaming still?"

I smiled down at her, bending over and taking her arms in mine. I lifted her with ease, marveling at how my strength seemed to be restored in this state, whether because it was all in the mind or because in her memory, I was this strong.

"I have to be dreaming." She laughed, but it crumbled halfway out.

I studied her, trying to decide how accurately this form reflected her in Mariande. There were dark circles under her eyes, her Mark stark against the middle of her forehead.

"We are in a dream state," I explained, hoping she believed me, "but the events we are experiencing now are no longer a memory."

"But it's a figment of my imagination," she said, but it bordered on a question.

I smiled at her, restraining the urge to hold her against me. "If you want it to be."

Another presence entered the dream, and I tried to maintain my composure as a golden, glowing silhouette carefully approached us. I drew my gaze back to Reva in time to watch her mouth open to say something, and yet nothing came out. Instead, moisture pooled at the corners of her eyes.

I reached out and caressed her cheek, my heart clenching as a tear escaped beneath my palm. "I know, aster. Oh, do I know."

"I'm sorry," she blurted around a sob. "I've broken all the

rules you gave me. So many people know what I am, and I just—"

I refused to let her blame herself for this.

"Hush, girl." I gripped her shoulders firmly, the gold form standing directly behind Reva now. It was time to test the boundaries of Fate in this state. "I told you I know. I know why you had to make these decisions. When you left, I instructed you to trust the touch of Fate."

"It doesn't make those choices any less frightening."

Gods, did I understand her.

I wanted to tell her so much about my life, how similar we truly were when we stripped away the titles and powers. I raised my fingers to her Mark, brushing along the scar.

"When the Darkness comes again—" The silhouette flared. Brightness bloomed behind my eyes, a sharp pain stabbing behind my eyes. "Marks will be revealed."

I was able to utter the prophecy, at least one line, without my ability to speak being hindered. Reva seemed disappointed, though. I sighed, my shoulders hunching.

"I grow weaker, aster." I dropped my hand down the side of her face, following her chin until I gripped it between my thumb and index finger. "You grow stronger."

She pondered that for a moment before saying, "I have two god-powers. Dionne is the fire… Well, I guess the core of the earth. We haven't figured out the other one yet. Do you know what it could be?"

I stared at the golden light, and I felt like it stared back. I wanted to tell her who she got the blue power from, that I believed her gift was from Asteria, but it still didn't make sense *to me.*

Reva's head twitched as if she tried to move, but a gold hand lifted and hovered above Reva's shoulder.

Like the Light.

If Reva had Asteria's powers, then I knew exactly who this was.

"The Gods mourn their children," I whispered, squinting.

"The Gods aren't here anymore, Karasi." Reva tried to move her head over her shoulder, but the figure's other hand shot out, glowing with the Light as it kept her head in place. "You taught me that."

The Gods were not here, but they were certainly somewhere, watching.

I tilted my head to the side as I looked directly into Reva's eyes. "She watches you."

"Who does?" Reva asked, her voice quivering.

The figure released Reva and shot out her hands, keeping them out of Reva's peripheral, and the flare of a white light lit up the dream space.

She was disrupting the dream state, waking Reva.

I smiled, hoping I could see Reva at least one more time. Then, the dream shattered in a white flare.

My consciousness restored as I slowly blinked awake, finding the fire dead before me and the house empty. I shook my head, trying to clear my mind, but I couldn't shake the internal instinct and the sixth sense I dealt with my entire life.

This golden silhouette hovered around Reva since the moment the blue god-power manifested. It went with

Reva when she left for Mariande, and it still watched her, stepping in to correct my moments of carelessness—when I wanted to tell Reva everything.

Danica had been watching Reva for a decade.

And she wasn't done.

BETRAYALS & GODS

After hearing about the attack on Mariande, I knew I had to talk to Reva again, despite not only Fate trying to limit me, but now Danica. The Gods never did anything for me or our world up until this point, so I refused to let them control us.

I shut my eyes, grateful Remy and Dahlia left for the night, and I dove into the mind-walking.

Reva's dream was more pliable now that she knew I could enter. My presence interrupted the dream she was having, morphing the setting into our home. The only difference was that it seemed my memory had chosen the home for Reva, a time long before she even existed.

It would've been when another Sirian woman lived with me.

"I'm not really dreaming, am I?" Reva interjected, scanning the walls.

Even if this was only in our minds, seeing her before me eased an ache that still hadn't left me since she did.

"It is a dream." I tilted my head, watching her gain her bearings. "Your dream and my memory. Last time it was your dream and our memory."

"*What memory is this?*" She peered down the hallway where her bedroom was, but I knew she wouldn't find her things there.

"Long before you showed up on my doorstep." I chuckled low, gesturing to the table, one I hadn't seen in hundreds of years.

I lowered myself into one of the chairs as Reva whispered, "There's something I want to ask."

I saw it written all over her face and the fidgeting of her fingers. Not only that, but being in her mind, I sensed the various emotions she carried into sleep. There was a great deal of anxiety and exhaustion, tinges of betrayal, hope, and a slight warmth I knew all too well.

The same warmth I once felt for one of her ancestors.

"I know, aster." I nodded, taking a deep breath. "I feel your turmoil. There are many emotions swirling inside of you right now. Some rather intriguing, but most concerning."

She laid her hands on the table, hunching in on herself. "I know who you are."

So that's what the betrayal was about.

"I suspected your research into your god-powers would lead to me." I looked toward the window, and I schooled my face as the gold figure flickered in and out.

"So, you are the Great Child." I dragged my eyes back to her and almost winced at the hurt in her eyes. "You're Sybil's daughter."

"Me being the child of a demi-god is what you're really upset about." I slouched into the chair, sighing. Out of all the things this child could ask me about... "Yes, Reva."

"So that makes you…" Even if she didn't vocalize it, I knew she did the math. Myths and legends said I was old, but there was only one person alive who knew exactly how old I was.

"I was born before the Sirians vanished from the world," I confirmed, realizing just how long it had been since I admitted my age. "I was born just after King Alrik was officially made King."

Tears welled in her eyes as she shook her head. "I don't think I will ever understand why you never told me that. You had to know I had both Dionne and Asteria's god-powers. I would've felt less alone, especially knowing that my own guardian understood—"

"You were never alone, child," I snapped, holding the claws back. I couldn't tell if I was hurt from her accusation or that she ever felt alone, despite how hard I tried to surround her with people who hid her secret. "My age never mattered, and even for the reasons you believe it would've, all I could do was raise you the way I had. You needed to go through life the way you did and the way you will in order to fight the Darkness."

She slammed her head into her hand, gently tugging at her hair. "Why?"

I reached across the table, brushing her elbow. "Fate demands sacrifice. That was established long before you and I ever existed. The sacrifice it will take for you to come to your power would never have transpired if your life did not play out as it has. You would have gone down an entirely different Path than the one you are on."

"Sacrifice?" The sound from her was a mix of a laugh and

a choke. "What sort of sacrifice? Haven't I sacrificed enough? I will never get to know my parents, and I had to leave the only family I've ever known… Hasn't that been enough?"

"Not according to Fate." I tried to add more, but Danica's golden form flared once in warning. "I wish you didn't have to know any pain, aster. Not like this."

"So, another thing you can't or won't tell me?" She snapped, her eyes burning through me.

I was done with this.

"I wish I had more time to explain to you the limitations of my gifts." I swore I could make out an angry frown on the silhouette as something within me tried to crawl at my throat. "My Magic has been a burden my entire life because it created walls between myself and the people I loved. Just because I knew something doesn't mean I got to speak its entirety. There are so many things I wish I could tell you that I know, aster."

Reva averted her gaze, but the tightness in her face relaxed as she looked out toward Orion's Lake. My heart broke when a tear slowly slipped down her cheek. I reached over and swiped her jaw, catching it.

"If you're the descendant of a demi-god and have lived to be over a thousand years old," she paused, her voice rough, "what does that mean for me? You lived while Sirians walked the earth. Do we have extended lifespans like Magics, and will I live long after all my friends are gone?"

So many images flashed in my head from her question, and I reeled, trying to keep up with them.

There were two outcomes for Reva as things stood, but they had similar Paths. I saw her aged with slight wrinkles around her eyes. Heads with blond and auburn and eyes with green and amber, a male with dark skin like mine, and a blond woman with a missing crown…

The friends she spoke of and the ones she wanted answers for.

Despite her two outcomes, I knew with certainty she would lose different ones depending on the route she took.

"The Sirians always lived mortal lifespans," I explained, trying to catch my breath. "Those who descended from the demi-gods were never any different. I cannot speak for two god-powers, however. As for your friends—"

Behind Reva, Danica's form raised her arms, and the house rumbled with a low growl. Reva shot up from her chair, but I glared at the glowing form behind her.

"Is this part of your memory?" Reva looked around the room, but she conveniently avoided turning around. "Is it an earthquake?"

"She is losing patience with me." I smirked on my face as I looked at Reva. "She doesn't want me answering any more of your questions."

"You mentioned a 'she' last time, too," she shouted over the deafening roar as Danica's fists closed. "Who are you talking about?"

I smiled, thinking about how angry the nickname made Danica last time. "There was always a reason I called you aster—"

In a blink, Reva vanished from the table, one minute there and gone the next.

Which only left me and the strange form of Danica

standing where Reva had been.

"Your mother knew when to talk and when to be silent." Danica's voice projected through the room, the sound like tinkling glass. "You would think she taught you better."

"Unlike my mother, I'm not your seer," I said, slowly rising from my chair. I studied the edges of her form where I thought I could see a distinction between her features, but once I thought I grasped them, I lost it all again. "What is your motivation, Danica?"

If the faceless form could narrow its eyes, I ventured she did just that as she snarled, "What do you mean by that?"

"You've been following Reva for nearly ten years, ever since her Asteria god-power developed," I explained, walking out from between my chair and the table. "In my thousand years of existence, I have never felt a single God on this plane until that day. Since then, you've hovered and trailed Reva wherever she goes. Why now? And why in this form?"

"You ask questions about things you do not need to know." It was a warning, but I no longer cared.

If Fate required my death, it was either by Danica's hands, or Danica couldn't harm me until it was officially my time.

"My life has revolved around Fate and its motives," I said quietly, shaking my head. "If I am to die for the cause, I want my questions answered."

"What would you like to know, Lemurian?" Danica's tone dripped with sweet poison.

I had so many questions, including what that term meant, but I needed to know about Reva.

That was all I cared about in the end.

"Why have you left this world?" I asked, strutting across the living space. "And how are you back?"

"Your mother once told a prophecy that threatened the very existence of the Beings on this plane," Danica said, her figure hovering off the ground. "The events that unfolded because of it forced some of us Lyrans to forge an ancient Lock around your Realm to keep you safe from the Lyrans who wished to harm it."

Lemurians and Lyrans, two terms without meaning to me other than Sybil saying the latter once. Again, I yearned to ask about them, but I needed to focus on Reva.

"Am I correct to assume all the Gods are on the opposite side of this Lock?" I spun slowly on my heel with an eyebrow raised. The figure nodded its head, the gold light flickering. "That's why you only appear like this?" I waved my hand up and down her body.

"If the Lock was not breaking, I should not be able to appear at all," Danica answered, and the hairs rose on my arm. "It seems the Lock was not made properly, and it has slowly broken down with every Being that tests its strength. First you, then the child who pulled the Aether from the Abyss, then Reva—"

"Wait," I interrupted, holding a hand up. "What do you mean me?"

I knew the child she spoke of was Tyra, but I was more curious about the name Danica labeled what we called the Darkness: Aether.

"Sybil did not see you coming," Danica said, which was something I already knew. "Once your powers came, she should *have left this world. The powerful must be few—"*

"For balance to remain," I finished breathlessly.

"Morana warned her," Danica seethed, gold light flashing once. "She did not want to leave you."

She did not want to leave you.

I pushed that aside because this conversation and knowledge came a thousand years too late.

"So why Reva?" I asked, blinking. "Why did you appear ten years ago, and why have you hovered since?"

Danica's light stilled, no longer waving or pulsing. She was far too silent, so much so that I thought maybe she would vanish. Alas, she stood there for I didn't know how long.

"Fine." I sighed, falling back against the couch. "Different question…"

I stared at the empty fireplace.

Danica appeared after Asteria's god-power came. Something about that day must have scared Danica just as much as it had me. Maybe I felt Danica's fear that day when I realized Reva shouldn't exist.

"Asteria didn't have any children, did she?" I asked instead, trying to meet what I thought were Danica's eyes. Her silence was enough. "How can Reva have Asteria's god-power then?"

"You should ask Morana that." Danica chuckled low, the sound skittering across my skin. "Your grandmother, the Goddess of Life and Death, agreed to reincarnate Asteria in some deal she struck with her so Asteria would forge the Lock."

"I didn't think that reincarnation was real," I whispered, shaking my head. "That doesn't make sense, though. Certain lines of the prophecy appeared just when Reva conjured her

god-power. A betrayal by Death, a Goddess born again…"

Saying the words out loud had old memories rushing into me with a force that knocked the wind from my lungs.

Never believe the history you have been taught.

"Asteria wasn't a demi-god." I stared at Danica's figure like I could read her face. Despite that, I felt her confirmation. "She was a full Goddess… Then Rod was her father?"

Danica laughed, but the sound was hollow, leached of any joy. "Rod was most definitely not her father."

The only other Gods were females. That meant there were more Gods we didn't know about. If that was the case, I was afraid of the following few questions.

Not for me, but for Reva.

"How does Reva challenge the Lock's integrity?"

"Reincarnation is something that transcends Fate," Danica explained, shaking her head. "Neither you, Sybil, nor Dola could have seen that Reva was Asteria reincarnated. Reincarnation is connected to Destiny, and that is beyond your abilities. It's why the prophecy changed when she conjured that power. It revealed her true soul.

"The Darkness you know used to be called the Aether. Before the Lock, Sirians wielded both. They did not distinguish between good and evil. They were powers, simple as that. Asteria was the true Goddess of Sirians. She did not just have the starfire, but she also could wield—"

"The Light and Dark," I finished for her. "Reva could very well wield both, then?"

"Hypothetically speaking, yes." Danica's light flared again, and I had to shield my eyes from the brightness. "She cannot, *though. I have watched her, and she can very well sense the Aether in others, but she doesn't know she can wield it yet and doesn't seem to have tried to. Should she do that…"*

Danica didn't need to finish for me to understand. The Lock wasn't just protection for those within it, but it was keeping something out, and I assumed it was these Lyrans Danica spoke of.

It was decided long ago, a prophecy given to Sybil. The powerful must be few for balance to remain.

The balance they spoke of was the integrity of the Lock.

"Too many powerful Beings could break the Lock," I whispered more to myself, slowly rising from the couch. "Reva is one powerful Being, and if she wields the Light and Dark, she will be a Goddess reborn. A Goddess within Aveesh."

"The Lock cannot sustain a full Lyran living within it," Danica said, her voice quiet but clipped.

"How do you suppose you'll keep Reva in check when I'm gone?" I narrowed my eyes. "Hovering over her every step of the way?"

"I may use your voice to appeal to her gradually," she said, her figure beginning to flicker out. "After that, the veil of the Lock is currently fragile enough that I can reach her just as you have reached her."

"That doesn't answer my question." A sly grin crawled up my cheeks, and I hoped Danica could see it. "How will you keep her in check? You don't know her as I do. She won't do something she doesn't want to. Not until she is ready."

A hum of indifference reverberated from Danica's form.

"She is not my daughter," Danica said, her form fading,

"but you would be surprised to learn how many qualities Reva and Asteria appear to share."

LILLIES & LOVE

I walked with Dahlia through Heridy, though I wasn't sure anyone still called it that. One hand held my cane, the other tucked into the crook of Dahlia's arm. I swept my gaze over the little stands and crumpled buildings, frowning because there was once a time when this village was a flourishing hub with a long-lost name on the throne.

Carraphim. The Carraphims had been on the throne.

Reva's family was on the throne, a single line that was buried amongst the masses long before I even existed.

"Reva," I said aloud, my gaze frantically searching the children running in front of the spouting fountain. "Where is she?"

"She's safe at home," Dahlia explained, except that didn't feel right. I could've sworn she was right beside me, but there was also the matter of the knight who came to take her away.

"The knight came?" I turned my head to Dahlia, searching her familiar blood-red eyes. "The one with green eyes?"

Dahlia smiled softly, patting my arm. "That exact

one."

I hummed as I swiveled my head back to the rather busy streets, except when I blinked again, there were the usual number of Magics in town, and the fountain was crumbled once again. A breeze curled through the air, carrying a sharp, burnt scent that startled me. I stopped walking, snapping my gaze to the west.

"*Darkness comes again,*" I muttered in a monotone voice, a chorus of voices echoing in my head endlessly. My hands trembled as the voices clawed at my head to get out. "*Fate demands sacrifice.*"

"Don't worry about it," Dahlia scoffed as if the balance of the world didn't hang by a single raven-black strand. "We sent Reva off to take care of it, remember? She's in Mariande and she's going to figure it out."

"No." I shook my head, a dread falling over me, dampening my cheeks. "She won't figure it out. She must continue the prophecy when I'm gone." My voice dropped from its manic fluctuation into the monotone again, "*A betrayal by Death raises the new Gods—*"

"Enough talk about the Gods, Karasi." Dahlia curved around my body, her hand still holding my arm as her other hand wrapped over mine on top of the cane. "You should enjoy the early morning air and the town. I know you grew up here, so I thought maybe you wanted to see it—whenever you're seeing it."

I nodded, trying to urge the voices to settle down, all of them mixing in a flurry: *the* voices, Sybil's, King Alrik's, Tyra's—

Brand.

You're no longer wild and untamed…

My eyes fluttered at the shadowy form standing beside Dahlia, turquoise eyes glowing.

"I didn't stay sane," I whispered. Another breeze took the form with it, leaving me with Dahlia again, who looked at me with so much pity it made my skin crawl. I snarled at her, "I'm over a thousand years old, woman. Did you expect me to stay sane?"

"I love it when the *you* I've come to know and love peeks out—"

The building beside us shattered, the force of the blast throwing Dahlia and me apart. I landed on my side, rolling through gravel as rubble rained down on me, pain shooting through my hip and ribs before going completely numb.

Screams rose from around me as my vision swayed, the fountain tilting at angles that churned my stomach. I coughed around the smoke, which only brought a deep ache back to my ribs, stealing my breath away.

I vaguely heard Dahlia shouting my name, but the screams and her voice meant nothing as the ground fell away from me, and my body was thrown upright into the air.

Except I didn't fall back down. I was suspended in the air, kicking my feet in the emptiness below me. My fingers instinctively shot out my claws, aimlessly grasping at nothing for my cane.

"Oh, how far the Great fall." An eerie, high-pitched

voice curled like smoke from below.

I dared a peek at the ground, my stomach dropping when I realized I was easily two stories above it.

A woman with blond hair stood before me, a devious half-smile stretching across her pale skin. Her eyes glowed pure white, as did her Mark and the veins beneath her skin. Her hand sat poised on her hip, palm up.

"Karasi!" Dahlia shouted from a few feet behind the woman. "Put her down—"

The woman flicked her hand as if she were shooing Dahlia, and Dahlia's body dragged across the pathway back toward what could only be described as utter madness.

Black tendrils shot from various angles, spearing Magics left and right. Multiple people wielded the Darkness, and I was reminded of a young, frightened girl who once looked into my eyes as her hopeless future flashed before me.

"You must be Sidra," I managed around a cough, my chest tightening. I placed my hand against my hip, where my weakened healing attempted to repair it. "I have to say, Fate never let me see how I would die, but this seems right."

"Is that what happens as we age?" Sidra asked, tilting her head. "We're just so ready for death?"

"When you've seen what I have," another cough interrupted my speech, "you'll be ready too."

"I suppose you and Death have been close friends for a long time." Sidra lowered me to the ground so I was closer to her, the tips of my shoes just touching the path beneath us. "Kingdoms rise and fall, friends come and go… Death has walked with you all your life, just as it has mine."

She studied my face, waiting for a reaction I supposed, but she wouldn't get one. I trained for a thousand years of neutrality.

It only angered her.

Black leaked into the glowing white of her Mark and eyes as thorns pierced my midsection, burning.

"Why did you never come for the hundreds of Sirian children forced into slavery at the hands of Teslin?" Sidra hissed, and I grunted at the tightness around my waist, the fabric dampening.

"Fate prevented me," I explained, although I owed her nothing. She was far too gone, driven mad by the Darkness and the power Phoebe's gift gave her.

"Fuck your Fate."

"It will be your fate, too." I winced as my chest twinged where the rib hadn't quite healed yet. "The powerful must be few for balance to remain."

Sidra cocked her head, her jaw twitching. "So are you, Great Karasi? Ready for death?"

I had one more thing I needed to do.

I took a deep breath before I felt a sharp spear of pain pierced through the middle of my chest, blooming across my limbs.

And then I begged my mortal body to hang on just a little bit longer so I could say goodbye.

Reva stood in the empty square that once thrived in Heridy, surrounded by buildings that sold pastries and ale. She walked forward hesitantly, and I wondered if she recognized where she was. She wore her nightgown again, so I glanced down at my own body to see if I would be covered in blood or black ink.

Except I was young again—the same age as Reva—dressed in the fashion of that time.

"Incredible what time will do to a place," I said, and Reva spun on her heel, the gravel crunching beneath her.

I suppressed my laugh as her eyes widened, her mouth dropping open while her gaze swept up and down my body.

"So, this is the Great Karasi the world first knew," she said gently. I thought of the last time I saw Brand, and I probably looked no different from then. "What is this place?"

I really looked at Heridy, trying to decipher when this memory was. My eyes caught the Black Avalanches in the background, the Abyss hovering at the peaks.

My mind chose the day Sybil left as the memory to place in Reva's dream.

"It's only fitting it would be this memory." I raised my eyes to Reva's. "You now know this place by a simple name. But long ago, it was known by another throughout the land, run by a family deeply influenced by your god-power."

Her brows twitched in confusion, but then she seemed to remember her history. "This is Main Town?"

I nodded. "A little less than a thousand years ago. Shortly after, the Sirians suffered at the hands of the Korbins."

Her face cleared of her frown as she suddenly said, "Karasi… I healed Clint."

"I know, aster." I smiled at the pride that swelled in my chest. I always knew she would, not just because of Fate, but because she was resilient. So, I told her. "I knew you would."

"I heard your voice." She stepped toward me, her hands clasped in front of her. "You told me to take my necklace off. When I did, something happened to my powers. They were easier to wield, but the burning I got from Asteria's power intensified. It was unbearable. What does it mean?"

Something invisible tugged at my sternum, and I wondered how much longer my mortal body could hold. I pressed my lips together, unsure of how much I could tell her now that I was in Death's domain—my grandmother.

"She told me she was going to use my voice to appeal to you."

Reva stilled, all fidgeting ceasing. "Why?"

My sternum tugged again, my heart pinching in my chest. I shook my head, trying to will my body back in the physical world to hold on. "My mother told me never to wear hematite pieces at a young age. She said they would mute my abilities, the ones I inherited from her, despite being the child of a demi-god."

I thought about how afraid of Sybil's wrath I'd been. She sternly told me once never to wear hematite, and I tried many times to use it or wear it.

It only ever burned my skin.

My powers couldn't be turned on and off like Reva's.

"I always had a feeling the hematite was meant to keep a leash on the abilities of the demi-gods. Why is beyond my knowledge and was a decision made far before my time. I was the final child born directly from a demi-god, although there were plenty of descendants of my cousins."

"So, it doesn't keep me from 'yearning for more'?" I curled my lip at that statement, wondering where she heard that outright lie. "Why did you let me wear it all this time?"

Guilt crushed me then, or maybe it was my heart failing me in my real body. I averted my gaze, hoping I could be honest for once. "I always knew who your god-powers came from, just as I knew it could not be my role to teach you how to wield those powers to their full capacity. I encouraged the necklace because I knew it was just as I said: a leash."

My girl no longer needed a leash.

"Leashes can be taken off." I smirked, raising my head. "I knew one day you would be ready for your full powers, and you would no longer need the hematite necklace to keep them at bay."

"When I took it off, the starfire overcame the Energy..."

My control slipped on the mind-walking as I was thrown into my body in a blink—a quick flash of Dahlia—before I returned to the memory.

"Asteria's power has always been an enhanced variation of the Light." I tried to smile, but the ache in my chest was becoming unbearable. "This power you call starfire is your Energy. The hematite is just able to separate it from your natural Sirian heritage. I'm sure the more you wield the starfire, *the more your body will acclimate to it and no longer feel its effects. But remember, while your starfire is unleashed without your necklace, so will be the firepower."*

"So, hematite is still useful when I'm not using my powers."

Something yanked at my sternum, my mind feeling as though it was being ripped in two.

I was out of time.

"You are the most powerful Sirian to walk Aveesh since Asteria herself." I grabbed Reva's hands in mine, speaking around the haze clouding my head. "The powerful must be few for balance to remain. Fate will demand sacrifice."

The feel of her hands in mine brought the control back, if only for a moment longer. I looked upon that beautiful face of hers, seeing all of her at once from the first moment I laid eyes on her to the day she left.

A tear slipped from her golden eyes, and I raised my hand to wipe it away.

"Why am I crying?" She whispered as I gripped her face.

I pulled her toward me, placing a gentle kiss against her forehead. A shock of pain went through my entire body before I held her at arm's length.

"You know why, aster.*" Something warm ran down my face. "The Stars have called you back home, my little orphan, but do not forget who you are."*

Brand's voice came to me then. Find those who can understand you and accept you as I have, who do not require your gifts, but your love.

I poked her chest, above her heart, as mine felt like it was being ripped from me. "Do not forget all those who have loved you."

"Mi leiron," the voice rang out, soft and unmistakable.

I slowly twisted around, and standing in the white expanse was Brand, old and wrinkled like the final day I had seen him.

"You did well," he whispered, stretching his hand out. "She is beautiful."

Tears dripped down my face as my eyes fluttered. Suddenly, my body felt as if it were floating, numbness washing over me.

"She's the greatest gift Fate ever gave me."

I knew then if I had to do it all over again, I would walk through this hell if it always led me to Reva.

I stepped toward him, accepting his outstretched hand. "Where are we going?"

"Wherever you want." He smiled, those turquoise eyes glistening. I looked back over my shoulder, but Reva was no longer there. "Karasi?"

I brought my gaze back to him, and I cupped his cheek in my other hand. "I'm ready, now."

A Message from Katie

I always knew I wanted to write Karasi's story and share the things this woman did before she knew Reva, and for a very long time, the woman was just as mysterious to me as she was to you. Somehow, despite the brief interaction with her and seeing her through Reva's memories, you all wanted to know about Karasi. I hope her story was all you could've asked for and you loved the tales of the old woman. I had fun writing this and getting to know who Karasi was before Reva, and seeing the similarities between them was touching.

This story was written in a deeper silence compared to any of my other books. I don't think I realized how much of Karasi's theme for her story spoke to me—we are all different people all through our lives. It is something I've used to get me through my life in some of the toughest times. She goes through loss, both from death and from the choice to protect herself before they left her. *This* spoke to me so deeply.

I also approached a lot of mental health representation that I do not often speak on. As mentioned in the trigger warnings, Karasi does practice a form of self harm to silence "the voices". I didn't initially plan on that, but as I wrote, it just sort of came into the story and I stuck with it. I will *always* write mental health into my fantasy stories, whether it's direct or indirect (the dementia-like Madness that plagues Sybil and Karasi). My generation is the semi-colon generation, and I know *far too many* who lost their lives or nearly lost their lives to suicide, which is why I also made the dedication to those who are battling their own inner demons—in whatever forms they come.

If you are reading this and that habit of Karasi's mental health stuck with you, remember that you are a living, breathing, beautiful soul on this planet. I know it's hard now, but your story is not over yet.

ACKNOWLEDGEMENTS

I'm going to keep it short and sweet, because as I mentioned in my little message, this piece was written in silence compared to the loud, public sharing of the main books in the series.

I first want to thank my grandma, Gran. You have always believed in my stories and my passion for writing, and I think so much of you came out in the "Crone" version of Karasi—both in this prequel and in *Darkness Comes Again*. You are all the good that I have put into Karasi, and her love for Reva was directly reflected in all the times you told me how much you loved me and how much I meant to you. *Forever and always.*

The next people I want to thank are all my readers who have been genuinely excited about this prequel story. I know how much you all wanted to see more of Karasi's story, and I was so happy to be able to deliver this to you guys. Thank you as always for reading my books, for being my ride or die readers, and for fueling me with the confidence I never knew I needed.

As alway, thank you to my editor, Sophie: we've come such a long way, and who knew this would be the *fifth* book of The Sirians Series that you would edit since we first connected late-2023. Thank you for sticking with me and my madness, and here's to the next few as we near the end of the series.

Lastly, to my husband, Jake: thank you for silencing the voices, even when you didn't mean to. Thank you for being my best friend and the true love of my life.

ABOUT THE AUTHOR

K.M. "Katie" Davidson is a fantasy romance author. Her authorial journey began as a young writer creating YA fantasy novels in composition notebooks and publishing them on Wattpad. After getting her Bachelor's in Creative Writing and Master's in English Literature—and abandoning 20+ book ideas—she finally sat down in 2023 and finished her debut novel, *Darkness Comes Again*, Book 1 of the Sirians Series.

Outside of writing and reading, Katie is a Content Marketer. She loves dance parties with her husband and dog, hiking, traveling, entertaining conspiracy theories (none more than aliens), collecting more rocks, and buying old copies of books published over 100 years ago.

For exclusive sneak peeks, character aesthetics, and more news, follow K.M. Davidson on social media: @kmdavidsonbooks

www.ingramcontent.com/pod-product-compliance
Lightning Source LLC
Chambersburg PA
CBHW050516110726
47899CB00005B/1483